Spy Notes

Judy Hutson

RWM
REBEL WORLD MEDIA

For my parents - Mary and Calvin Hutson
To my husband Emmanuel Awartey and my son Omar - who gives me
everlasting support.

A Note From Judy

Thank you for picking up *Spy Notes*. Before you meet Johnny Harrington on her first mission, know that there's more of her waiting for you—a free origin story, *The Making of a Spy*, that reveals the secret she carried long before any of this began. You'll find it at the end of the book. For now, turn the page and enjoy the ride.

Chapter 1

09:35 Heathrow Airport London

Johnny Harrington raced through the airport, weaving and dodging through the crowd while glancing at her phone, which was on fire with messages. As she neared the gate, she answered her phone breathlessly, "Jerry, I'm practically there. No, definitely not. I'm getting on this plane. You never spoke to me." She hung up before he could respond.

Panting as she entered the door, Johnny was greeted by a flight attendant who smiled warmly and took her Moncler jacket. "Welcome aboard, Ms. Harrington." The thud of the heavy plane door closing behind her confirmed her status as the last passenger. She trudged to her first-class cubicle and sank into the plush leather seat as the chief steward announced, "Boarding complete."

As the plane began to taxi, Johnny gratefully accepted a glass of champagne. The chaos of her day melted away with each sip, and she drifted off to sleep before she could even finish the sparkling drink.

****

A sliver of light from the cabin coaxed Johnny's eyes open. She slid the window shade up and gazed out the plane window at the azure waves below, rushing to meet the white sand. *In less than an hour I'll finally be in that water.*

"We're getting ready to land soon," the flight attendant's voice broke her trance. Johnny turned to her. "Thank you." She smiled as she pushed the button that transformed her bed back into a first-class seat. The guaranteed premium tickets were the only reason she'd taken the side trip to London before heading to Barbados.

Checking her hair and make-up, she released a deep sigh. At least two weeks without having to take crisis calls in the middle of the night. *He's somebody else's problem for now.*

She tried not to think about the missed messages and all the calls she'd ignored as she hit the off button before rushing onto the plane at Heathrow. Now Naïve, one of the most famous music artists in the world, was on his way back to rehab in New York, and she was spending the holidays here on the island.

The bright sun and soupy Caribbean air hit Johnny as she descended the airplane steps. The familiar fragrance of human moisture melding with wilting foliage welcomed her as she walked across the tarmac to the airport's arrival area. She closed her eyes and took a deep breath before entering the building, sensing the warmth of being home. A glance over her shoulder assured her all the pressures and worries of her fast-paced life in the music business were behind her on the plane returning to London.

Although she hadn't been born in Barbados, her heart lay on the island. Memories of her childhood vacations with her parents, learning to swim in tranquil blue water with her uncle after her parents returned to New York, deepened her connection to the place. Christmas days spent going from house to house and partying with friends on the island gave Johnny the confidence to call Barbados home.

The trade winds blew Johnny's blonde kinky curls away from her face but didn't ease the heat from her Burberry cashmere hoodie and Moncler jacket around her shoulders. Through the terminal window, she could spot passengers—one with the ubiquitous raincoat and umbrella—waiting to board the return flight to London. She entered the terminal, sweat oozing from her body, and glanced around, pulling her clothes away from her skin. *Where is Lockwood?* The moisture slowly dripping down her body gave a sensation of swimming in hot soup, but hopefully, he was here to give her the VIP treatment through customs—the beginning of her restful vacation.

 ****

Chapter 2

14:55 Bridgetown Barbados

Philip Lockwood stood under the swaying palm trees while his officers removed the dead body next to the kilos of cocaine, the latest confiscation from the area. The fresh scent of the salted sea water flowing onto the shore usually calmed him. But not now. He shook his head. Human remains and kilos of cocaine. Both treated the same. Carted away in separate vehicles. Clasping his folded hands behind his back, he rocked back and forth on his feet. *How had it come to this? There had always been drug problems here. But this was different.*

"Sir, the final tally of the bags," said a young Black policewoman.

The furrows in Lockwood's brows deepened. He read the report she'd handed him.

The coroner approached. "Do you know the cause of death?" Lockwood asked.

The ennui in the coroner's eyes was visible. He gave a perfunctory nod over the body. "From a first look, blunt force wound to the head. But he was probably dumped into the jet ski a few days ago."

"Why do you think that?"

"I don't think he was killed on a jet ski in the middle of the ocean and there are beginning signs of bloating in the body."

Lockwood gave a deep sigh. "I need to see a full autopsy report as soon as it's complete."

"Sure, no problem." The coroner walked back to the van.

"Make sure the jeep is escorted to the armory and the bags are recounted before they're placed inside," he said to the policewoman.

"Yes, sir."

As she darted away, memories of his own young officer years flashed in his head. Back then, the biggest problem the island's British-born Police Commissioner usually dealt with was British expatriates complaining about natives stealing fruit from their trees.

He shook his head as he looked around. *Who would have imagined I would become Police Commissioner? And that an all-Black police force would be dealing with much bigger problems and protecting the same homes now owned by Bajans?*

The vibration of his phone interrupted his thoughts.

"Lockwood here."

"Sir, you told me to remind you when it was 3:30," his secretary's voice streamed into his earpiece.

"Thank you, Ms. Braithwaite. I'm heading to the airport."

As Lockwood drove, passing the festive lights on the houses, he tried to feel the spirit of the season. A smile crept up on his face. Those former cane fields, the same ones in which he'd played as a child and later lost his virginity, were now a highway. He nodded to himself. Yes, the island has changed, but some things will always be the same.

After entering the terminal, he observed the natives rushing to greet returning relatives. Tourists taking a break from North America's and Europe's fierce winters searching among the mountain of suitcases for their luggage. Lockwood grinned when he spotted

Johnny in her high heeled Prada boots and Moncler jacket falling off her shoulders, schlepping through the crowd, dragging her carry-on luggage behind her. He might not know the labels she was wearing but could tell the cost of her entire outfit was probably a month's salary for one of his officers. Although she returned to the island every year, he still saw the precocious little girl in the beautiful young woman's face. *Can't believe she is a young woman. Like the daughter I never had.*

"Welcome back, Johnny." He hugged her and took her hand luggage.

"It's so good to be back."

"Let me have your passport. You can wait here while I take care of your documents," Lockwood said.

"Thanks." Johnny handed him her passport, admiring her old family friend's wavy salt-and-pepper hair, which accented his light brown complexion as he turned away. As he trekked through the airport, Johnny noticed two police officers rushing toward him. He pulled them to the side, his jaw clenched and hands clasped in front of him as he listened to whatever they told him. He disappeared behind an office door before returning in no time with her documents and the rest of her luggage.

"How's the family, Johnny? Everyone is well?" Lockwood inquired as they strolled to the car.

"Yes, everyone's fine, thanks. Hope I didn't interrupt your day. You look like you're pretty busy."

"Not anything more than usual."

Johnny's instinctive people-reading skills told her the weariness in his eyes betrayed his words. Always through the eyes. That was how she discerned the artist who was about to go on a drug binge or the lecherous executive who would put her in a precarious situation— and how she survived in her business.

As soon as Lockwood got in the car beside her, Johnny pressed him. "I saw those officers run to you. It looked serious."

Lockwood put his head out the window to yell hello to an acquaintance before he faced Johnny with a smile. "Just some police business in the area. The young officers are always trying to make a good impression."

It didn't get past her how he diverted the conversation by giving her the latest news about mutual acquaintances. *I'll let it slide for now.* She soon became distracted gazing out the window at the beautiful red and white poinsettia swaying among the exotic hibiscus which grew in abundance around the island. *I love this. It never gets old.*

"This is the new Princess Highway we're heading towards," said Lockwood as they entered the roundabout. "It might not have been completed last year when you were here." He pointed out to the horizon. "You take it straight from the airport to the West Coast."

Johnny shrugged. "It makes the trip from the airport faster, but I miss seeing the little white houses along the way and the cows and goats in the open fields. Barbados's quaint charm is the reason visitors become addicted to this country."

Lockwood glanced at her. "Things are changing a lot and, in more ways, than you might realize."

Johnny raised an eyebrow. She studied him. "What do you mean? Does it have something to do with your business at the airport?"

He stared straight ahead. "Oh, it's more than just the physical changes to the island. People's attitudes are also different. Sometimes for the better. Sometimes not."

Several acres of the namesake trees surrounding the sprawling Flamboyant plantation was Johnny's first sight_as they drove up the graveled courtyard to the house and closer to her favorite childhood spots. Flamboyant's veranda surrounded the house on three sides, each with doors opening out towards floral grounds that brought a cool breeze from the sea.

Johnny smiled. Flamboyant was almost as old as her family's lineage on the island. The remnants of the island's oldest sugar mill where she played as a child were still on the edge of the plantation land. The sound of the car brought Elizabeth Harrington, trailed by yapping dogs, out of the house. Her aunt approached them with an air of the British aristocracy.

Johnny rushed to hug her. "Welcome back, Johnny." Elizabeth said.

"I couldn't wait to be back here." Johnny gushed. She pulled away, surveying her aunt's attire.

Elizabeth's fine brown hair was now scattered with hints of gray, but that didn't take away from her beauty. The orange background in her printed organza shirtdress complemented her copper skin, while the full skirt with billowing sleeves of the dress made her look like a rich lady of the leisure crowd. How does she stay so elegant in this sweltering heat?

"I see you forget about me when your relatives come home," Lockwood teased Elizabeth, as he gave her a friendly peck on the cheek.

"Oh Philip, you are part of the family. How can I possibly forget you?" she replied in a sweet British-fringed Barbados accent. "Come, leave your bags," she said to Johnny. "Leonard will bring them in."

Lockwood winked at Johnny as she whispered "thank you" before Elizabeth intertwined their arms and led her into the house.

Johnny glanced over her shoulder and smiled at the ground's caretaker. "Hey Leonard. You're still looking good. How's it going?"

"I'm still here surviving as long as the good Lord wants me to stay," he answered in his strong, country-accented voice.

He closed the entrance gate that was always open before he picked up the bags. Leonard never appeared to age. His tall, lean body and jet-black skin belied his advanced years. But that gate had seemed heavy for him to close. Maybe the years were finally catching up with him.

She missed her childhood days when Leonard would tell her all the folklore of the island. Now he treated her with more distance, the same respect as her aunt in public. But at least they still always had their private chats in the kitchen when she shared his favorite Godiva chocolates she brought from New York.

Johnny beamed as she entered Flamboyant and took in the entrance hall. As she walked past one of the sitting rooms, she paused. Everything was still the same. She stared at the oil portrait of the Harringtons' pale-faced, British-born patriarch, wondering why he didn't smile. The much smaller portrait of his dark-skinned, Barbados-born wife had finally been found and placed next to him.

All of the original 19th-century mahogany furniture Barbados was renowned for throughout the West Indies was perfectly arranged. The loveseats, with their cane backs and curved arms—behind which she'd hidden during games of hide-and-seek—were polished to a fine shine. Walking up the curved staircase, Johnny recalled how she used to sneak out and slide down the banister with glee.

"Your regular room is ready for you," Elizabeth said as she opened the door and walked toward the four-poster mahogany bed. The transparent white batiste material draped around the posts swayed in the tropical breezes coming through the large, open shuttered windows. The bed was the reason this was Johnny's favorite room.

She ran her hand along the thick post, remembering how for years her parents wouldn't let her stay in it, fearing her restless sleep and its height from the ground. When they'd finally deemed her the right age, the room became hers whenever she visited.

"I saw Leonard shut the front gate. I've never known it to be closed during the day," Johnny remarked.

Elizabeth walked to the balcony door and tied back the curtains before she faced Johnny. "Some extra precautions Phillip suggested," she said with a wave of her hand. "Why your uncle takes him so seriously sometimes, I don't know. Now, Johnny, I've already set aside a schedule of events and parties coming up during your visit. You might not want to attend all of them, but I've put a small star next to the ones you shouldn't miss."

Of course you did. Johnny's eyes followed her aunt as she flitted around the room. Then she picked up the schedule from the side table. "The same ones as usual, I see."

"The first party is this evening, here at Flamboyant. Of course, we expect all the regulars, so take out what you plan to wear. Clara will collect it from you to be pressed. I suggest you rest this afternoon so you'll be fresh for this evening's event."

Elizabeth glided toward the door. "I'll be downstairs if you need anything."

"Okay, thanks." Johnny had hoped for a relaxing evening on her first night back at the estate. She should have known. It was the Christmas season. Since Elizabeth and Charles were part of Barbados's elite society, people expected them to give their annual parties. At least staying up later would help her get over the jet lag.

She ambled out onto the balcony and glanced over the vast, lush land with the plantation's namesake trees surrounding the estate. Johnny instantly thought about the most relaxing thing to do instead of resting in her room. After changing, she sneaked out of the house using the back staircase, hoping Elizabeth wouldn't see her.

Chapter 3

16:00 Paradise Beach, Barbados

The road to Paradise Beach was lined with the island's short sea grape trees, their full, waxy green leaves bearing big, juicy grapes. Johnny gazed at the colorful bougainvillea flowers cascading down the walls of the old Canard estate house. Long vines of the bearded fig tree, which gave the island its Portuguese name, darkened part of the path. During her childhood, she would hurry past them because of the tales of spirits that lived in them. Now she appreciated the shade they provided.

Johnny picked a quiet area to take a leisurely swim and placed her towel on the soft, white sand. She glided into the water as though performing a religious ritual, immersing herself in its tranquil blueness. Enveloped by the warm sea, a calmness slowly covered her.

The waves rolled over each part of her body, caressing and bathing her, washing away all the pressures of unreturned emails and midnight crisis calls.

She waded further into the ocean and lowered her head before starting butterfly strokes. After a few laps along the shoreline, she stopped and faced the sun, allowing its rays to warm her brown skin, her eyes riveted toward the horizon.

"Hey, Johnny!" The voice shouting from the shoreline pulled her to attention. She twisted to squint at a tall, slender, dark figure, and immediately a smile spread across her face.

She moved closer to the shore. "Winslow! How did you learn I was here?"

"I always know the moment you step on the island," he responded with a sly grin.

Her face lit up. Winslow wasn't only one of the best detectives on the drug task force but also her most precarious relationship. "Hope you aren't using police resources."

"Only if it gives me time to be close to you." He took off his shoes and walked to the edge of the water. "Are you going to come out of there, or do I have to come in for you?"

Johnny treaded water. "I haven't been in long enough. It feels too good to come out now. You, of all people, should understand. You love the sea even more than I do."

He held his arms out toward her. "I haven't seen you in a year, so grant me this one wish. Only for a minute. Then you can go back in."

She rose out of the ocean and pushed the kinky coils cascading down her shoulders away from her face.

Winslow pulled her toward him. "It's crazy how you are more beautiful as each year passes. You keep trying to run away from me. One day, you'll come to your senses and realize I'm the only person who can put that smile on your face."

"You're holding me too close." She coyly pushed away from him. "You're going to get wet."

A warmth flowed over her body as he flashed his smile—the same smile that had given her peace after she'd ended a volatile relationship back home. He had taken her away from so many of the pompous affairs, to the dismay of Elizabeth, and shown her a simpler life in Barbados.

She teased him as her hands ran over the top of his head. "Don't have it on today?" It was their joke about his fisherman's hat—the one he always wore as they raced around in his speedboat by day and removed at night before they lay on the sand roasting fish by a campfire.

They would gaze at the stars dotting the dark sky as he stroked her hair and whispered, "Stay with me. I'll stop the world for you." He made her breathe a little slower and her body become lighter, but it wouldn't last.

Eventually, she would have to return to reality without him. Her world took the good-hearted like a beast capturing its prey, devouring and churning them in its immense maw until nothing was left but a shell of the former person the beast tossed aside.

She would never want to see Winslow lose himself in her world. Living a simple life with him for two weeks had worked perfectly, but how long would she last without the adrenaline of her fast-paced lifestyle? If Johnny left her world, she would eventually become the beast of prey that would destroy him.

"I'm on duty, but I had to see you. Sit for a few minutes. Tell me what's going on in your life."

She picked up the towel. "And waste the taxpayers' money by hanging out?"

"I'm always working. It's been harder now than ever," said Winslow as he looked toward the horizon.

She stopped drying herself. "Are you working on an exciting case?"

"No, but they're more difficult ones." Winslow's tone turned solemn. "Things aren't as easy as they were before."

She squinted at him. *What isn't he telling me?* The intrigue, the details and tidbits he usually shared—although against the department's rules—were what she loved. This part of his work fascinated her. But his face lost its usual glow as he continued to avoid her questions.

"Are you holding out on me? Don't tell me you've stopped trusting me after all these years."

He drew her closer to him. Brushed his hand along her face.

"Of course I trust you. You should have no doubts in your mind about my feelings for you."

"I love to hear about your cases."

Winslow moved aside. "I persuaded you out of the water to talk about you, not me." His reaction convinced Johnny he had no intention of answering her questions. Just like Lockwood this afternoon. *Something is going on and it doesn't seem good.*

"Oh, everything is the same," Johnny said. "Naive finally released his new music, so we'll be on tour next month."

One thing Johnny hated to do in Barbados: talk about her work. It brought New York too close to her paradise. "Aunt Elizabeth is having her big annual party tonight so I'd better return before she notices I'm gone. Are you going to drop by?"

"You know that crowd isn't my thing. Since you're on a curfew, I'll give you a ride back to Flamboyant."

She scoured the area. "Where's your bike?"

He put his arm around her shoulders as he pointed. "It's beyond the trees."

They headed in the bike's direction. Johnny felt Winslow's eyes consuming her from head to toe. The same look he always gave her before he talked about marriage. *Please don't start that conversation again. Marriage would only ruin what we have.*

No matter how many times she tried to persuade him their different worlds wouldn't meld, he ignored her. She stared at his back as he walked towards the bike and placed his leg over the seat. *He would never be okay with my career, no matter what he says. I won't let him destroy this.*

"Which road do you want me to take, the beach or the main road?"

She placed her bag in the baggage compartment and jumped on.

"The beach road, of course."

Winslow peeked over his shoulder and winked at her. "The beach road is a longer way to Flamboyant."

She grabbed his waist. "I know."

Winslow's motorcycle dodged between the trees on the beach path. The wind blew Johnny's hair dry, while the brine from the salty sea air reminded her of the first time on the bike with Winslow. It was the same carefree vacation when she sat behind him, holding him tight as they rode around the island.

That year, she learned to love life on the ocean. She'd gone from squirming at the fresh catch to eating it straight from the sea. They would sail on Teamie when her dark cloud hovered over. Somehow, he knew the salt from the sea air and the ocean breeze would lift her mood without saying a word. His intuitive ability scared her more than she wanted to admit.

He stopped the bike in Flamboyant's circular courtyard and took off his helmet. "Here you are, safe and sound. When will I see you again?"

"I'll call you sometime this week," Johnny answered as she got off the bike.

Winslow's face changed as his shoulders slumped and he lowered his gaze to the ground. She bent her head to meet his eyes. "You can find me at my favorite beach every day, so drop by when you have a break."

His face broke into a big grin. "Then I'll see you tomorrow."

As he rode away, Johnny shook her head and ran up the steps to the house. *Winslow is still the same Winslow. Using his guile to make me feel guilty.*

"We were wondering where you were, Ms. Johnny." Elizabeth smirked as she greeted her at the door.

"I went for a quick swim. I thought it would help with the jet lag. Plus, I couldn't relax inside on such a beautiful day."

"Well, I hope you've decided what you want to wear tonight. If you're hungry, go into the kitchen. Clara is preparing plenty of food."

Johnny's flip-flops slid under her feet because of the remaining water and salt on her skin as she moved toward the stairs. "I want to take a shower before I have a snack. I'll be down in about an hour."

The suds from Elizabeth's fresh citrus shower gel left Johnny's skin extra clean. She wrapped her wet hair in a towel and put on her plush white terry-cloth robe, finally in total vacation mode. Clara had already unpacked her suitcase and hung up her clothes in the closet.

She flipped through her dresses before pulling out a white linen sheath—the naturally wrinkled material was part of the chic. No need for Clara to press it. Johnny placed it on the valet rod above her gold stiletto sandals before going down the stairs decorated with imported holly and twinkling white lights.

The kitchen was a vast area, fully equipped with top-of-the-line appliances. The room was filled with the extra staff Elizabeth had hired, running around in frantic turmoil. At the kitchen's entrance,

Clara darted around, giving instructions to the staff. She stopped as soon as she spotted Johnny. "I've prepared a small sampling of tonight's menu for you. Here, take this dish and go sit in the breakfast area. I'll bring some more over."

Thin, dark-skinned, and lively, Clara was gifted with the country's elixir of youth, hiding the fact she'd worked for the Harringtons for more than twenty years.

As Johnny headed toward the nook, she caught a glimpse of her uncle and Lockwood down the hallway, their heads close in a tense conversation. She stopped and lowered her head, nibbling on the fishcake puffs on her plate while she took side glances at them.

Lockwood had been here for hours. *Why was he still around?* Johnny started to walk toward him to say goodbye.

The police commissioner handed an envelope to her uncle as he gave her a side glance, pivoted, and rushed out the back entrance. Johnny squinted her eyes and slowly ate the last fishcake puff while watching Lockwood's car leave through the hallway window.

Chapter 4

19:00 Flamboyant Estate Barbados

Charles Harrington disappeared into his office for a few minutes before meeting Johnny in the hallway with his usual jovial manner.

"Johnny, welcome home." He strode towards her. "It's wonderful to see you." He took a step back. "Let me look at you. Ah I see you're keeping fit. How're William and Irene?"

Johnny hugged him. "Everyone is doing okay."

"As you see, we are ready to start the holiday festivities." Charles thrust out his chest as they walked back inside the kitchen. The estate was his pride and joy. With love and tender care, he had made his home one of the most prestigious plantation houses on the island.

"William and Irene should come and spend the holidays one year. It would be nice to have your parents and the entire family here for Christmas. After all, it's not like we don't have enough room," Charles continued in his proper British accent. Johnny stared at the dashing figure facing her. Built like an American linebacker, he had the grace and style of a man born to the manor.

"How's business, Uncle Charles?"

Charles shrugged. "It's as good as to be expected in these

economic times." Clara handed him his afternoon cocktail. "Thank you, Clara."

He faced Johnny. "Are you still traveling around with those insane pop stars?

"Yes, I'm still with Naïve. But enough about me, tell me what's happening on the island. I've heard there've been quite a few changes."

Charles took a sip of his cocktail. "There are always changes. You don't expect things to stay the same. If the country wasn't changing, there would be no progress."

"But it appears some changes aren't so good." She watched his facial expression as she leaned against the wall.

"What do you mean?" Charles swiveled the ice in his glass and sat in the breakfast nook. Clara brought a small crystal bucket of ice and a small plate of appetizers to the table.

"I've been getting that impression from Winslow and Mr. Lockwood." She continued to focus on his face. Since Charles was an influential business owner in Barbados, he was in contact with all the political bigwigs. He knew the pulse of the country.

"Oh, Johnny, you should know better than to take Winslow seriously. He will always exaggerate a situation because he wants to impress you." Charles added some more ice to his cocktail as he avoided her stare. "And Lockwood, as I've said before, has used the hyperbole at times"

What is going on? He had never talked about Lockwood or Winslow like this before. Charles was the one person at Flamboyant who liked Winslow because of his solid reputation on the force. And he always bragged about how Lockwood had always been on point since his schoolboy days.

Something wasn't right. Why is he being evasive?

"I better head upstairs to get ready for tonight before Aunt Elizabeth takes off my head."

"Yes, you know how particular your aunt is. By the way, Johnny, don't worry about the politics here." He lifted his glass towards her. "You're on vacation. Barbados will always be Barbados." _Does this attitude have something to do with the envelope Lockwood gave him?_

On the way to her room, Johnny passed the open study door. Lockwood's envelope was on the empty desk. Maybe some of the answers are in there. She entered the room and had just placed her hand on the envelope when a voice behind her said, "Are you looking for something?"

Johnny swiveled to face Charles, smiling at her with the whiskey tumbler still in his hand.

"I was looking for some paper or a pad to jot some notes down."

He strolled over, took one of his company's pads out of the top drawer of his desk, and handed it to her. Then he picked up the envelope.

"Do you need some pens as well?"

"No, this is fine." On her way toward the door, she tried to read the return address on the envelope against his chest, but was unsuccessful. I'll come back later during the party.

****

Outside Johnny's bedroom balcony window, the sun was setting, coloring the sky in a glowing orange. She double-checked her makeup and outfit, ready to be inspected by Barbados's elite.

At the bottom of the steps, she surveyed the guests who had already arrived. All of the usual suspects. Everyone will be busy. Perfect time to look at the envelope. She made a quick turn and headed toward her uncle's office.

Johnny placed her hand on the door handle. It wouldn't move. She stared at the doorknob. *This door has never been locked before.* Without success, she tried to turn it again. Her eyes darted around as she heard her aunt's voice. *Damn it. I can't stay any longer.* She returned to the main party area, determined to get into the office later that evening.

As she entered, a server greeted her with a glass of champagne. Over in one corner, she spotted the Prime Minister, jovial as usual, with his beautiful wife in a gold bias-cut silk crepe dress lying tastefully on her toned body.

On the other side of the room, the famous British actor James Hurley, in a royal blue velvet jacket with a silk ascot and matching pocket square, was talking to Derrick Worth, the British High Commissioner. Hurley spent every Christmas holiday on the island and never missed the Harrington parties.

Johnny moved toward the veranda, greeting the familiar guests. Since the Harringtons' dinner parties were usually buffet-style, they had set the entire veranda with small tables for dining. Each table was laid with white linen tablecloths and small floral centerpieces composed of red anthurium lilies and white poinsettias.

Around every centerpiece were name cards for the seating. Elizabeth was meticulous in the seating arrangements for her parties, so Johnny peeked at the different tables to see with whom and where she would sit.

"Oh, there you are." Elizabeth studied Johnny's linen sheath and Jimmy Choo gold stilettos. "You look beautiful. There are some people I want you to meet, so come along." She took Johnny's hand and pulled her like a child. "And stop trying to peek at the tables." Elizabeth had a mischievous twinkle in her eye. "You know I like everyone's dinner partner to be a surprise until they are seated."

Elizabeth led her across the room.

"This is my niece from New York I've been telling you about," Elizabeth told a group of guests. *Probably the yearly stragglers that Aunt Elizabeth always invited to her parties.* They were usually first-time high-society visitors from London—a fun, eclectic group ranging from friends of the Royal Family to ultra-wealthy people of questionable means.

Sir Landon, who regularly dines at Buckingham Palace, questioned Johnny about how exciting it was to work with such a big music star. No matter their status, they still wanted to know the behind-the-scenes gossip of celebrities. As they chatted, her mind drifted away from the conversation. She gave furtive glances around the room for a viable escape. *I hate this.*

Johnny would rather be at the dentist than continue this conversation. Barbados was her respite from her hectic life, and she didn't want any reminders to break the spell of her tranquility. Her eyes caught sight of another unfamiliar man. *Who is that?* The tall, lean figure with a golden hue emanating from his brown complexion confidently worked the room. He greeted many other guests, so she concluded at least some attendees knew him.

She noticed him working his way around the room and the pleased response of each person he encountered. Definitely a charmer. Heads turned in his direction. Johnny immediately noticed the European-tailored suit made of fine linen as he moved in her direction. *This vacation is becoming more interesting.* Johnny turned to the group and took part in the conversation so he wouldn't notice her observing him. He made his way up to Johnny's cluster.

"Oh Henley, welcome back," said the man to her left. "Good to see you. How long have you been on the island?"

"I arrived yesterday so I could attend a meeting this morning," Henley said. His proper British accent held a tinge of the Barbadian lit.

He faced Johnny with a grin. "I don't believe we've met. My name is Henley."

Lady Stanfield smiled as she pulled Henley into their cluster. "You haven't met? Let me introduce you two. Henley Williams, this is the Harrington's niece, Johnny Harrington, from New York."

He nodded. "Nice to meet you. Did you get here before the Christmas rush?"

Johnny placed her empty flute on a passing waitstaff tray. "I arrived this afternoon from New York."

"So, you're here for the holidays?" asked Henley.

"Yes." *He has a nice smile to go with his suave moves.*

"Henley, can you come here for a moment?" The British High Commissioner summoned him from across the room.

"Will you please excuse me?"

Johnny gave a coy smile. "Why, of course."

Johnny searched for Elizabeth among the guests and pulled her to the side. "Aunt Elizabeth, who is Henley Williams?"

"Yes, Henley, you haven't met him before?" Elizabeth tilted her head. "Adorable, isn't he?"

Johnny shook her head. "You didn't answer the question."

Aunt Elizabeth ran off the information like a human Wikipedia.

"Henley runs Caribbean Airways European division. He lives in London and is unattached."

Johnny rolled her eyes. "I didn't ask about his marital status."

Elizabeth gave a European double cheek kiss to a guest walking by them. "I know, but thought you might be interested in the additional information."

"Is he a Bajan? He sounds very British. But I detect a trace of a West Indian accent."

"He was born in Barbados and moved to England with his parents when he was a child. Henley comes from a distinguished family, but most of his relatives no longer live in Barbados. Is there more information I can give you that you didn't ask for?"

"No, I think that's enough. I'll find out anything else I want to know from the horse's mouth."

"I'm sure you will." Elizabeth smiled, turning to glide towards another person. Johnny mingled with a group of guests but kept Henley in her peripheral vision. In an instant, the stifling scent of lilac encompassed her. *Oh no, she's here.* Her heart raced the same way it had the first time she encountered the odor, as a child trapped in a dark closet. She closed her eyes for a quick moment, then swung around, fully cognizant that Vera was behind her.

Chapter 5

19:30 Flamboyant Estate Barbados

"Hello, Aunt Vera."

"Johnny, you're looking well," said Vera, glassy-eyed with her usual martini glass in hand. Her stilettos were too high, as was the haute couture dress from last season—not quite appropriate for a woman her age. "So nice that you are here for the holidays. Let me look at you." When she stepped back to observe Johnny, she fell backward. Johnny barely caught her before her aunt fell onto a passing server.

"I'm fine." Vera brushed herself off and straightened her dress before placing her arm around Johnny's waist—more for stability than for an embrace.

She addressed the group. "I've known Johnny since she was a little lady. Always a precocious child. Had a memory like an elephant. She could remember every detail in the room." Vera stumbled as she turned toward Johnny. "Do you still have that memory?" Johnny could tell from the powerful stench of alcohol emanating from Vera that this wasn't her first drink.

"I think you should sit down, Aunt Vera. You seem a little tired. Please excuse us," Johnny said as she escorted her aunt out of the party. She found the door to her uncle Charles's office ajar and steered Vera toward the couch. The suffocating scent of her aunt's lilac perfume brought back the shroud of darkness that had surrounded Johnny when Vera locked her in the closet. She closed her eyes for a quick second to rid her mind of the memory.

"Just lie down for a little while, Aunt Vera." She glanced at the desk; it was now bare except for a crystal tumbler left on the side.

"Do you still have that memory?" her aunt repeated, slurring the words.

"Yes, Aunt Vera." Her aunt smiled as she slowly closed her eyes.

She placed a throw over Vera, then moved the strands of gray hair that covered the weary face of a faded beauty. She stared at her aunt with mixed emotions of pity and disgust before leaving the office, closing the door behind her. Pity for a wasted life. Disgust for allowing a man to be the reason.

Johnny returned to the party area, surveying the crowd for Henley as Elizabeth shook her famous dinner bell.

"Dinner is ready," Elizabeth announced. "Will everyone please go to the dining room for the buffet."

Johnny pulled her aside. "I just put Aunt Vera in the office."

Elizabeth shook her head with pursed lips. "Thank you. I'll go check on her in a minute."

After preparing a plate of macaroni pie and stewed chicken, Johnny sat at her assigned seat and began friendly chit-chat with her dining companions when Henley appeared next to the empty chair beside her.

"I believe this is my assigned seat. I was about to get a drink. Can I get you something?"

"Yes, thank you, one of those tropical punches."

Henley returned to the table with the drinks.

Johnny sipped her drink casually as she peered past Henley. "Is this a quick visit for you?"

"About the same time as you," said Henley. "But I have to go to a few meetings while I'm here."

She tilted her head and smiled. "So, you're combining business with pleasure."

"I'm trying to." Henley leaned closer to Johnny. "In fact, you can help me by letting me take you out tomorrow. I have a meeting in the morning, but I'm free in the afternoon."

Johnny smiled. "I like to spend most of my days on the beach, so if you're not a sun and beach lover, I don't think I will make good company for you."

Henley leaned back in his chair. "That's no problem. I know a perfect beach that most people don't know. We could meet at two o'clock."

"That sounds perfect." *He doesn't look like much of a beach person, but it could be an interesting day.*
****

Lockwood checked his office clock in disbelief over the lost time. *Wasn't it only four-thirty a few minutes ago? Now it was after seven o'clock in the evening.* He was expected at the Harringtons' dinner party over an hour ago.

Instead, he was at his desk fixated on the phone, hoping the call he'd been waiting for would come in before he left. His mind continued to go over his conversation with one of his most trusted informants. A big drug shipment was expected to come into the island earlier in the afternoon.

He had his undercover agents in place all day, but they'd seen nothing unusual. He never missed a Harrington party, especially the seasonal holiday events. His absence would arouse unwanted questions. A late appearance would be better than no appearance. Lockwood called his head field agent to get an update on the situation. "Henry, Lockwood here. How's it going out there? Anything yet?"

"Not a thing so far, sir. Everything's quiet."

"I'm heading to the Harringtons' dinner party. If anything happens, call me." Lockwood said.

"No problem, sir. Will do."
****

"It really is a beautiful night," Johnny told Henley as they strolled around the lit pool. "I love when the sky is clear. Lit by the stars. We don't get to see stars in New York City. At least not the ones in the sky." Beaming as she gazed at Henley.

"I can't believe we never ran into each other before tonight. How many years have you been coming to the island?" asked Henley.

"For many years, since I was about eight years old."

"It's so strange that we've missed each other since we seem to know many of the same people."Johnny faced the garden and pulled one flower. "Probably because we come at different times of the year. Do you ever travel to New York?"

"I'm frequently in and out of there. It's a great city. So much to do and see."

"Henley, Johnny, there you two are. We're about to serve dessert," called Elizabeth from across the pool.

"Okay, we'll be right there." Johnny moved toward Henley. "We better go in before she sends out the army for us," she said in a low voice.

They strolled toward the door. Henley stopped Johnny before they entered the main room. "Before we get distracted with other people, I want to make sure we're still on for tomorrow."

"Of course, I'm looking forward to it." Johnny grinned. She peeked at him from under her eyelashes as she joined the other guests. This should be fun.

"Johnny, I can see that you have already partaken of some of Barbados's sun this afternoon. You don't waste any time, do you?" Lockwood shook Henley's hand. "Nice to have you back again, Henley. Are you here for business or pleasure?"

Henley focused his gaze on her. "Hopefully both, with some help from Johnny."

"It's the holidays, you should make some time to relax."

Johnny redirected the conversation. "How's Mrs. Lockwood? I didn't see her with you."

"Oh, you know my wife. She doesn't like the social circuit."

"Of course," Johnny said. She's probably not feeling well again. For years Madeleine Lockwood's mental illness had been something Lockwood tried to keep a secret on the small island.

"I would love to drop by to see her before I leave["

Lockwood nodded. "She loves talking to you."

Charles Harrington jaunted towards the group. "Glad you made it, Lockwood. We were wondering where you were."

Lockwood gave Charles a friendly tap on his back. "I had to finish some work before I left the office."

The silent vibration of his phone made him remove it from his pocket. Henry's number flashed on the screen.

"Please excuse me; I need to take this call." He rushed to the library, hoping this was the call he's been waiting for all evening.

"Lockwood here."

"Mr. Lockwood, this is Henry. You need to come down to McCullers Cove immediately."

Lockwood heard ocean waves in the background. "What's going on?"

"I feel you should see for yourself."

"Okay, I'm leaving now." Lockwood hurried back to the party already dreading the excuse he would use to remove any suspicion for his abrupt departure.

Chapter 6

20:35 Flamboyant Estate Barbados

"Oh, there you are. We missed you earlier tonight." Elizabeth took Lockwood's arm and led him to the main drawing room.

Lockwood stopped. "Elizabeth, I'm sorry, but something has come up at home I have to attend to, so I need to leave."

"Is Madeleine all right?" Elizabeth whispered to Lockwood with a sympathetic gaze.

"She's doing fine, but sometimes----well, you know----she gets a little edgy," said Lockwood.

"Of course, I understand. Please give her my love.

****

Lockwood sped along the winding roads. *What did Henry find?* McCullers Cove's beautiful stretch of beach on the island's west coast was one of Lockwood's favorite spots. The calm sea waves hitting the shore serenaded him as he drove fast on the dark and dangerous roads, guided only by the headlights of his car through the labyrinth of cane fields. As he drew closer to the beach, the headlights from the police vehicles blinded him. Lockwood parked his car and located Henry.

"What's happening here?" Lockwood asked.

"It's over here," Henry led him to a cave.

The cave at McCuller's Cove was a small inlet that many Bajan lovers claimed as their own. Memories of illicit pleasures returned as Lockwood lowered his head to enter the opening. When he squinted to adjust to the darkness, he saw a body lying on the sandy ground—it was the informant who had given him the drug shipment tip.

He moved next to the CSI officer. "How long has he been dead?"

"Probably about twelve hours." The officer removed his disposable gloves. "It seems they hit him in the head from behind. There's no sign of a struggle, but there are also bruises around the neck."

"Mr. Lockwood, look at these." Henry pointed toward some markings on the ground. "Since the tide was low, water hasn't entered the cave to remove them. It looks to me as though a small fishing boat was in here. You can see that somebody dragged the boat out of the cave."

"Probably to sail to a bigger getaway boat. Our men would never have suspected a small Moses." Lockwood bent down to inspect the markings in the sand. "There are hundreds of Moses with fishermen in them all day and night. We don't have enough men to search everyone. They are taking over our island."

Lockwood's eyes narrowed. "Maybe someone who knew Dalton gave us the tip and killed him." He stood up and went over to look out of the cave before returning to Henry. "I want to keep this out of the press until we've done more investigation. Did Dalton have any relatives on the island?"

"Only an aunt. The rest of the family lives in England. They sent him here to get away from his druggie friends in London." Henry sighed. "Isn't it ironic?"

Lockwood's brows furrowed. "Well, we don't want his aunt to know about his involvement with drug dealers. Let's say we found his body washed up on shore." He paused. "Tell her the department will investigate and pay for a proper funeral. That should ease some of her questions."

"Yes, sir."

Lockwood turned to exit the cave but stopped to take one last look at the body. *Dalton had gotten into a little trouble now and then, but he didn't deserve to die like that.*

****

Johnny walked the grounds of Flamboyant while the guests danced under the moonlight. She wanted to savor the cool Caribbean air. The colorful Christmas lights drew her toward the street, and she meandered along the gravel by the front entrance. Perched on a hill, Flamboyant offered Johnny a panoramic view of the island below and the clear, starry sky above. The serene chorus of cicadas was suddenly interrupted by the explosive roar of a motorbike. She spun around. Winslow.

He took off his helmet and squinted as he gave Johnny a hard smile. "Tired of the party already?"

"No, it's a lovely party. I just needed to get some fresh air." She knew Winslow could see right through her with his unsettling x-ray perception. It sometimes annoyed her. She hated the idea that he could read her happiness—or lack thereof—better than she could. He shouldn't have that ability, but he did. And it scared her.

Winslow leaned on his bike. "You should have sneaked away like I asked you to. We could be at Paradise Beach right now, watching the waves."

Johnny sniffed, stepping away from the bike. "Don't be silly. Why would I want to miss one of the biggest social events of the year to lie on the sand?"

Winslow folded his arms and shook his head. "I don't understand why you keep running away."

"I'm not running away. In fact, I'm standing right here talking to you."

He moved toward her. "You're not running away physically, but mentally, you're running with the speed of a panther, trying with all your effort to pull your soul from me." His gaze pierced her under the star-filled night sky.

"My soul belongs to me. I'm the only one who decides where it stays," Johnny snapped. Almost immediately, she regretted her harsh tone. "I'm sure you didn't come over here to argue with me."

"No, I didn't. In fact, I'm here to see Mr. Lockwood."

Johnny glided her hand over the bike as she passed along the side. "He left about twenty minutes ago."

Winslow jumped back on his bike. "Do you know where he went?"

"I think he told my aunt he had to go home because of Mrs. Lockwood."

"I've got to go, but I'll call you tomorrow." He started the motor and rode away. Johnny watched the motorbike disappear downhill. *Why is he in such a rush? That's not like him.*

The same nagging feeling that had surfaced earlier with Lockwood and her uncle returned, persistent and unwelcome. Johnny shook it off and turned back toward the party, the lively music and laughter calling her away from her thoughts.

****

Winslow called into headquarters and drove straight to McCullers Cove after leaving Johnny. *Lockwood probably got the tip!*

"What happened here?" Winslow asked Lockwood as he watched the attendants put a body into the ambulance.

"It's Dalton Thomson. Hit from behind. He was left in the cave. We found markings from a small fisherman's moses."

"I have a feeling someone knew he gave us a tip. Damn." Winslow shook his head. "I'm the one who convinced Dalton to give us information. He wanted to turn his life around." Winslow clenched his jaw as he closed his eyes. "He wouldn't be here if it wasn't for me."

"It's not your fault. Dalton made friends with some dangerous characters. He knew the consequences. It was his decision. If he hadn't made it that decision, he still might have ended up this way."

Winslow narrowed his eyes. "I'm just as guilty as his killers."

Lockwood pulled him away from the other officers. "Winslow, last time I talked to Dalton, he said he was on to something big. Some tips from London. This is much bigger than we think. They probably used the moses in the cave as an inconspicuous getaway vessel to take the person or persons away from the scene."

Winslow shook his head. "He had to know whoever it was. He wouldn't come here alone to meet someone he didn't know."

"I consider you one of my best officers, Winslow," Lockwood said. "You'll probably be Commissioner one day. You're someone I trust. This investigation needs to be a priority. Top secret. Whoever killed Dalton is our link to the drug shipments coming onto the island."

Winslow veered his face away. *I have to find his killer.* Watched the waves with their whitecaps gleaming by the moonlight. A single tear streamed down his face. "He was my half-brother."

Chapter 7

13:30 Flamboyant Estate Barbados

Slivers of sunshine streamed through the wooden slats of the window shutters, softly awakening Johnny from her restful sleep. She rolled over to check the time. It was one thirty. She had overslept. Johnny jumped up and hurried to get ready for her two o'clock date with Henley.

"Good afternoon Ms. Harrington. You woke up later than your usual time," said Clara.

Johnny poured herself a glass of water before sitting at the table. "I was up pretty late at the party."

"Well, as long as you slept well." Clara placed a table setting in front of Johnny. "Can I get you some breakfast?"

"I'll have some tea and a few of your delicious pumpkin fritters."

"How did you know I made pumpkin fritters?" asked Clara with a snicker.

"When have you not made fritters for my first breakfast at Flamboyant?"

"Do you want some eggs and ham with the fritters? Don't tell me you're watching your weight because you're always the same petite size."

Johnny glanced at the kitchen clock. "I'm running a little late. Someone is picking me up at two, so I'll have the pumpkin fritters and tea."

Clara waved her arm. "Uh, whoever it is, will probably be late. You know how Bajans are with time." Johnny ate breakfast while she gave Clara the latest gossip from the previous night's party.

"Good afternoon, Ms. Johnny. Mr. Henley is waiting for you in the library," said Leonard as he entered the kitchen.

"Thank you, Leonard. Can you please tell him I'll be there in a couple of minutes?" Johnny raised her eyebrow towards Clara with a crisp nod.

"Um, if he is a Bajan, he must have lived overseas for many years to become so timely," Clara said with a deep, singsong Bajan accent.

"You are right about that. He lives in London now. So, I will give you that."

Clara lifted her head with confidence. "I know what I'm talking 'bout."

Johnny took her last bite before getting up. "I better run upstairs. I don't want him to think I run on Bajan time."

****

"Ms. Johnny says she'll be with you in a little while," Leonard informed Henley as he stopped by the library's entrance.

"Thank you." Henley ambled over to the bookshelves and surveyed the selection: Brontë, Melville, Dickens, all leather-bound with gold leaf edges. Henley loved this type of room—the dark wood paneling, the burgundy leather armchairs, and the massive mahogany desk. Charles had decorated the space as though he'd transported the furnishings directly from an old English men's club.

"I hope I haven't kept you waiting too long." Henley turned as Johnny approached, her coils bouncing lightly around her head. Her colorful sarong skirt accentuated her shapely figure, and her gold metallic bathing suit shimmered against her mahogany-brown skin.

"No, it hasn't been that long. I love waiting in this room, looking over Charles's collection of the classics. Are you ready?"

"Yes. I've got my suntan lotion and sunglasses, so I'm ready for an interesting day at the beach. After all, you promised to show me some beaches even the locals aren't familiar with," Johnny said, raising an eyebrow and pursing her lips.

"And I plan to live up to my promises. So, I think we should be on our way."

Johnny's face lit up as she spotted the shiny red mini-moke parked outside, its convertible top down. *The perfect ride! I hope Aunt Elizabeth isn't looking out the window.*

Henley's expression grew serious as he opened the door. "I hope you don't mind, but I rented a mini-moke for our expedition. Although some people frown on them, they're the best vehicles for navigating the country's back roads."

"I've always wanted to ride in one of these. Now I'm finally going to get my chance. But let's hurry before my aunt sees us. She would have a fit." Johnny laughed as she jumped into the mini-moke.

"I thought for our first stop we should visit Mullins Bay in St. Peter's. It's one of my favorite beaches. Have you ever been there?" Henley asked as they drove off.

"Yes, it is lovely, but hardly an unknown beach," Johnny teased.

Henley tilted his head and grinned. "The day is still young."

As they left the parish of St. James, Johnny admired the roadside view of some of the island's most luxurious and elegant hotels. Henley eventually parked the mini-moke to the side of the road, and they walked onto the white sandy beach toward Mullins Beach Bar, a quaint wooden house on stilts.

"Would you like something to drink?" Henley asked.

"No, I'm heading into the water, but you can get something while I go for a swim."

Henley's eyes lingered on her as she dropped her sarong to the sand and ran into the water. The sunlight danced off her metallic swimsuit, making her look like a golden mermaid surrounded by a brilliant light. Johnny swam gracefully, her movements fluid and natural, each stroke mesmerizing Henley.

When she emerged from the water, she rushed over to him, water dripping from her hair and glistening on her skin. "Aren't you coming in? The water is lovely. I love to swim at this time of day when it's not too hot or too cold."

Henley leaned back, a sly smile on his face. "I've been enjoying the view."

Johnny glanced around. "Which view?"

"Why, you, of course. Do you always cause such a sensation when you go swimming?"

She patted herself dry with a towel. "I don't know what you're talking about, but I do know you're missing a wonderful swim."

Henley rose and took the towel to dry her back. "Well, I think we should start heading to the next beach. After all, I have to live up to my promise."

As they drove deeper into the countryside, the scenery changed to miles of cane fields full of golden stalks waiting to be harvested. Scattered among them were wooden chattel houses painted pink and gray. The mini-moke rocked and jolted as it navigated the gravel roads, the occasional hole causing Johnny to grip the side handle tightly.

"You're right about the mini-moke being the best car for this trip," Johnny said, laughing. "I don't think regular cars could survive these roads."

Henley battled to keep control of the vehicle. "I'm sorry about the bumps, but after heavy rainfall, these country roads wash away. We'll hit the East Coast Road soon—it's smoother than this."

When they reached the East Coast Road, the ride leveled out, and Johnny took in the breathtaking view of the turbulent Atlantic Ocean. Savage waves crashed dramatically against the rugged Bathsheba coast, a stark contrast to the tranquil waters of the island's west side.

"Can we stop along this beach?" Johnny asked, her eyes fixed on the water.

"This isn't a good place to swim."

"I just want to sit for a while and watch the sea."

"There's a perfect spot a mile ahead. I've made lunch reservations at the Atlantis Hotel," Henley said.

She cocked her head. "Is that old hotel still around? Their restaurant's reputation for authentic Bajan food is world-renowned."

"Yes, it's still around. Here's a perfect spot to enjoy the coastline." Henley parked the mini-moke and retrieved a blanket from the trunk.

"You've thought of everything, haven't you?" Johnny teased.

Henley leaned in, smiling. "I told you I was going to promise you a perfect beach day."

Right away, Johnny noticed the stark difference between Bathsheba and the west coast beaches. She lay on the blanket, her gaze fixed on the waves. Her damp coils blew away from her face in the sea breeze. Henley studied her as she stared in serene reverie, the setting transforming her into a beautiful, living Botticelli statue against the backdrop of the wild ocean.

He laid down beside her. "A penny for your thoughts."

Without facing him, she replied, "You can save your money."

"Well, something must be behind that contented look."

"It's the sea. It's the only thing in this world that can soothe my soul." She rolled over to him with a perplexed look. "You know the sea is an oxymoron. Although it is a stable force, it changes every day."

He rested on one elbow, facing her. "Is that also a sign of your personality?"

"I don't know; maybe it is." Johnny traced a finger along the sand. "I guess the best answer to that question would come from the people who know me."

"Or the special person who knows you best?"

"There isn't a special person, but many special people in my life." Johnny sat up and gazed down at Henley. "Does that help to answer your question?"

Henley placed his hands behind his head. "What question?"

"The not too-subtle one about my romantic relationships."

He sat up. Lowered his eyes, with his chin dipping down. "I didn't think I was being obvious."

"Since we're touching on personal relationships, how about you?" She faced him with a twinkle. "Is there someone special in your life?

"No, I don't have the time to devote to a relationship. My work keeps me pretty busy."

"What is your line of work?"

"I'm sure your aunt gave you the information already, hasn't she?"

"What makes you think that?" Johnny raised an eyebrow. The corner of her lip tilted up. "Are you so conceited, Mr. Williams, that you think people sit around and talk about you?"

"No, but I know Bajans, and they are thorough gossips. You probably asked your aunt about me at the party because I asked one guest about you."

She bent back on her elbows. "Oh, you did, and what did you find out?"

"I was told that you live a glamorous lifestyle, traveling around with a pop star as his publicist. You're also known to drive half of Barbados's male population crazy."

"The first part of your information is true, but I would have to say the second part is quite exaggerated," said Johnny as she laughed.

Henley focused his eyes on her. "Well, I can see why people would believe the rumors." She rotated her eyes to the horizon. "Well, I learned you're the head of the Caribbean Airways European division, and you come from a family with a prominent background who moved to England when you were a boy."

"Your facts are all correct. You found out quite a lot of information for someone who doesn't spend their time discussing another person," Henley said with a chuckle.

Johnny faced Henley and nodded. "Touché."

Time flew by as they talked about all the different European places; they both had visited and their favorite haunts.

"We've been talking for a long time, and it's almost time for our lunch reservations. Did you bring a change of clothes?"

"Yes, they're in the car, but where would I change?"

Henley rose and stretched out his hand. "I have a friend who lives down the road. I told him I would be in the area, so he's expecting me to drop by. We can shower and change there."

Chapter 8

14:30 East Coast Highway Barbados

They drove off the East Coast highway and onto a narrow side lane that led to a palm-lined road. After about a mile on the road, Johnny viewed a plantation house on a hill. The circular courtyard led to a two-story white brick edifice. At the side of the house, she caught sight of a small building attached to the main house.

A chill went down her spine from the thoughts of slaves cooking in the smaller edifice. On the staircase to the house, Johnny noticed the pineapple sculpture on the banister's head. Only a few of the original plantation houses still had the pineapple.

She remembered how her uncle told her about this ancient symbol of Barbados' original aristocracy. It was a sign of welcome and wealth. The wide brick staircase ended at an arched opening towards the verandah. A young servant opened the door.

Henley greeted him with a smile. "Good afternoon. Could you please tell Mr. Ashton that Henley is here? He's expecting me." Johnny surveyed the house furnished with the usual colonial- style furniture. *Definitely not part of the nouveau riche, but they spent money to preserve this house.*

"Henley, my boy. How are you?" A tall, stout man approached them. Then faced Johnny. "And who is this beautiful young lady?"

"Nice to see you, Howard," said Henley as they embraced. "This is Ms. Johnny Harrington, a friend of mine who's visiting from the States. Johnny, this is Howard Ashton, a dear old friend of my family."

"I think we met many years ago when you were a teenager at your Uncle Charles' house. It's a pleasure after so many years," said Howard as he kissed Johnny's hand.

Johnny took a step back. "I'm surprised that you remember me. It's been so long."

"I don't want to be rude, but I know I told you I'd drop by since I was going to be in the area. The truth of the matter is that we can't stay. We have reservations at the Atlantis, so we need the use of your house to change," said Henley apologetically.

"No problem, you know you are family. I'll have Edward show Ms. Johnny to the guest suite. You and I can talk before you change. We'll have time since women usually take a while to get ready," said Ashton as he winked at Johnny. "Edward will help her with anything that she may need."

"I won't take very long," said Johnny, as they led her away.

"Don't rush. I want a minute to talk to Henley. After all, we don't see each other that often." Ashton smiled at Johnny as he closed the door behind her.

"Would you like a drink?" asked Ashton as he poured himself one.

Henley sat in one of the big high-back chairs. "No, thanks."

Ashton laid back against the mahogany desk. "How's the family?"

Henley fiddled with the paperweight on the stand next to him. "They're all fine."

"How's business?" Ashton inquired.

"Expanding and doing well. Especially the European/Caribbean route.".

Ashton's tone turned from jovial to serious. "That route is vital to this island. We must do whatever it takes to hold on to it."

"Don't worry, there've been a few problems, but we're correcting the situation."

Ashton ambled behind the mahogany cane back seat, glared out the window. "Barbados is the most important hub to the region and Europe. We can't have any problems, minute or otherwise, which would place this area at risk." He pivoted to face Henley. "You have a promising career, Henley. I have complete confidence in you. I'm sure you wouldn't let the family down."

Ashton halted the conversation. His genial manner returned as he rotated toward the opening door. Johnny entered wearing a short white halter dress and gold flat thong sandals.

His face lit up. "My dear, you look lovely. Henley is lucky to have such a beautiful luncheon companion. I don't blame him for cutting our afternoon visit short."

Henley rose from his chair. "I'll give you a few minutes to pursue one of your favorite pastimes----flirting with young ladies while I change."

"I'll be only a few minutes," Henley whispered to Johnny with a wink before he left the room.

Ashton walked over to the bar stand. "Would you like a glass of wine, my dear?"

She relaxed on the settee. "Yes, thank you."

"I hope Henley hasn't left you with the wrong impression of me. I'm quite harmless, but I am a true aesthete." Ashton sat next to Johnny and handed her the glass of wine.

"I think you're charming, Mr. Ashton."

"Oh, please don't make me feel older than I am. Call me Howard."

Johnny raised her wineglass to him. "Okay, Howard."

"Now, tell me how Henley was lucky enough to meet you."

Johnny took a sip of her wine. "We met last night at Flamboyant during my aunt and uncle's party."

Ashton nodded. "They invited me, but I had some unexpected business that had to be taken care of right away. Too bad, or maybe I could have given Henley a little competition." Ashton bent toward Johnny. "I say a little because if I were younger, he wouldn't have a chance."

Never allowing an opportunity to flirt past her, Johnny said, "I think you still could give Henley a run for his money."

"You're kind and beautiful. That seems to be quite a rare combination these days." Henley walked into the room wearing white linen pants, a white batiste shirt, and noticed how Johnny had already completely charmed Ashton.

He smiled to himself. "Well, I see I'm back just in time before I lose my date."

"See, I told you not to underestimate yourself." Johnny smiled at him as she rose from the seat.

"Henley, you must bring her back for a longer visit," Ashton said as they walked to the door.

He kissed her hand. "You're quite an enchanting young lady. Please come back again."

Johnny kissed him on his cheek. "Thank you for your invitation. It was a pleasure seeing you again after so many years."

As Johnny got into the mini-mote, Henley sidled over to Ashton. "I'll call you during the week with any update." Ashton's eyes turned to stone. "Make sure you do." They drove off as a vintage Aston Martin car approached the house. Johnny swiveled around, observed a man getting out of the car, and Ashton greeting him before they entered the house.

Chapter 9

15:00 St. Joesph Barbados

"We're so close to the Atlantis. What do you say we take the local road, heading back to the East Coast highway, instead? That way, we'll see more of the countryside," Henley said.

Johnny shrugged. "You're the entertainment director today, so I'm in your charge."

They sped on, enjoying the scenery of the rocky shores. Colorful wooden chattel houses built at the mouth of the gully. The abundance of tropical trees surrounding the homes. Orange, mango, coconut with their intoxicating perfume from ripened fruits permeating the hot tropical air.

"Hold on. The road is rocky." Henley took control of the minimote like a rodeo cowboy riding a steer. At last, the Atlantis hotel came into view.

"That's quite a ride." Johnny's face flushed.

"Just think of it as an unusual local apértif,"

They parked, exited the car and immediately greeted with a heaping glass of sweet-smelling rum punch at the entrance.

"Wow, this is nice," Johnny took a sip.

"Good afternoon Mr. Williams. Welcome back. May I direct you to a table?"

"Thanks George, glad to be back." Henley smiles.

He led them to their seats, Johnny surveying the restaurant as they went. It had a distinct 60s era flavor to it, white oval-back chairs pushed under green felt card tables, with the black coral fans adorning the walls alongside worn fishers's nets.

They approached a wall partition with a huge orifice where the diners viewed the sea.

"One of our best tables," the server comments. The outside balcony surrounded the entire building.

"The view from this hill is beautiful." Johnny pointed toward the shore. "Those two massive rocks where the waves constantly crash... like mother nature's own sculpture."

The server approached the table, and Henley turned to Johnny. "Do you mind if I order for you? For someone visiting after a long absence, the Atlantis Special with Chardonnay is the perfect dish. It gives you a sample of several authentic Barbados cuisines."

She nodded. "Like I said, you're the director today."

The server returned to the table. "Two Atlantis Specials and two glasses of your best Chardonnay."

Johnny shot him a coy glance. "Are you trying to get me drunk? First the punch, now you're ordering wine."

Henley's eyes darted toward his silenced cellphone as it lit up. "If I were trying to get you drunk, I would have ordered an entire bottle. Just trying to give you the taste of the area and an exquisite Chardonnay to go with it."

He nodded; eyes focused over Johnny's shoulder. "Can you excuse me for a minute?"

"Sure." Johnny's eyes followed Henley. He walked over to another table, where he shook a man's hand. Johnny noticed Henley's phone flashed, then turned dark. She slid her hand across the table, keeping her eyes fixed on Henley, and touched the dark phone. The face illuminated, revealing a pineapple background with a blue message tab on the screen. Johnny leaned forward and peered at the phone, trying to read the message.

In her peripheral, Henley was returning to the table. She leaned back, hoping the phone would darken before he reached her.

"I'm sorry about that, but business sometimes interrupts when you least expect it."

"Yeah, I definitely can relate." She stared into her glass and swirled the straw in her rum punch. "But you can make it up. You still haven't told me much about yourself."

Henley smiled. "I thought you found out most of what you wanted to know from your aunt."

"Just the basic facts, not the tantalizing details. You've told me the different places you've visited, but not anything about yourself."

Henley sipped his drink. "There isn't that much to tell."

"I can't believe that a worldly man like yourself doesn't have a fascinating story."

Johnny tucked into her fried flying fish with pickled breadfruit, rice and peas, while she tried to learn more about Henley covertly. She cocked her head to the side, focused on him, as she slowly slid the rum punch cherry from the toothpick into her mouth.

"Where did you say you live in London?"

"I didn't say. I'm hardly in my flat. Heathrow is more of my home."

"But you must have some favorite restaurants. You don't seem to be one to cook at home." Johnny knew his type. *He probably has an expense account with a tab at some of the trendy restaurants in London.* If he picked one of the usual ones, she knew most of the maître d's and could get the inside scoop.

Henley's eyes fixated on Johnny's lips, toying around the cherry's left-over toothpick.

He grinned. "I make a mean pilaf. You seemed to have enjoyed the rum punch. Let me order you another one." He waved the server over.

"No, no. This is really enough." The server was at the table before she said the second no.

"Are you sure?"

Johnny raised her head to the server. "No, thank you. Nothing else."

When the meal ended, she knew as much about Henley as when she started

****

"Mr. Lockwood, we assembled everyone in the conference room for the meeting. Anything else you need?" asked Ms. Braithwaite.

"Thank you, Ms. Braithwaite, but that will be all for now." Lockwood called a meeting to inform his head officers of the importance of tightening the foot and horse patrol on the beaches. *I don't want any suspicion about Dalton's death.* He entered the conference room with a determined face to fool the men he had trained to detect deceit and lies.

Lockwood stood in front of the seated audience. "Good afternoon, gentlemen. As you know, we found a body last night in McCuller's Cove. We must step up security on the beaches." He pointed to the Barbados map on the wall. "Tourism is the bloodline of our economy. We can't have dead bodies turning up in caves around our beaches. This is endangering our primary industry." Lockwood folded his arms behind his back. "We've tried our best to keep the press at bay while investigating this murder. There must be twenty-four-hour shifts on the beaches. I immediately canceled all vacations."

"But sir, many of the officers have made plans with their families," an officer pleaded.

"This is our busiest tourist season, and our guests must be able to feel safe and if that means we must make sacrifices, then we must.

Are there any more questions?" The sullen faces were silent. "Then that's all."

Lockwood watched his head officers dispersed from the room. *Could one of them possibly be a mole?* He handpicked most of them. He was there when they brought a new life into the world and held them when one left. Did one of them betrayed him? The thought rankled him. After all, being a member of the force was one of the plum positions on the island. Lockwood's mind returned to the days when the elite officer corps comprised only white upper-class Englishmen.

He turned and stared at the portrait of the first Black Barbadian who became part of the officers' corp. It was a big event on the island. Hedley Jones is in Barbados's history. There is even a street named after him in Bridgetown. Again, he understood life is not the same as it used to be in Barbados.

Lockwood walked out of his office. "Ms. Braithwaite, I'm going out."

She peered over her glasses. "But you have another appointment in an hour."

He peeked over his shoulder as he strode out the door. "I'll be back in plenty of time."

Lockwood took a drive on the new highway up the West Coast and then diverted into the hinterlands by some of the cane fields. His journey ended at one of the local rum shops. A small wooden shack hugging a tidy home.

His eyes and ears consumed the daily activities of one of the island's ubiquitous establishments. Gossip sputtered out of the patron's mouths as the buttery cheese cutter sandwiches entered. A young boy lugged bags almost equal to his weight, overflowed with plantains, yams, and palm oil, on its way to a grandparent. And of course, the main revenue - sturdy drinking glasses lined up like soldiers dressed in the amber liquid the island is famous for.

He walked up to the door-less wooden shack and said to the proprietor,

"A Banks beer please."

"Ya wanna glass to drink it ere or ya takin it wit ya," she asked in the country Bajan singsong accent. Lockwood returned to his native melodic vernacular and replied,

"I'll take da bottle and drink it ere." Lockwood fitted in perfectly with his native cotton business executives's shirt, known locally as a shirtjack. He quietly absorbed the surrounding political conversations. Since Lockwood was a frequent visitor to the various rum shops, he received the same treatment as any of the regulars.

He swigged his beer and heard the rumble of an approaching motorbike. It became louder before it stopped right behind him. He turned and watched the driver stop and dismount from the bike. The opaque black helmet covering the driver's head made his face indiscernible as he approached the bar.

"Hello Mr. Lockwood." A mumbled sound comes from the helmet as it is being removed.

"Hello my boy, what brings you to these parts of the island?" Lockwood asked Winslow.

"I usually like the peace of the countryside." Winslow scanned the area. "It reminds me of the Barbados I knew of when I was a schoolboy."

"Yes, the countryside still has a lot of the old charm. It even reminds me of my schoolboy days and believe me, that's many donkey years," said Lockwood as they both laugh at the old Barbados term. Lockwood waved his hand toward him. "Take a seat. Would you like to have a beer?"

"Sure." He sat on a stool next to Lockwood. The surrounding patrons were oblivious to Lockwood and Winslow as they spent the next twenty minutes bantering back and forth.

Lockwood rose. "I have to run back to the office for my next meeting." Winslow and Lockwood continued their congenial conversation as they sauntered to his car.

As soon as they were beyond the earshot of the other patrons,

Lockwood faced Winslow. "This is the plan. You're going to be fired by me because of insubordination. The cause will be your continuous contempt for the way the Thomas investigation is being handled. After the firing, you'll let people know how you despise the police force. Talk about how you are looking to revenge the way they dealt with your half-brother. Hopefully, this will invite the people we are trying to find to welcome you into their circle."

Lockwood turned and stared beyond him. "But I must warn you I cannot help you if you run into trouble. I'll have to denounce you to the force in order for your undercover role to be believable. You can keep in contact with me on Ms. Braithwaite's line. She's the one person I know I can trust on the force."

He handed the number to Winslow. "Memorize the number and throw it away before you leave. I suggest you call me from burner cellphones and call between three and four in the afternoon when most of the staff are out of the office."

Lockwood leaned closer to Winslow. "You will use the code name Spider. Ms. Braithwaite and I will be the only people to know your identity. I suggest you tell no one about this assignment, not even relatives. Barbados is a small country and there are too many ears on too many walls." He stepped back from Winslow. "You're not obligated to take this assignment. It will be very dangerous and you will not have the back-up of the force."

Winslow's stern face stared straight ahead. "When can I get started?"

"We can start as soon as I return to the office."

Lockwood squinted at his watch. "Meet me back at headquarters in about an hour." He smiled. "That's a good time for you to burst into my meeting with your insubordination."

"I'll be there."

"Good luck," mumbled Lockwood under his breath. He watched Winslow ride away, hoping he wasn't sacrificing one of his best men.

Chapter 10

16:00 Atlantis Restaurant Barbados

Johnny finished the last piece of her coconut pie and gazed at the crashing waves below the balcony.

"Did you enjoy the meal?" asked Henley. "It was delicious. Everything was delicious. You were right about the wine. It was exceptional."

Henley's face lit up with a smile. "Glad you enjoyed it, but I still have to fulfill my promise to take you to a beach that is very exclusive."

"I didn't think that you still planned to follow through."

"You'll see I always follow through on my word", said Henley as he signaled the server for the check.

"The beach is on the East coast so I'll take the highway instead of the local roads. It will save us some time. I would really like you to see this beach before the sun sets."

The mini-mote hugged the narrow roads as they entered the parish of St. Peter and turned into an even smaller winding road.

Johnny surveyed the unknown area. "I didn't know this road existed here. It's so close to McCuller's Cove. How could I have missed it?"

"There aren't too many people who know this area, not even the natives." At the tip of the winding road, they came to a dead end.

"Let's get out here. The walk is steep," Henley said, stepping out of the mini-moke.

Johnny glanced around but didn't see anywhere obvious to go. Henley walked to the edge of the hill and began descending a narrow path. "Be careful," he cautioned, extending his hand toward her. She hesitated before taking it, letting him guide her down the precipitous walkway.

At the bottom, the view opened up to a hidden inlet from the ocean, surrounded by a dramatic fjord. The rocks, covered in frangipani and vibrant bougainvillea, cascaded down the walls like a natural masterpiece. Johnny gasped at the breathtaking scene, almost stumbling into Henley's arms.

Their eyes met, and she felt a warm surge ripple through her body. The pounding of her heart seemed so loud it drowned out the other sounds of the beach—the gentle lapping of the water, the distant chirping of birds. For a moment, she could only feel the rhythm of her heartbeat and the intensity of his gaze.

She gently pulled away and smiled awkwardly. "Thanks for saving me from a nasty fall." Turning away, Johnny sat on a nearby rock, hoping he didn't notice how flustered she had become.

Henley stood behind her, sensing her unease. "So, what do you think about the view?" he asked softly.

"It's magnificent," Johnny replied, her eyes fixed on the horizon. The sky was awash in the orange glow of the setting sun, its light illuminating the walls of the fjord in fiery hues. The scene was so serene, so otherworldly, it felt like a moment suspended in time.

They sat quietly, both succumbing to the magnificence of nature's surreal hour. Henley finally broke the silence. "I wish we could stay longer, but once the sun touches the horizon, it descends quickly. We'll be in total darkness climbing back up the hill."

Reluctantly, Johnny stood as Henley took her hand again, guiding her back up the path. When they reached the car, he asked, "I hope I didn't disappoint you with my beach itinerary today?"

Johnny shook her head and smiled. "Not at all. It was wonderful."

As they drove back to Flamboyant, the atmosphere in the mini-moke was quiet but companionable. They both admired the Christmas lights flickering on as dusk turned to night, illuminating the charming houses they passed. The silence between them wasn't awkward; it was the kind that spoke of mutual contentment.

When the mini-moke pulled up to Flamboyant's entrance, Johnny leaned against the car door. "I had a wonderful day. You make an excellent entertainment director," she teased. "I would definitely recommend you for the job."

Henley leaned toward her, a glint of humor in his eye. "Would my recommendation be good enough to spend time with you again?"

"Definitely," Johnny replied with a coy smile.

"I'll call you tomorrow. I have meetings during the day, but please keep the evening hours open."

"I'll try," Johnny said, her grin widening as she walked toward the house.

Henley watched her retreating figure for a moment before starting the car. *Definitely a different modus operandi,* he thought as he drove away, already anticipating their next encounter.

###############

Winslow rode his motorbike swiftly on the Princess Highway. His mind flashed back to the day's events. Lockwood's plan seemed to start out perfectly. His truculent interruption of Lockwood's meeting seemed to convince everyone that he deserved to be fired. After all, he smiled to himself, no one in the force would ever dare accuse Lockwood of carrying out an incompetent investigation. Yes, he thought as the cool evening wind blew against his body; he did a fine acting job, but now, he better get to the Harrington's house to talk to Johnny.

This will not be a simple job. I can't possibly tell her the truth.

Even though he trusts her, this job is too crucial and too dangerous for her to know the facts. He could never risk her life. But he definitely had to tell her something. *Since Lockwood is a friend of the family, he might just tell her about the termination.* Winslow felt he had to deflect some of the negativity from the rumors. Johnny would surely ask a lot of questions. It would be better for him to talk to her first. His bike stopped in Flamboyant's graveled courtyard.

"Good night. Is Johnny in?" Winslow asks Clara.

"Come inside and I'll see if she's upstairs."

Winslow sat on one of the rattan chairs. "I'll wait on the verandah."

"Suit yourself," replied Clara tersely. She never approved of Johnny hanging around with Winslow. He seemed well mannered but in the strict social code of Barbados, he would never do as a proper suitor. Johnny was a little girl when she first visited the Harrington's and Clara fell in love with the rambunctious and precocious child.

Clara remembered being a little worried when Winslow and Johnny seemed to get too close for her comfort. She smiled to herself as she thought of Henley. Now, Johnny's attentions are being directed to a more suitable candidate.

Winslow leaned back and gazed out at the view. He always felt more comfortable on the Harrington's verandah than in their sitting room. *It's just like sitting in a museum exhibit. You're afraid of breaking something.* He had some of his best conversations, he remembered, sitting with Johnny on the verandah until the early morning. This is where they became so close, he could feel her soul become part of him.

"Winslow, where are you.?" He heard Johnny's voice pulling him out of his deep thoughts. "What? Why are you asking me that question?"

"Well, you certainly weren't here. I called your name twice before you answered me. She tilted her head and squinted at

Winslow. Is there anything wrong?" Johnny watched his tall, wry frame move close to her.

"I'm all right," he told her, but his dark, fine-featured face betrayed his words.

"Well, I don't believe you. Something is wrong."

"The only thing that's wrong is I haven't heard from you. I'm gonna make sure I get you to spend time with me." He took her hand. "Just push all those other guys to the side for a day. I have my boat fixed. We could go sailing tomorrow."

Johnny couldn't deny his pleading look. "Okay, tomorrow sounds good."

Winslow would have preferred to go right away, but it was getting late and Johnny didn't particularly like sailing when it was dark. Lockwood had his monthly meeting with the staff, which lasted very late in the evening, so he would not be visiting the Harringtons tonight.

"Let's start early. I'll be there at 8:00am." He drew her close to him. "Just you, me, and the sea." He kissed her on the forehead and then left before she could ask him any more questions.

Chapter 11

08:30 St. Michael Barbados

The sun had risen only a few hours, but the day was already hot when Winslow and Johnny set sail. The boat was just as Johnny remembered it. Winslow kept his 19-foot pride and joy, *Teamie*, in impeccable shape. The freshly painted and glossy hull gleamed under the sun, her sails swayed proudly in the wind, and the decks were spotless. Winslow had been overjoyed when he bought *Teamie*. He'd gotten her at a fantastic price from a foreigner down on his luck. Although it had cost him most of his savings, he'd felt it was worth every penny.

Winslow had lovingly maintained the teak wood, preserving it from the ocean's relentless elements. Yes, Johnny thought with a smile, *Teamie is a beauty—and the real competition for any woman trying to capture Winslow's heart.*

The wind was with them as they set sail under a bright blue sky. Johnny's hair blew wildly around her head as she felt the salt of the sea on her face and tasted it on her lips. She watched Winslow work the sails, his movements as practiced as a maestro conducting an orchestra. Sailing Teamie was more than a task for him; it was an act of love, a partnership between man and vessel.

Johnny reclined on the deck, letting the sun warm her skin, but her eyes were drawn back to Winslow. His slender frame moved deftly along the deck, his jet-black skin glistening in the sunlight. Each movement of his well-toned muscles seemed perfectly choreographed, like a living sculpture in motion. Yet something about his expression was off. His face lacked the usual serene glow it wore when he was sailing. *We're beyond the shore, but he's not relaxing. He's not letting Teamie do her job.*

Winslow's eyes stayed fixed on the horizon. "Be careful. Don't take too much sun. I don't want your auntie vexed with me."

Johnny sat up, her gaze locking onto Winslow's. "I'm fine, but what about you? You didn't answer my questions last night, and there's nowhere to run now."

He avoided her eyes, busying himself with the sails. "I wanted to tell you myself before you heard any rumors. I've been... disagreeing with some of the superior officers, so I'm taking a little time off."

Johnny frowned. *This isn't like Winslow.* He was the ultimate professional, easygoing yet devoted to his job—a man who loved what he did.

"What happened?" she asked, her voice tinged with concern.

Winslow turned toward her. "Do you trust me?"

"Of course, I do."

His eyes searched hers. "I mean, do you *really* trust me? Do you believe in me and know the kind of man I truly am?"

Johnny felt a knot form in her chest. "You know I do, but what—"

Winslow interrupted; his tone urgent. "Listen, Johnny. No matter what you might hear or see, if I mean anything to you—if I've ever meant anything to you—please, don't ask any more questions. You know how I feel about you. When the time is right, I'll tell you everything. But until then, promise me you won't ask."

Johnny studied his face, his agitation a stark contrast to the calm confidence she was used to.

"If that's what you want, then I won't question you," she said softly, hoping to soothe him.

Winslow moved closer and kissed her deeply, the intensity of it pulling at her soul. For a moment, she surrendered to it, her heart racing in time with the waves around them. Then she gently pulled back, her voice steady but tender. "We'd better stop before the moment gets the best of us."

Winslow smiled faintly and laid his head in her lap. For the rest of their journey, they made casual conversation, *Teamie* rocking them gently into a languorous state. In that perfect world—just the sea, the boat, and each other—they found a fleeting sense of peace, untouched by the troubles of the outside world.

But as Johnny stroked Winslow's hair, a shadow lingered in her heart. She couldn't shake the feeling that she was losing him. Yet even in her deepest fears, she couldn't imagine the extent of the loss to come.

###########

Riding on the back of Winslow's bike, Johnny unconsciously held him a little closer than usual. They rode in silence, engulfed in the bike's serenity speed. The sights swiftly passed around them. At the bottom of Flamboyant's courtyard, Winslow noticed Lockwood's car.

"I better let you off here," said Winslow as Johnny lifted off the bike.

"This was a perfect day," said Johnny.

"I'm glad, and will you remember what I told you?"

"Yes, I'll keep my promise."

Winslow smiled. "I'll call you later on this evening."

Johnny remembered her date with Henley. "I'll probably not be here.".

"Okay, I'll call you tomorrow and maybe we can go sailing again," said Winslow before he kissed her goodbye. Behind the roar of his bike's engine speeding away, Winslow's mind floated back to Johnny on his boat and how the day ended with his deceit. The sight of Lockwood's car in the courtyard assured him she would be told a different story. *It's better I don't see her until the assignment is over.*

Lockwood stood on the verandah as Johnny walked away from

Winslow's bike. *I thought he wouldn't see her anymore. Not only could it jeopardize the assignment, but also her life.* He won't allow that. Johnny approached him with windblown hair and a glow one only gets from the sun and the salt of the sea.

"Johnny, you look like a little sea urchin," said Lockwood jokingly. Aware of her disheveled state, she said, "You know what a day of sailing can do for you."

"Which boat did you go on?"

"The Teamie."

"Hum, isn't that Winslow's cruiser?"

"Yes, it is."

Lockwood's expression became serious. "I suggest that you be careful with him."

"Why would you say that? You know Winslow is an excellent sailor."

"I'm not warning you about the sailing. It's his recent behavior."

"What do you mean? Are you referring to the minor disagreement he's been having with some of your officers?"

"Is that what he told you?"

"Yes."

Lockwood shook his head. "It wasn't a minor disagreement with some of my officers. It was a big fight in front of my officers with me." He recanted the story about Winslow's attack on him. Johnny sat down, astounded at what she was hearing. *Why would Winslow lie? But I've never known Lockwood to lie either or be unfair. What is really going on?*

As the days passed, Johnny spent her mornings at the beach and afternoons looking for Winslow. After a while, she knew he was definitely avoiding her. Finally, she talked to his mother. Johnny hesitated as she climbed the steps of Winslow's small wooden bungalow.

She only talked to his mother a few times and always with Winslow at her side. Each time they met; she hugged Johnny with a warm smile but now she would have to question her about Winslow. *How can I question her about her son? But I have no other choice. I need to talk to Winslow.* Johnny knew in the West Indian culture; the sons are always beyond reproach in their mother's eyes.

The small living room with its oversized mahogany furniture seemed to get smaller as Johnny sat and told Winslow's mother her concerns.

"I don't know what going on with da boy," Winslow's mother said with a thick Barbados accent. "I hardly see him anymore. He's in and then quick, so he's gone again. And to tell ya da truth, I am worried also. But he doesn't give me da chance to talk to him."

Winslow's mother wrung her hands. She swayed back and forth in the chair. "He had such a good job with da force. I don't understand how he could throw it all away." Her eyebrows pinched together as she shook her head. "He always thinks so highly of you, maybe you could talk to him."

"I want to, but I just can't seem to reach him. Do you know where he goes during the day?""I don't know. But I know every day he takes his windbreaker. He used to take that only if he was going fishing on the boat at night." *At night. That's where I can find him. On his boat! Winslow docks his boat at the same place on the beach in the evening.*

Johnny knew she would have to make an excuse to cancel her usual dinner date with Henley. It wouldn't be easy. Their evenings together, which were becoming a ritual, would need a good excuse to allow her to change plans. She tried to ease Winslow's mother's anxieties, bid her goodbye, and left with the determination to talk to Winslow that night.

Chapter 12

20:00 St. Michael Barbados

When Johnny returned to Flamboyant, she called Henley and excused herself from their dinner date. She explained that her family was planning to have dinner with an elderly relative in the countryside. It was a better excuse than feigning illness—it eliminated the possibility of him stopping by to check on her.

After quickly eating and giving her reason for not dining with Henley, Johnny changed clothes and headed for the beach. Winslow had docked Teamie within walking distance of Flamboyant, and Johnny told her aunt that she was taking the bus to visit a friend. Otherwise, her aunt would never allow her to walk the beach alone at night. It was risky, but she had to talk to Winslow tonight.

The floodlights from several beachfront properties illuminated parts of her path as her feet sank into the warm, damp sand. Ahead, she spotted Teamie docked just past an enclave of trees. The area beyond was dark and unlit. She rushed toward the boat, entering the enclave as a blanket of darkness wrapped around her. The stillness felt suffocating, and she quickened her pace.

Her only guide was the faint gleam of light from *Teamie,* her focal point. The sound of her breathing and the crunch of branches underfoot were the only noises breaking the silence. Suddenly, she stumbled against a rock, pausing briefly to steady herself—but the crunching sounds continued.

Someone is nearby.

Johnny's pulse quickened. She walked faster, but the footsteps behind her matched her pace. Fear gripping her, she broke into a run, her heart pounding as the brush behind her seemed to grow closer and closer. *I have to reach the end of this enclave. I can make a dash to Teamie.*

She burst out of the trees and started toward the boat when a hand clamped down on her arm, yanking her back. Without looking, she thrashed, trying to break free, but the grip was too strong. She felt herself being pulled back into the darkness. *I can't be pulled back in. Someone has to hear me.*

Johnny opened her mouth to scream, but a hand covered it. Instinctively, she bit down hard. The hand released instantly. She tried to run, but the grip returned, this time shaking her to turn around.

"What are you doing here?" demanded Winslow.

Johnny froze, her breath ragged. "What are you doing?" she shot back.

"I should be asking you that question," he replied tersely.

"I was coming to see you! For days I've been looking for you, and you keep avoiding me. I even went to your mother—she's worried about you too. What's going on? Why did you lie to me about the argument at your job?"

"You shouldn't have talked to my mother," Winslow snapped. "And you shouldn't be here. You know better than to walk alone on the beach, especially in this dark area." His grip tightened on her arm. "Does your aunt know you're here?"

She pulled away. "Don't change the subject. Tell me what's going on."

"Shush. Don't say a word," Winslow hissed, pulling Johnny

behind a tree. His head turned sharply toward Teamie. Three men approached the wharf, their voices low but urgent as they gestured toward the boat.

Winslow gripped Johnny's arms tightly. "Listen to me carefully. I'm going to the boat to talk to those men. When they leave, I'll come back for you. Stay here, by this tree, and don't move. Do you understand?"

"No, I don't understand! Why can't I come with you?"

Winslow's eyes bore into hers. "Remember the promise you made to me? You said you would trust me, no matter what. Please keep that promise. I don't have time to explain, but don't make a sound. Just stay here."

Reluctantly, Johnny nodded. Winslow released her and strode quickly toward *Teamie*.

Hidden behind the tree, Johnny watched the scene unfold, completely baffled. Winslow and the men conversed, their gestures fast and jerky. One of the men shoved Winslow up against the side of the boat.

Something is wrong. I can't just stand here. What are they doing to him?

Fear prickled at her, and instinct urged her to run to Winslow's aid. But his words echoed in her mind. *Stay here. Don't move.* She clenched her fists, rooted to the spot, her eyes fixed on the group.

For what felt like an eternity, Winslow placated the men. His tone was low, but his body language radiated calm authority. Finally, the men walked away, disappearing into the shadows.

Winslow climbed onto *Teamie* and lingered on the deck.

Why isn't he coming back? Did he forget about me?

Johnny's heart pounded as she waited in the suffocating silence, her confusion and fear mounting with each passing second.

After a few minutes, Johnny concluded that he probably didn't want to take the risk of the men returning. *Or is he expecting them to return?* A few minutes later, she watched Winslow head back to her.

"Let's go, I'm taking you home." He grabbed Johnny's hand and hurried out of the enclave.

She tugged away from him. "Wait one minute. Don't expect that you are going to take me home without explaining what went on just a few minutes ago."

"Oh, those are just some friends of mine."

"What sort of friends do you have? Do your friends usually push you around like that?"

"We were just having a friendly argument. Why, were you worried?" Winslow asked as he pulled Johnny towards him in an embrace.

He whispered in her ear. "I know you care for me a lot more than you're willing to admit."

Johnny, not wanting to get into another argument with Winslow, pushed away. "Let's go, it's getting late and I don't want my aunt to get worried." During the walk home, she could tell that something was terribly wrong, although Winslow tried in vain to assure her. They made plans to meet the next day but Winslow never came by Flamboyant. It became clear he was avoiding her. But Johnny wasn't willing to waste a short vacation chasing after Winslow. *I'll eventually catch up with him on Old Year's Night.*

##########

Old Year's Night is the highlight of the holiday season and Barbados puts forth her best to bring in the new year with an all-night festival. Everyone goes from one house party to another throughout the night until the sun rises. In the morning, party-goers end up at various homes that are designated "morning houses," where there are four course breakfasts.

Although Barbados is very class conscious, there are certain places on Old Year's Night where there are no social barriers, and everyone celebrates together. Barbados's elite, rich visitors, as well as the average native, make sure that their celebratory journey includes a stop at Enid's for flying fish cutters and the sweet Red Juicy soda.

Or at Verna's for a taste of her traditional good luck meal of blackeye peas and rice, pickled pig's feet, souse, and blood pudding. The entire island seems to pass through these two spots, right after the Old Year's Night fireworks display in Queen's park. Johnny is certain she will meet Winslow at one of those places.

The Harrington's Old Year's Eve party is the season's most coveted invitation. Barbados's elite make sure that Flamboyant is the place where they ring in the New Year. Preparations for the night start two weeks prior, but just like the last day before the opening of a show, Flamboyant is full of activity and frenzy.

By the afternoon, the decorators are buzzing around the house, putting the final touches on the flower arrangements. Clara is supervising the extra staff with the setting of the tables. In the evening, Flamboyant is a radiant jewel sparkling from the decorations and the festive aura surrounding the house. By nine o'clock, people dressed in their finest attire fill Flamboyant. As Johnny walked around greeting and chatting with the guests, she glanced around, wondering why Henley has not arrived yet.

****

Henley sat languorously on the settee as Ashton fixed drinks. Although he portrayed a calm exterior, Henley slowly rubbed his right temple as he awaited the end of this unscheduled visit, hoping he could still get to the Harrington's before midnight. But one thing Henley learned about Ashton, never let him think you are anxious about anything. He feeds on that emotion and eventually manipulates it to control a person.

"Do you have big plans for Old Year's night?" Ashton asked casually as he handed Henley his drink. "I'm going to drop in at the Harrington's party."

"Oh yes, the Harrington's party is always spectacular. I intend to drop by myself. They always go all out for Old Year's Night. I'm sure you'll be escorting that lovely young Harrington girl. She's quite charming as well as beautiful. A rarity to find both qualities in a woman these days," said Ashton with a twinkle in his eyes.

"Yes, of course she will be there."

"I don't want to keep you too long from the festivities, but there seems to be a matter of concern with our Barbados operation. The company thinks that there might be a problem in our system. They are working on finding exactly where it might be located and to eliminate it immediately. You could help the situation."

"Ashton, you know that isn't my forte, so I don't know how I could help them," says Henley as he focused on the ice swirling around his glass. "I'm sure you're quite aware of how important Barbados is to the company," snaps Ashton.

"I told them you would be available for questions, since you know this area better than anyone else in the company."

"Of course, I'll help them if I can."

Ashton's face lit up with a smile. "Good, I'm sure they'll contact you soon. Don't you know it's bad manners to keep a beautiful woman waiting? You better finish that drink quickly and get to that Harrington girl."

Chapter 13

13:55 Flamboyant Estate

Johnny's chiffon and organza dress rustled as she danced with Lawton Bridges. Lawton, one of the top lawyers on the island, craved Johnny. He drew her closer, and they danced the traditional West Indian grind to the band's calypso song. As soon as the band stopped, Johnny quickly pulled away and excused herself before the band started the next song. As an old friend of her uncle's, it would be impolite to refuse his request to dance, but it wouldn't be impolite to get away before his advances became lascivious.

Johnny discreetly glanced around for Henley but didn't see him anywhere. It was nearly midnight, and she couldn't believe he hadn't arrived yet. A chill ran down her spine as thoughts raced through her head of accidents on the dangerous roads during Old Year's Night. She shook her head. *I will not let my imagination spiral out of control.*

"Ladies and gentlemen, it's almost time to countdown to the New Year," the bandleader announced.

"Fourteen seconds, thirteen seconds."

"Where is Henley?" asked Elizabeth as she walked toward Johnny.

"I don't know. I haven't heard from him."

"That's strange, but come on, the other guests are gathered by the band."

"Ten seconds, nine seconds." People gathered closer to the band with their New Year's horns and hats, counting along with the bandleader.

"Seven seconds, six seconds." Johnny's eyes kept darting around as she joined in the countdown.

"Five seconds, four seconds." Lockwood entered the room and joined the countdown. He greeted Charles and nodded hello to Johnny.

"Three seconds." Ashton entered, greeting Lockwood and Charles.

"Two seconds." The guests blew their horns with anticipation.

"One second. Happy New Year!" Everyone kissed the people around them. The band played *Auld Lang Syne*. The voices of people saying "Happy New Year" surrounded Johnny. It became a continuous echo heard throughout the island. The fireworks from the harbor lit up the sky. Johnny became part of the whirlwind of people kissing and wishing her a Happy New Year.

"Happy New Year, Johnny."

She heard this greeting above all the music and other greetings. It stood out alone among the cacophony enveloping her. Johnny turned around quickly to see Henley standing and smiling at her. He pulled her tight to him.

"Happy New Year." She embraced him. He drew her so close that she could feel his heart beating quickly. Then he kissed her lightly on the lips several times until it slowly developed into a deep, soulful, long kiss. They kissed as though they were the only ones in the room, unaware of the surrounding people. She became light-headed as they kissed. A kiss so long that she wasn't breathing on her own anymore. They were breathing as one, a symbiont whose one breath was the key to each entity's existence.

"Hey, leave some of those kisses for me," said a voice that broke her hypnotic state. She pulled away from Henley, and for a quick second, they both stared at each other as though they had just met. A hand took Johnny away, kissed her Happy New Year, and led her into the other revelers, giving New Year's Eve good wishes. She got caught up in the crowd and separated from Henley. Her head was still spinning as she greeted each person with New Year's wishes and glanced around for Henley. She felt an arm tug her out of the crowd. Henley rushed her toward the back patio. They walked out into the garden. He drew her close and kissed her again.

"Let's go someplace where we can be alone," Henley whispered into her ear. He kissed her lightly on her face. Johnny became speechless. He captivated her. The idea of Henley sweeping away all inhibitions frightened her.

"I can't leave the party," she stuttered. "They will all start asking questions and wonder where we are. Especially Aunt Elizabeth."

"If they miss you, will that really be so bad?" Henley whispered in her ear. Johnny felt herself melting into his arms and answered quickly, "You know how Bajans are. It would be a big insult to leave so abruptly." She released herself from his arms and took his hand. "Come on, Henley, let's go back into the house." He stopped her right before they entered. "You can't keep running away, Johnny."

Old Year's Night slowly turned into New Year's Day when Henley and Johnny arrived at the Braithwaites for their first breakfast of the year. Again, the same people who enjoyed the festivities at the Harringtons and Enid's gradually but steadily came to feast on a traditional New Year's Day breakfast of eggs (fried, boiled, omelets), smoked ham, coconut bread, pumpkin fritters, and assorted tropical fruits (mangoes, bananas, figs, oranges).

After greetings, flutes filled with mimosas clicked to toast the New Year. They enjoyed the morning feast. While Johnny talked with the other guests sitting next to her, she remembered she had not seen Winslow the entire evening. She missed having a New Year's drink along with sharing their favorite fishcakes together.

****

Lockwood was also not one of the breakfast guests. Someone else occupied his usual seat where he would exchange acerbic quips with the Braithwaites. This New Year didn't start on a good foot for him. One of his officers called him to come to Buccaneer Beach. He was sure it wouldn't be a good sign, but he didn't expect this. How will he explain this to everyone?

Chapter 14

15:00 Flamboyant Estate

Johnny woke up from a brief nap with great anticipation for the late New Year's Day lunch. Although it was a regular event during the holiday festivities; this time it would be different. Henley would be there, and she was looking forward to continuing the scenario that occurred between them.

As she prepared herself, she detected voices coming from downstairs. Johnny dressed quickly, thinking it might be Henley who arrived early to pick her up. She entered the drawing room, surprised to see Lockwood and her uncle, heads bent while in a whispered conversation. She approached them. They turned to her with solemn faces.

"Good morning, everyone. Why such sad faces on this beautiful morning?" she gleefully said as she greeted each one with a kiss on the cheek.

Charles's drawn face accompanied his solemn tone. "Lockwood has brought some bad news."

Johnny could feel the tension in the air. She tried to lighten the mood with her hesitant but nervous response. "Don't tell me the New Year's lunch is cancelled."

"No, it's a serious matter, so you better sit down," said Charles. Lockwood explained how his visit to Buccaneer Beach discovered a body believed to be Winslow's. Johnny listened in disbelief. The body had Winslow's cross on it, but it was so deteriorated that they couldn't identify the remains.

Her mind faded away. He continued with how a witness saw Winslow at Buccaneer Beach a few days ago. Stunned, Johnny's mind raced back, trying to remember the last few hours that she saw Winslow. *When was the very last time?* The evening he rode to the house looking for Lockwood? The time they spent on the boat? During the New Year's Eve festivities? *Or did I see him? Was he at Enid's?*

She thought about how she must have seen him somewhere and how it must be a mistake as she rushed out the house, running, her feet carrying her on a bus while her thoughts centered on Winslow and the passengers starring at her as she got off the bus and walked along the coast road, ending up on the beach, racing towards Winslow's boat hoping to see his silly hat again.

She tried to get on Teamie when a police officer stopped her. "Miss, you can't go up there," he shouted with a strong Barbados accent. "This boat is off limits to the public."

"I'm looking for the owner of this boat. Have you seen him?" asked Johnny.

"Miss, this boat is part of a crime scene. No one except the police are authorized to go on board." The police officer crossed his arms. "Questions about this boat have to be dealt with by the Constable."

"A crime? What crime?"

"There's been a murder, Miss. Any more questions will have to be resolved by the Constable." Before he could finish his sentence, Johnny ran away from the boat. She continued to run in no direction. *I have to find Winslow. There has to be a big mistake. Maybe I saw him on New Year's Eve. I just can't remember. Everything was moving so fast. Henley was late, then it was midnight. I saw everyone at Enid's. Wasn't he there?* Her brain is running so fast that she stopped and held her head, hoping she can slow it down. *Collect your thoughts.* Johnny tried to remember.

But no matter how hard she tried; her mind wouldn't confirm what never happened. It was almost dark before Johnny stopped searching for Winslow. When she finally arrived at Flamboyant, Henley was among the people waiting for her. "Here she comes," said Leonard as she approached the house. Elizabeth ran towards her. "We were so worried about--------." Before she could finish her sentence, Johnny fell into her arms, sobbing uncontrollably. Elizabeth held Johnny and walked her to the bedroom. She put her to bed and closed the door.

"I think we should just let her rest. She's just in shock. They were very close." Elizabeth shook her head. "It's such a tragedy. I must send my condolences to his mother."

"Are you sure she'll be okay?" asked Henley.

"Yes, a good night's sleep will do her a world of good," answered Charles.

Lockwood placed his head in his hands. "I really didn't mean to upset her. If I had known she would have taken it this hard, I would have tried to break the news a little easier,"

"Don't worry Phillip. It's not your fault. There isn't any good way to break that type of news," said Elizabeth as she placed her hand on his arm.

For the next couple of days, Johnny wondered around in a daze. She couldn't bear to return Henley's calls. It felt like she was betraying Winslow.

She stayed near the house and walked on the beach. When Charles gave her the information about Winslow's memorial service, she listened with no emotion. She had no intention of going because she didn't want to believe he was dead. Elizabeth and Charles, still worried, tried to find out what they could do to help, even though Johnny assured them she was okay.

But both of them knew that was a lie. She hadn't gone in the sea since she found out about Winslow. Every day, she walked along the shore as the sea beckoned her to submit to its advances. But she wouldn't heed its call. After a week, she finally spoke to Henley. He was leaving in an hour on unexpected business but promised to call her in New York. There was no disappointment with his sudden departure. In fact, it relieved her. She was running out of excuses not to see him.

On the day of Winslow's memorial, Charles and Elizabeth were a little surprised that Johnny would not attend the ceremony, but they didn't press the issue. They both believed Johnny was in a fragile state and didn't want her breaking apart in Barbados. *God forbid if they have to call her parents to come and get her. What a horrible scandal that would be!*

Johnny sat by the pool after Elizabeth and Charles left. She instructed Clara that if anyone called, she wasn't available. *I refuse to go to a funeral for someone who isn't dead. I know in my heart and soul Winslow is still alive. Why didn't I look for him on New Year's Eve?* She used two fingers to swiftly stop a tear from escaping down her cheek.

Clara sighed and shook her head as she placed the newspaper and a cup of tea on the poolside table. Johnny flipped through the pages, barely looking at them, when her eye caught a message in the personal column. In bold capital letters: *SEA PRINCESS IT'S OKAY*.

She immediately picked up the phone to call Lockwood. "Mr. Lockwood, please. It's Johnny Harrington."

"I'm sorry, Ms. Harrington, but Mr. Lockwood is at a memorial service. Do you want to leave a message?"

"No, thanks. I'll contact him later." The call ended before she finished her sentence. *Those Americans are always in such a hurry,* Mrs. Braithwaite thought as she shrugged and put away her message pad.

Johnny ran up the stairs past Clara, who stuck her head out of the kitchen, shaking it as she watched Johnny bolt by. Johnny changed into a pair of dark slacks and a blouse and raced back downstairs.

Where did Charles say the memorial was? Why didn't I write it down? Think, think. There were only a few places for a memorial in Barbados. Charles probably wrote it on his phone in the study! She ran to the study and picked up the notepad he scribbled on during calls. Nothing. Damn! She rummaged through the wastebasket, tossing paper aside. Still nothing. As she left the room, her eyes landed on a piece of paper on the side table: Westbury Chapel, written on today's date.

She decided against asking one of Charles's drivers to take her and instead opted for the bus to avoid being seen.

During the bus ride, she resolved to make Lockwood give her a straight answer. No more evasiveness. She would speak to him alone, without Elizabeth or Charles finding out. She didn't want them thinking she had finally fallen apart. Johnny checked her watch. If she timed it correctly and approached Westbury's back entrance, the memorial would just be ending.

****

Lockwood made polite chit-chat with acquaintances as he left the chapel, but his thoughts were consumed by Winslow. He understood better than anyone the risks that came with the job. Yet losing one of his best men felt like a punch in the gut, knocking the wind out of him. He still couldn't piece together exactly what had gone wrong. Winslow had checked in with Ms. Braithwaite as usual the day before the accident.

He wouldn't have made a stupid error that cost him his life. This wasn't an accident. Winslow had been an expert sailor and swimmer. Could it have been an inside job? But Ms. Braithwaite was the only person who knew about the undercover operation. Lockwood trusted her implicitly. And then there was the body—unidentifiable, no dental records for Winslow on the island.

Lockwood, deep in thought, unlocked his car door. Just as he opened it, Johnny rushed toward him from behind a tree.

Lockwood instinctively scanned her. He had observed everyone at the memorial—it was an old habit to note faces, knowing murderers sometimes attended their victims' funerals. Johnny, in her casual attire, would have stood out starkly among the sea of mourners dressed in black suits. Her sudden appearance sharpened his focus.

"Johnny" he said, his tone calm but guarded. "What are you doing here?"

Lockwood squinted and cocked his head. "Johnny, I didn't see you at the memorial. Were you there?"

"No, I came to meet to you." It made perfect sense from their last meeting why she wasn't at the memorial. Her rapid speech with small beads of sweat on her forehead made him weary of upsetting her again.

He opened the car door. "You could have come to my office. In fact, I'm going back now. You can come with me."

Johnny jumped in front of the car door. "No, this couldn't wait. I had to find you right away. Winslow is alive." Lockwood didn't know if this was part of her grief or rather, she had finally fallen apart. Either way, he trod the ground lightly with her.

Lockwood placed his hand on her shoulder. "I know it has been hard for you to come to grips with his death. It's been hard for me too. After all, he was one-----------."

She pushed his hand off of her shoulder. "No, you don't understand. I know he's alive because I got a sign from him." Lockwood gave her the same blank stare a psychiatrist would give to a hysterical patient.

Johnny closed her eyes and took a deep breath before continuing. "I was reading the newspaper this morning and saw the personal ads. In big bold letters, I saw Sea Princess. I'm Okay." Her speech came out rapid fire again. "Winslow's nickname for me was Sea Princess. I know you think it's probably a coincidence. But don't you think that would be a big coincidence, especially on the same day as his memorial? He knew I'd be upset and probably put the ad in the paper."

Lockwood sighed. "Johnny, I wish it were true. But Sea Princess could be the name of a ship or anything. You know how those ads are."

She paced back and forth. "I know, I know," she said as she tried to regain her composure, "but I know this is Winslow."

"Johnny, if this was true, why won't he just appear? Why would he be hiding and making people suffer and grieve over him?"

She stopped pacing and stood in front of Lockwood. "Look, Mr. Lockwood, I know you think Winslow went rogue, but he didn't. There was something else going on. The last time I spoke to him, he kept telling me no matter what happens, just trust him and trust that I know the real Winslow. Something else was going on."

Johnny told him about the incident she saw on Teamie. Lockwood thought she might have a point. He wondered if Winslow had found something out and had to go further undercover. If he did, it would be foolish of him to give a signal to Johnny and not contact him first.

"To put your mind at ease, I'll contact the newspaper. I can investigate the ad and find out who placed it. I'm sure it will be some lovesick person behind it. About the Teamie incident. I'll definitely investigate that further for more evidence. Maybe there were other witnesses."

He finally stepped inside his car. "Now can I drop you home?" Lockwood hoped that this would help to stifle Johnny's questions for a little while. He knew how inquisitive she could be. He didn't want her asking too many questions or finding out answers. Answers that could endanger not only the investigation, but maybe her life.

"Yes, I would appreciate it." During the ride, neither one of them discussed Winslow. Each one had their own purpose for not continuing the discussion. Lockwood, because he didn't want Johnny to ask any more questions and Johnny because she had her own agenda. This is the first time she felt distrust towards Lockwood.

She saw the sudden look of surprise on his face when she mentioned the ad. Although the expression changed quickly and he tried to ignore her theory, she saw his reaction. He believed there was something to it. Johnny had a friend at the paper. An old family friend who was always very kind to her. She planned to do her own investigation. So, they continued the ride in an uncomfortable silence.

Chapter 15

10:00 Bridgetown Barbados

The next day, Johnny called Mr. Cumberbatch at *The Ledger* newspaper. He had worked at the paper for about twenty years and had known the Harrington family even longer. Johnny would occasionally talk to him at the Harrington parties, but he was a quiet man. She could never figure out why he came to the parties. Johnny often observed Cumberbatch as he walked around, exchanged a few words with Charles and Elizabeth, and nodded hello to the other guests. Most of the evening, he would sit quietly in a corner, observing everyone.

Charles once told Johnny that Cumberbatch came from a poor family and had worked his way up from reporter to Editor-in-Chief. Despite holding the highest position at the country's largest newspaper, Cumberbatch still felt insecure around people he perceived as his social superiors, still seeing himself as the poor boy from Darrington village.

It flattered Cumberbatch to hear from Johnny. While she occasionally made time to talk to him at the Harrington parties, he had always felt it was just a polite gesture. Still, her attention brightened his evenings. She was the only woman besides his mother who had ever paid him much notice. So when Johnny expressed interest in touring *The Ledger*, he didn't think twice about her sudden curiosity in the newspaper business.

After lunch with Johnny, Cumberbatch was walking on air. Succumbing to Johnny's charms—her light touches on his arm, her laughter at his jokes—his head was in the clouds. He didn't think twice when she showed an interest in how personal ad information was stored. When Johnny "forgot" her bag in the archive room and took a moment to return to his office, he didn't notice at all. For him, it had been one of the best afternoons he'd had in a long time.

****

As Johnny thanked Cumberbatch and gave him a quick kiss on the cheek before heading to her car, she left him standing at the door, his mouth slightly open, with a dreamy, faraway look in his eyes. Driving home, her mind was consumed with the information she had just uncovered, and she waited for Lockwood's call.

Lockwood knew he had to keep Johnny's curiosity in check, no matter what it took. When he initially told her there was nothing behind the ad, he thought that would be enough. But her persistence —her insistence on meeting him—put him on edge.

When she kept calling, even after he brushed her off, he knew he needed a solid reason to put distance between them. Then Haiti provided the perfect excuse. The Haitian government had requested him as a consultant to help structure a new police force. He had to leave right away. By the time he returned, Johnny would be safely back in New York, and the situation would have defused itself.

This is perfect, he thought, as he returned her call.

"Hello, Johnny, this is Mr. Lockwood. How are you?"

"Just fine. Have you found time to meet with me yet?" Her tone was sharp and to the point.

"That's why I'm calling. I'm sorry, Johnny, but I have to fly to Haiti on business. I'm leaving today, and I'm afraid by the time I get back, you'll be gone."

"Look, Mr. Lockwood, this discussion shouldn't be over the phone, but I know what you told me was a lie," Johnny replied, her voice laced with steel. "I did my own investigation, and it wasn't a love-struck couple sending messages. Someone sent that ad anonymously with a cash payment for a month's worth of ad time. Why did you lie? What's really going on? If you refuse to tell me, I'll hire private detectives to find out about Winslow."

The silence that followed felt like an eternity, though it was only a few seconds. Lockwood struggled to recover from the shock of her words.

"Johnny," he finally said, his voice measured, "there are things I can't tell you. And even if I could, I'm leaving right away. Just forget about all this private investigation talk. It'll be a waste of your money. You're young. You'll get over the grief."

But Johnny wasn't convinced, and Lockwood could feel her resolve harden through the short silence that followed.

"Mr. Lockwood, I won't stop here. This is for Winslow's memory and reputation. I have some extra days left. Either we talk in Haiti or I'll just hire a P.I. from New York." The last thing Lockwood wanted was more inquiries about Winslow before he could truly investigate the situation himself.

"Okay, I'll be staying at El Rancho hotel in Port-au-Prince."

"I'll call now to get the next flight out."

Johnny told Elizabeth and Charles that she was going to Haiti to visit a friend for a few days before heading back to work. They were sorry she was ending her visit earlier than expected. But they thought it was a good idea for her to get away from Barbados and the memories of Winslow. There are no direct flights from Barbados to Haiti, so Johnny had to fly back to Miami to catch a flight. She spent the entire 3 hours pondering her conversation with Lockwood.

At first, Johnny needed to find out the truth behind Winslow's disappearance for the sake of his reputation. Lockwood's strange behavior was like a fledgling fire under her curiosity. When she mentioned hiring a P.I., it was a bluff. *But he took it. And quickly.*

Why? There must be a reason he can't take any risks. He even agreed to meet in Haiti. The flame under her curiosity became a full blaze.

Chapter 16

12:00 Port-au-Prince Haiti

Johnny arrived at Port-au-Prince airport on a bright day. As the plane doors opened, she inhaled the familiar Caribbean air. Walking across the hot tarmac toward the terminal, she noticed the similarities to Barbados's airport—the same welcoming sounds of a Caribbean band playing upbeat music. But once she stepped inside, the similarities ended abruptly.

After clearing immigration, total chaos surrounded her. The baggage claim area featured the familiar rotating conveyor belts, but instead of passengers waiting patiently for their luggage, people jostled and pushed for the best positions.

Skycaps climbed on top of the conveyor belts, their limbs agile as they maneuvered to retrieve luggage for passengers who had enlisted their services. Unlike Barbados, where the travelers were an international mix, most visitors in Haiti appeared to be returning Haitian residents.

Humongous suitcases were dragged off the conveyor belt, bumping into anyone in their path. *What the hell is going on? This is madness!* Johnny braced herself as luggage smacked against her legs, and strangers stepped on her feet. *I've got to get out of here.* Finally, she managed to flag down a skycap to retrieve her bags and escape the chaos. Clearing customs only brought a fresh wave of bombardment from aggressive taxi drivers and begging children.

"Madame. D'argent, d'argent, s'il vous plaît. Une dollar."

Luckily, Johnny's French was decent enough to navigate the situation. She chose a taxi driver who ushered her past the children and opened the car door for her.

"Je veux aller El Rancho Hotel. C'est loin ou près?" she asked, hoping it wasn't far.

"C'est près. C'est quinze minutes d'ici."

"Bon. Allons."

Johnny was relieved. The driver said El Rancho was only fifteen minutes away, and it was where Lockwood was staying—a perfect choice.

As with most private estates and hotels in Haiti, El Rancho was surrounded by an enormous wall. After passing through the gates and driving up the long driveway, Johnny arrived at a cluster of white brick buildings exuding a 1930s charm. A black-and-white marble walkway lined with tall dome lights led to the reception area.

The hotel had an open design, with no doors leading in or out of the main structure. Beyond the reception area were two swimming pools, rooms with glass patio doors on the first floors, and opulent balconies on the upper levels.

In her room, Johnny quickly changed and called the front desk to reach Lockwood. The phone rang for several minutes, but there was no response. She left a message: Having lunch in the hotel restaurant.

The poolside restaurant was expansive. Johnny observed swimmers sipping drinks while floating in the water. A small concrete area nearby looked like a dance floor used in the evenings. Tables were placed strategically around the pools, offering a pleasant view. It was the perfect vantage point for Johnny to spot everyone entering, including Lockwood. To avoid appearing too obvious or overly available, she brought a book to read during lunch.

After an hour, she was engrossed in her book when a familiar voice interrupted her.

"It's so nice to run into you here."

Johnny looked up to see Lockwood, dressed sharply in a cream linen suit with a matching straw fedora. *Why wouldn't he want anyone to realize he knows me?* she wondered. *Okay, I'll play along.*

"May I join you?" he asked.

"Why, of course. I would be delighted," Johnny replied smoothly.

The server approached immediately, but Lockwood waved him off.

"I hope everything was well when you left," he began.

"Yes, it was," Johnny replied curtly, not in the mood for small talk.

"I was just coming from a meeting when I got your message," Lockwood added.

Johnny leaned forward, her patience thinning. "Mr. Lockwood, can you now answer my questions?"

"This really isn't the right place or time," he said evasively.

Johnny's voice dropped to a firm tone. "Mr. Lockwood, I flew all the way to Haiti, and it wasn't to hear you say that. If not now, when?"

"There's a party being given by one of my colleagues tonight. You could come with me, and we could discuss it there," he offered.

Johnny leaned back in her chair, unimpressed. "At a party? Come on. How will you even get away from the other guests? I think you're just trying to brush me off. Maybe I should just head back to New York and go with my original plan."

Lockwood hesitated, his composed demeanor briefly faltering. Johnny had backed him into a corner.

"Believe me, I'm not brushing you off. It will be the safest place for us to talk. There are a lot of ears at El Rancho." "More ears than at the party?"

"It's just not more ears, but unfriendly ears. If I don't give you your answers by tonight. You can go to New York tomorrow and do what you planned."

Since her original plan was a bluff tactic, she had no other choice than to agree.

"Okay, what time should we meet?"

"Let's meet in the lobby at four o'clock. The Haitians believe in early soirees." He rose from his seat. "Anyway, I hate to rush off, but I have another meeting to attend."

"See you at four." Although four o'clock was only a few hours away, it was an eternity for Johnny.

Lockwood was in the lobby promptly at four o'clock waiting for Johnny. As Johnny descended the steps, Lockwood noticed every eye watching her walk toward him. "You look beautiful, as usual."

"Thank
you."

"The hosts are sending their driver to pick us up. It's only about twenty minutes away."

Along the winding roads, the beautiful houses were next to homes that are little more than shacks made of plywood, some with no doors, just a curtain for privacy. The further up the mountain, there are fewer shacks and more of the beautiful homes surrounded by gates. At the summit, they drove past elegant estates. Each house had high iron gates to keep out intruders, poverty, and despair of their fellow countrymen.

They approached an area where the roads immediately transformed into paved roadways. An open gate had a guard at each side. The driver stopped, identified the passengers, and allowed to enter. The car drove up a long road that ended in a circular gravel driveway at the entrance of the massive house. Inside, the house is airy and tropical, with all white furniture surrounded by antiques that the discernible eye can tell are quite valuable.

At the back of the estate, Lockwood and Johnny stroll by tents filled with tables elaborately laid with flowers and food. Servers in traditional black-tie uniforms roamed the grounds carrying flutes of champagne. A biracial woman came towards Lockwood, floating in the air, with her chiffon dress billowing behind her.

"Mon Cher, welcome. I'm so glad you are here." Her pure French sounds very different from the broken Creole language that most of the natives speak.

"And who is this beautiful lady?"

"Madame Toussaint, I would like to introduce an old family friend, Ms. Johnny Harrington."

"Enchanté, mademoiselle Johnny. Welcome to my home. You are quite beautiful." She turned to Lockwood and winked. "Are you sure she's just a friend?"

"Yes," responded Lockwood with a laugh. "She's here for a brief rest before going back to the States. We ran into each other at El Rancho."

"Well, whatever the reason, I'm glad you brought her to my party. I love to be surrounded by beautiful things and beautiful people. It makes life so much more pleasant, n'est pas?"

"Bien Sur", replied Johnny.

"Oh, you speak French, even more delightful. I must introduce you to some of my other guests."

Before she could whisk Johnny away, Lockwood interceded, "We just arrived, Marie. Let's settle down with a drink first."

"D'accord, but I will be back later." Then, as fast as she floated in, she floated away on her cloud of chiffon.

Chapter 17

20:00 Montagne Noir Haiti

"Marie is quite a character and a social force in Haiti," Lockwood told Johnny as he took two glasses of champagne from a passing tray.

"Let's walk around the grounds. She has some of the most exotic flowers in her garden."

Johnny followed Lockwood, curious why he wanted to show her flowers, as they sipped their champagne. They strolled leisurely, the music from the six-piece band playing softly in the background. Lockwood pointed out several types of flowers, but then the conversation took a sudden turn.

He darted his head from side to side, lowering his voice. "Johnny, Barbados has been going through some unwanted changes. The island seems to be infiltrated by an excessive amount of illegal drugs. We found our informant, who had a strong lead, dead earlier last week. That informant turned out to be Winslow's half-brother."

"A half-brother? I didn't know he had a half-brother. He never told me."

"None of us knew until his death. Of course, it devastated him. Someone leaked information about his brother. I needed to find an undercover officer I could trust. Winslow was the only one, and he volunteered for the duty."

Johnny sat on a garden bench, her glass trembling slightly in her hands. "That's why he kept telling me to trust him."

"Yes," Lockwood said, sitting next to her. "But I had to discredit him to keep both of you out of danger and to prevent you from blowing his cover."

"I would never do that."

"Not intentionally, of course, but you don't know who you can trust."

"So, he was undercover when he was reported missing?" Johnny asked.

"Yes, that's why I had to stop you from investigating. It could be very dangerous for you. I didn't think you would be so efficient in your investigation into the personal ad."

"So, I was right. He is alive. I knew it was Winslow who wrote that ad."

"Johnny, we don't know that for a fact. If Winslow were alive, why wouldn't he try to contact me? He's on an assignment. He would contact me or Ms. Braithwaite, the only other person who knows about his undercover status."

"I don't know why," Johnny said, her voice filled with conviction, "but I know it was Winslow. Maybe he can't contact you. Maybe he needs help."

"If he needed help, he wouldn't have sent a personal ad, Johnny. Plus, there was no guarantee that you would even read the paper."

"I know everything you're saying makes practical sense, but I just feel that he's alive."

Lockwood sighed. "Well, Johnny, let me continue to investigate the situation. I trust you'll keep all this information between us."

"Of course," she replied, a sly smile creeping onto her face. "Because now I'm going to help you."

"What?" Lockwood's eyebrows shot up.

"It only makes sense," Johnny began nonchalantly, as though

discussing a floral arrangement at the party. "You don't have anyone you can trust to continue the investigation. So why not use me?"

"Johnny, this is not some party whodunit game. This is real life and very dangerous. It's not just about Winslow. This is the drug trade. The problem isn't limited to Barbados—it leads all the way to Europe."

Johnny jumped up from the bench. "That's perfect! The next tour will be in Europe. I can help investigate while I'm there."

Lockwood stood, crossing his arms and glaring at her. "I don't think you understand. First, what and who would you even be investigating?"

"Well," Johnny said with a casual shrug, linking her arm in his as they strolled toward a pond, "you can give me that information."

For the next hour, Johnny tried to convince Lockwood that he should use her for the investigation. While he dismissed much of her reasoning as impulsive and naïve, a small part of him couldn't ignore that some of her points made sense. As reckless as she was, Johnny had determination—and sometimes, determination could make all the difference.

She will be in Europe, traveling in a business capacity among the rich and elite crowd, so she would be the least suspicious. She's right about not having any other person I can trust. He had run out of officers and even if he could dredge one up, they could never fit into the sophisticated European crowd.

She really was the only one he could trust and an ideal candidate. *But she's so inexperience and almost like family.* He thought he must be crazy, desperate, or both to even contemplate involving her. As they continued to walk around the grounds, she pleaded her case to him. He continued to dissuade her from her plans, but they were sounding more and more workable to him. *Some of the best spies in history, or even ones used today, are ones that were ordinary people with very little or no training. But what if anything should happen to her?* Could he face himself or her family?

Suddenly, jolted out of his thoughts when Johnny said, "If you don't agree, I can always just do a brief investigation of my own. It's not just Winslow, I love Barbados. It's like my home and I have a selfish interest to keep it as special as it is."

"Johnny, what will you do if you come across a situation that you can't handle?"

"Call you," she said with a mocking smile. "I'm not trying to catch criminals. Just be your eyes and ears in Europe and keep you informed of every detail. You might as well agree. Won't I be in more danger by investigating without your help?"

"Okay, Johnny, I really don't like this, but you're a hard bargainer. I know your family would kill me if they found out."

"Well, we just won't tell them."

****

Lockwood waved goodbye to Johnny as she walked on the tarmac, uneasy with the tasks that lie ahead of her. He has to be sure to keep her out of danger. The people he informed her about were basically just jet-setters that are suspected of dabbling in low-level drug sales, not any top echelon people. He instructed her to inform him of their movements, but never approach them. Deep down, Lockwood is uncomfortable about the whole situation. Johnny can be impulsive, and he will not be there to monitor her. If he didn't give her some type of task, she would be on her own and completely out of his control. He had no other choice.

Johnny is exhilarated, as the plane lifted off the ground, not only to leave Haiti but also with the task she has before her. She knew Lockwood was trying to protect her by giving peripheral information to investigate, but she made other plans. Johnny was sure she could do more without being in any real danger. And it would be all worth it. She planned her own mission. Find Winslow before it's too late, clear his name, and help save her paradise Barbados.

Chapter 18

19:45 New York City

From the moment Johnny landed in New York City, she became engulfed with the hustle and bustle of putting an international tour together. Jerry, her assistant, whom she considered more than a colleague, was at the airport in the company car waiting to pick her up. Most people were afraid of Jerry's acidic wit or in awe of his impeccable style and grace.

As Jerry exited the car, Johnny smiled at the stylish man she had a secret crush on until she found out he was gay. His slender athletic body and model good looks had women straining their necks to glimpse at him as he passed. Johnny found this all amusing since their stony stares at her were a waste of time.

"*Daarhling*, you look radiant as usual when you come back from Barbados. I could just knife you with envy for the first week. You look so golden," Jerry said as he hugged her. "Tell me all about the trip. And why are you coming back from Haiti instead of Barbados? You had some romance this time around? I know it had to do with some romantic entanglement. Otherwise, why would you cut your trip short and go to Haiti, of all places?"

"Believe me, my trip to Haiti has nothing to do with romance. Not this time." Johnny explained to Jerry about Winslow's apparent death and how she went to Haiti to mourn before she returned home. Although she trusted Jerry implicitly, she couldn't get him involved in her imbroglio. At least not this time. Her story about Winslow was the only way to quell Jerry's suspicions about her trip to Haiti. He understood their relationship, so he wouldn't find it strange that she left Barbados quickly.

"How awful for you. A death, right after New Year's Eve. And for it to be Winslow. I just can't believe it."

"It was very difficult. But the tour will be the best thing for me right now."

"So much is going on and a lot to be done before the tour. You will have your hands full." Jerry linked his arms with Johnny. "And there's so much gossip that I have to update you about. The holidays always bring more than just cheer and merriment."

Johnny was glad to have Jerry around. No matter how hectic or awful life sometimes could be, he could always make her smile or laugh. *It is going to be very difficult to keep my mission from him. He's very intuitive and good at sniffing out secrets.*

"Are the first dates and venues secured for the tour? I know there were some discrepancies before I left. I should have called, but I got all caught up and..."

"It's been all taken care of. You'll have a couple of days to get used to this cold weather before heading to London."

As Jerry continued to update Johnny on the business aspects of the trip, she gazed out the window. She was grateful to return to New York, but it just didn't seem the same to her. Her mind went back to Winslow and Lockwood. *What should be the first move?*

"Hell-*lo!* Are you with me or are you still in Haiti? I know you were supposed to be grieving, but are you sure you didn't have time for just a brief romance?"

"What did you say, Jerry? I'm sorry, but I'm still a little tired from the trip."

"There's a fabulous party tonight at Rea's, but I think the best thing for you, my dear, would be to get a good night's rest."

"Yes, I think you're right. After all, I'll be flying out of here in a few days."

The following days were so hectic for Johnny that Winslow was almost completely out of her mind. She had meetings all day regarding Naive's tour and interview schedules, then in the evening, she went to Naive's rehearsals.

By the time she got home, she was usually so tired; she didn't have time to think about anything except sleep. This was the schedule until she was back in the Escalade, heading to John F. Kennedy Airport in London.

"You have your flight and hotel confirmation?" Jerry asked, going through his checklist.

"Yes, I have everything."

"Did you change Naive's suite at the Connaught? You know how he only likes the penthouse suite?" asked Johnny.

"Yes, it's done."

Johnny turned to face Jerry.. "I think this will be a wonderful tour for Naive. It will definitely help his record sales and help to revive his career. His sales have been sagging a little lately."

"And that's not all that has been sagging. Did you catch those bags under his eyes?"

She laughed at Jerry's remark. "You can be so catty."

"Just stating the facts, dear, just the facts."

"I guess I'll get a brief vacation from you until we meet up in Paris," Johnny said flippantly.

"I know that you'll miss me dearly, but don't worry, we always make up for it in Gay Paree." After Johnny checked-in, she waited for Naive in the first-class lounge with Jerry. During the wait, they ate crudites while discussing the tour. They became so preoccupied with their conversation; they didn't notice how late it was. She turned to the clock on the wall and the time made her aware that Naive still hadn't arrived.

"I hope he doesn't miss this plane."

"We sent the regular car service and the driver that usually gets behind him about his timing," sighed Jerry. "I better call the office and see if there have been any messages from him." While Jerry made the call, Johnny ordered some tea. As the server walked away, Johnny's eyes opened wide with surprise at the man who walked towards her.

#######

Naïve's naked body laid prone on the bed, as he lifted his head slowly and squinted at his phone. He closed his eyes and flopped his head back down, facing the opposite side. Finally, that damn ringing noise stopped. After a few minutes, the ringing noise made him open his eyes to face a naked female body lying next to him. He lifted his head and squinted, trying to identify the woman next to him. A loud knock on his bedroom door lifted him from his stupor.

He answered in his toughest street voice. "Who is it?"

"It's Jimmy. From the car service to take you to the airport." Naive sat up on the bed and picked up his phone to check the time. He rose and almost tripped over the empty Hennessy and Veuve Clicquot bottles as he stumbled towards the door.

He cracked it open and peeked out. "Yo, Jimmy, give me a few and I'll meet you downstairs." After hearing the elevator door to his penthouse close, Naive shook the body on his bed. "Yo, yo, you gotta get up."

****

"Why Johnny isn't this a wonderful surprise? Are you taking the flight to London?" asked Ashton.

"Yes, I'm traveling on business with Naive. He's starting his European tour out of London."

"Oh, so that was who all the commotion was about when I got out of my car. I'm not too familiar with these new stars, but I recognized his face."

"Did you see him right outside?"

"Yes, he was signing some autographs as he was trying to enter the building."

"Jerry, I think you better go outside. Ashton said he just saw Naive trying to get into the building." Jerry ended his phone call and rose out of his seat. "I'm heading out there right now."

"This is a surprise. The last time I saw you was during New Year's Eve. Were you in New York for very long?" asked Johnny.

"No, I really just stopped over for about two days before heading to London. Now I'm so glad that I stayed over for a few days. It was worth it to see your beautiful face again."

"Are you going for business or pleasure?"

"A little of both, but at least now it will start off with pleasure since you will be on the same flight."

"Unfortunately, I'll probably not have any time since I'll be traveling with Naive."

"I completely understand, my dear. When business calls, one must always answer."

"Will you be visiting Henley while you are in London?" asked Johnny.

"Oh definitely. He might be jealous when you tell him we met on the flight."

Johnny gazed over Ashton's shoulder, looking for Naive.. "I hadn't planned on talking to him. I'm not sure that I would have the time. Plus, we haven't kept in contact since I last saw him in Barbados."

"Nonsense, my dear. I know Henley would be very disappointed if he heard you were in town and didn't even pick up the phone to call him. I'm sure you can find a few minutes in your busy schedule to have at least a quick chat.

Henley was probably traveling, and that is why he hasn't contacted you. You know the time differences and all that. But believe me, if he was in New York, there is no way he wouldn't get in contact with you."

"I'm going to try my best."

"Where will you be staying?"

"At The Connaught."

"If you don't mind, I would try to give you a ring and maybe meet for tea if your schedule allows?" asked Ashton.

"Sure."

"British Airways flight 201 is now boarding first-class passengers only," said the announcer.

"I better see what is taking Naive so long."

"Yes, my dear. Go ahead, I'll see you on the plane."

Johnny opened the door to leave the first-class lounge. She spotted Jerry coaxing Naive along as he stopped to sign autographs from fans.

"Naive, are you ready for the trip?" Johnny linked their arms and brought him into the lounge, as she gave Jerry a side-glance.

"Sure. Why not?"

"They're boarding the plane, so I think we better head to the gate."

"Okay, but I want to use the bathroom before we go," said Naive.

"t's right over there," pointed Jerry.

As Naive walked away, Johnny asked Jerry, "How is he?"

"He seems okay, but you know how he can be," Jerry said with a shrug.

Naive was usually nervous before a tour, but Johnny could tell he was more so than before. Both of them are aware he needs this to boost his record sales and revive his career.

Naive walked towards her. "All set?" asked Johnny

"Yeah, I guess so."

"Ok, let's get moving."

"Hope you have a pleasant flight and I'll see you in Paris.," said Jerry as he gave Johnny a European kiss on each cheek.

"Yes, and please make sure they confirmed all the transportation arrangements in London.

"Don't worry. It's done. Just relax while you still can on the flight and have a glass of champagne for me."

Chapter 19

09:35 London

The flight was smooth and calm. Air travel was always the most relaxing part of a business trip for Johnny, and night flights were her favorite. They offered uninterrupted time to think, away from ringing phones and endless meetings. She enjoyed the quiet of this flight, especially since Naive usually slept through the entire trip. But not this time.

Although Ashton sat a few rows ahead, he made her uncomfortable. He hadn't bothered her during the flight—in fact, she could almost forget he was there. But something about his presence unsettled her, and she couldn't figure out why. *Could it be his link to Henley? she wondered. That's probably it. I didn't leave things with Henley the way I wanted. But what else could I have done?* Her thoughts shifted to Winslow, her grief still fresh. *Maybe I should call Henley and let him know I'm in town. But that can wait.*

That wasn't her main concern. Her focus was on finding information for Lockwood. She still had no idea how she would do it, but her determination to try was unwavering. These thoughts were her last before she drifted off, lulled to sleep by the purring engine of the plane. She didn't wake until the gentle clinking of the flight attendants' serving carts rolled down the aisle.

Johnny lifted her window shade slightly, squinting as the bright sunlight tried to pour in. Rising, she headed to the bathroom to freshen up.

"The true test of a beautiful woman is how she looks in the morning," said Ashton as she exited. "And you definitely pass the test."

"I doubt you'd feel that way if you saw me before I went in," she replied, smiling politely.

"I'm sure I would have."

"You're too kind. Did you get any sleep?" she asked.

"Just a few winks. I never sleep well on planes."

"Good morning, everyone," came the captain's voice over the intercom. "This is your captain speaking. We'll be landing at Heathrow Airport in about 20 minutes. The weather is…"

"I'd better get back to my seat," Johnny said, stepping past Ashton.

"Yes, please don't let me keep you," Ashton said as he entered the bathroom.

Returning to her seat, Johnny glanced at Naive. He hadn't moved, his sleeping mask still covering his eyes. She hated to disturb him when he seemed so peaceful, but it was better to wake him before the plane landed.

"Naive, the plane's about to land. I think you'd better go to the bathroom and freshen up before they turn on the seat belt sign," she whispered.

"Yeah, okay," he grumbled, removing his mask.

"How long before we land?"

"About twenty minutes."

"I feel like we just got on this plane. Is there any black coffee?"

"I'll order some while you're in the bathroom," Johnny said.

As Naive shuffled off, Johnny walked to the flight attendants' station to get his coffee. On the way, she passed Ashton's seat.

"Johnny, can I speak to you for a moment?" Ashton called.

"Sure, Ashton, but I need to get coffee for Naive."

"This won't take long. I just wanted to ask if you'd like to meet for tea."

"Sure, Ashton. That would be nice. I just don't know when, given the schedule. But you can call me at the Connaught."

"I'll definitely do that," Ashton said with a smile.

When Johnny returned to her seat, Naive was back, wearing his sunglasses and leaning back against the headrest.

"Naive, here's the coffee you wanted," she said, handing him the cup.

"Thanks," he murmured, barely lifting his head.

Naive hated transatlantic flights. The jet lag always took a toll on him. He longed for a private plane for the tours, but his management never agreed to the cost. *Maybe this tour will finally be the boost I need, he thought. After all these years playing dives, I deserve a private plane. Maybe I can work it into my next contract. I'll talk to my lawyer about it.*

"Naive, are you awake?" Johnny asked.

"Yeah, I'm up," he replied groggily.

"Your coffee's getting cold, and the fasten seat belt sign just went on."

############

After clearing customs and getting the luggage, Johnny was relieved that the car was on time. London's weather was the usual dreary sky. But although it was the middle of winter, the temperature was mild. The thing Johnny loved about London was the weather in the winter. No harsh winds and snows like in America.

The Connaught's uniformed doorman with his top hat and white gloves opened the door.

"Welcome back Ms. Harrington", the doorman greeted her with his clip British accent. "And you too sir", he nodded to Naive.

"Thanks Gerard. It's nice to be back," said Johnny.

"Ms. Harrington and Mr. Naïve, it's so nice to have you back. I hope your flight wasn't too terribly overbearing," the concierge greeted them.

Johnny started signing the check-in paperwork. "It was surprisingly pleasant."

"Yeah, as pleasant as going to the dentist," added Naïve.

"Don't you worry. We'll make amends for any inconvenience you've had."

"Your favorite suites are ready and your luggage is already on its way up."

To Johnny, Royce seemed like a concierge from one of the old 30s movies. He is the stereotypical British valet and butler all in one. Sometimes he could be too obsequious, but his highly efficient manner and second sense knowledge of guests' needs makes up for it.

"Johnny, I'm heading up to my suite", said Naive as he headed to the elevator.

"Okay, I'll call you later."

"Ms. Harrington, you have several messages", said Royce. All of them forwarded to your voice mail in your suite. Naive's was also sent to your room. I thought he might not want to be disturbed as soon as he arrived", whispered Royce to Johnny.

"Thanks Royce. You always know what's best."

"Of course, Ms. Harrington. We are here to please. Will there be anything else?" "No, I'll just head up to my suite and answer these calls."

Johnny's suite was as large as some apartments. The warmth of a blazing fire in the fireplace and a silver tray with warm scones and a pot of tea on the living room table greeted her as she entered. The familiar antique furniture and homey sofa made her feel relaxed, as though she had returned home instead of to a hotel. That is the beauty of the Connaught, thought Johnny.

Johnny listened to her messages. It was the usual calls from the concert promoter, the record company, and various invites for Naive while he was in town. But there was one message that was not familiar to her. Although the person didn't ask for Naive, Johnny thought it might be one of his friends.

She returned the calls, set up rehearsal schedules and meetings, and gave Naive his messages. When Johnny gave him the last message, Naïve wasn't familiar with the person either. Johnny decided she would return the call later on that day. But for that moment, she took a walk around London.

Chapter 20

15:00 Mayfair London

The day was dreary, but it couldn't obscure the stately Georgian architecture that dominated the Mayfair area of London. Johnny enjoyed browsing the art galleries, especially the Timothy Taylor Gallery on Carlos Place. Occasionally, she would make a small purchase if something caught her eye, but today was different. Jet lag hung heavily over her, and she decided to head back to the hotel.

As she walked, a feeling of unease crept over her, the kind of instinctive sensation that someone was hovering nearby. Johnny instinctively quickened her pace. Turning a corner, she felt a tap on her shoulder. Her innate New Yorker defense mechanisms kicked in as she spun around and stepped back.

"Ms. Harrington?" the man inquired, staring at her with concern. "I'm so sorry if I startled you."

"Do I know you?" Johnny asked assertively, eyeing him cautiously.

"Ms. Harrington, again, please forgive my intrusiveness, but I've been trying to reach you. My name is Rogers Caruthers."

The tension drained from Johnny's body. "Oh, you were the one who left the message. I wasn't sure if it was for me or Naive. I didn't recognize the name, and you didn't leave a business affiliation. By the way, how were you able to identify me? I don't remember meeting you."

"Since I didn't receive a call back, I decided to visit your hotel and see if I could catch you as you returned. Mr. Lockwood provided me with a description of you and some of your vital information."

"Oh, so you work with Mr. Lockwood?"

"No, I wouldn't say I work with him," Caruthers replied with a chuckle. "Let's just say he's an old friend who asked me to do him a favor."

"Did he give you any information to pass on to me?" Johnny asked in a low voice, leaning in closer.

"No, nothing so mysterious," Caruthers replied, his voice matching her whisper, but with a mocking tone.

"Did Lockwood inform you about the entire situation?"

"Yes, he told me everything. Including your heroic aspirations," he said in his mocking upper class British accent.

"Are you here to help me or not?"

"I'm here to keep you out of trouble. But if you need my assistance, I will be available for you."

"Are you in the police force?," Johnny asked him but knowing the answer as she surveyed his Savile row suit and conservative Burberry raincoat.

"No, but I believe I'm qualified to give you any help that you may need."

"How do you know Lockwood?"

Caruthers pulled his raincoat collar up. "It is rather chilly out here for an inquisition? Why don't we go have some tea? It is that time. You must remember you are in London."

Caruthers hailed a cab to take them to The Ritz hotel. As they got into the cab, Johnny thought how Caruthers is the epitome of the British gentleman with his slender built bowler hat, and the ubiquitous London umbrella.

. . .

"Hello Mr. Caruthers. Your table is ready," said the maître d' as he led them through Ritz's Palm Court.   Caruthers greeted many acquaintances as they walked towards his table. Johnny loved the Palm Court's gilded mirrors and marble. When a person entered the Ritz, they felt like they are being taken back to another era of time.

"You are very sure of yourself to make reservations. Suppose you didn't run into me?

Caruthers pulled out Johnny's chair. "I have a standing reservation for tea. I guess you can say I'm a creature of habit."

"What are your other habits? Rescuing woman, you believe will be in distress?"

" I think it is time we order tea." He glanced up and the server approached the table.

"Is there a particular tea that you prefer? Or would you like to see the selection?" asked Caruthers.

Johnny surveyed the room. "I'll take Darjeeling."

"My usual", he said to the server.

"How many years have you've been coming here?"

"More years than I'm willing to admit."

Johnny still couldn't figure out his age and his answers were not helping her. Although she thought he might be a contemporary of Lockwood, she still wasn't sure.

"Now Mr. Caruthers, tell me how you know Mr. Lockwood. Are you an acquaintance of the family? Although I thought I knew most of Lockwood's family. But you could be a long-lost relative that I've never met."

"No, in fact, I don't think I've ever met any of Lockwood's family. Just say I'm an old acquaintance of Lockwood. We go back many years together."

"Where did you all go together?"

"Oh, my dear many places. Too many places to talk about."

"Mr. Caruthers, I thought you were going to tell me how you're qualified to help me."

"Oh, here is our tea now. I was wondering what was taking them so long. They are much quicker than this." Two servers appeared with sterling silver teapots, silver tea trays with scones, tea sandwiches cut in perfect triangles without crusts, and small pastries.

The servers placed the silver pots with clotted cream and various jams in front of them. Next to the silver teapots and the Ritz's Hotel emblem tea settings, were the silver tea strainers. Napkins were laid on Johnny and Caruthers laps before the waitstaff left.

"Ms. Harrington------"

"Please, call me Johnny."

Caruthers poured Johnny's tea through her strainer. A black string bracelet peeked beneath his French cuffs.

"Lockwood knows that I've been in London for many years and traveled in many circles. And while traveling in these social circles, I've become acquainted with various people. He believes I can answer questions you may have or give you any type of help while you're here."

"I'm sure he told you to keep an eye on me."

"Well, yes, he mentioned it."

"Mr. Caruthers ----," Uhm, he didn't say to call him Roger. The formality of the British,

"Mr. Caruthers what is that you do?"

"Let's just say that I'm a jack of all trades."

"And a master of none?" said Johnny. Whatever business he's in, it must be profitable because his Savile row tailored suit screams old money.

"Well, I don't know how you could help me." Johnny realized Caruthers was going to be evasive, so it was a waste of time asking him personal questions. After twenty minutes of stilted conversation and jet lag gradually taking over, Johnny found herself getting aggravated.

"I just wanted to introduce myself and let you know I'm here if you need me."

"This was very pleasant and I appreciate your time but I realize I should return to the hotel."

"Let me pay the bill and walk you to a cab."

"That's okay. It's not too far, so I think I'll walk."

"I don't think you want to do that. You may not have noticed but it is raining outside." She glimpsed out the window as the rain poured on the panes. Caruthers called the server and signed for the bill.

"Are you ready?" He asked as he returned the bill to the server.

"Yes"

Caruthers turned to the Ritz doorman. "We need a cab."

"It will be a few minutes, sir. Take a seat in the lobby. I'll let you know when it is here."

"Let's sit over here," Caruther said as he led her towards a couch.

"Where will Naive be performing?"

"At the Hammersmith Odeon," said Johnny as her eyes followed the people walking through the lobby. As Caruthers tried to make idle conversation, Johnny hoped the cab would arrive soon to end his effort.

"I've read a lot about his upcoming concert in the papers. I don't listen to his music so I 'm not familiar with his work."

"He's very good." "Sir, I have a cab waiting for you." As they trekked to the door, Caruthers stopped Johnny and said, "By the way, I'm sure you'll get an invitation to the Hawthornes party. They throw some of the biggest soirees in London. There is always an eclectic crowd---writers, artists, high society, intellectuals, and anybody who is anybody in London. I consider it a good place for you to be on Thursday."

"Why?"

"You want to be the next Mata Hari. I'm sure you'll figure it out." The doorman held an umbrella over them as he opened the cab door. Johnny stepped into the cab and Caruthers closed the door behind her.

"Do you need a ride?"

. "No, but thank you for a lovely afternoon."

"I hope you'll take my advice about the invitation."

"Will you be there?"

"You never know where I'll pop up," said Caruthers before he walked away from the cab.

Chapter 21

18:00 Connaught Hotel London

Johnny watched the raindrops trickle down the cab's window as London blurred past her. Succumbing to jet lag, her eyelids drifted closed.

"Miss, this is the Connaught," the cabbie's cockney accent roused her. She startled awake, paid the fare, and closed the cab door behind her. On the way to her room, the concierge handed her an envelope. Too overwhelmed by exhaustion to read it, she stuffed it into her bag.

Inside her suite, she sank onto the couch and tried to stay awake by flicking through the television channels. The last thing she wanted was to fall asleep and disrupt her adjustment to the time zone. The television voices blurred and slowed. Her hand on the remote stilled, then went limp as her eyes closed.

Amid her dreams, she heard bells ringing in the distance, growing louder and closer until she woke with a start to the shrill sound of the telephone.

"Miss Harrington, your car is waiting for you," the front desk informed her.

She glanced at her watch: 8:00 p.m. *Instead of a few minutes, I've slept for hours.*

"There must be a mistake. I didn't order a car."

"It's a car sent by the Hawthorne residence for you and Mr. Naive."

Johnny retrieved the envelope she had stuffed into her bag earlier and opened it. Inside was an invitation to a party at the Hawthorne residence that evening for her and Naive.

There's no way Naive would want to go out tonight, she thought, *and I'm still recovering from jet lag.*

"Please let them know we won't be using the car."

"Yes, Ms. Harrington."

Johnny walked out onto the terrace and gazed at the London evening skyline. Back in the living room, she picked up the invitation again, noticing the gold leaf trim and the gold pineapple symbol in the corner—the same symbol she had seen at Ashton's house in Barbados. She thought about what Caruthers had said about the party.

Without hesitation, she dashed to her bedroom to prepare.
****

Johnny entered the Connaught lobby dressed in a simple black sheath, a cascading pearl necklace draped around her neckline, and black Manolo Blahnik pumps. A trench coat was draped over her arm. At the front desk, she reminded the concierge not to transfer any calls to Naive's room. *He's probably already taken Ambien, so he won't notice I'm gone.*

As she stepped outside, the doorman noticed her waiting and immediately called over a black cab.

"Where to, Miss?" asked the cabdriver.

"28 Hyde Park."

The cab weaved through London's winding side streets before arriving at a townhouse across from Hyde Park. The modest exterior belied its spacious interior, revealed by a grand foyer. A desk at the entrance checked her name, and a butler relieved her of her trench coat.

Johnny followed the butler down a hallway toward a large wooden door, which opened to reveal a grand ballroom filled with people. In one corner, a small jazz quartet played softly. Waitstaff approached her with trays of wine glasses. Johnny took one and began strolling through the room, scanning the faces as she moved. Some were familiar.

Sitting by the window with his usual glum face was Bérnard, one of Europe's well-known intellectuals. Right next to him was Dominque, the world renown painter. Across the room, an international screen actress, currently involved in a romantic scandal. Johnny smiled, thinking how glad she is that Naive didn't attend the party.

She imagined Naive heading straight to the actress to begin another imbroglio she would eventually need to clean up. A tray passed by with canapes and Johnny was just about to take one when a voice behind her said, "Stay away from the scotch eggs, you never know how fresh they might be". She turned around to Caruthers, taking a sip of his wine while he surveyed the room. "Interesting room, wouldn't you say?"

"I see you made the party."

"Didn't I say, you never know where I might turn up." Caruthers glanced around the room. "Where is your ward?"

"If you are talking about Naive, he should be in his room resting up for tomorrow."

An elegantly dressed woman walked towards them and Caruthers smiled at her. "Katherine, you look younger and more beautiful every time I see you. How do you do it?", Caruthers greeted her with a European double cheek kiss. Her eyes quickly scanned Johnny. She said to Caruthers, "And who is your lovely companion?".

"Oh, you haven't met yet? This is Johnny Harrington, impresario extraordinaire, who works with Naive. Johnny, this is Katherine Hawthorne, the most important hostess in London."

Katherine glanced around and said, "Oh, is Naive here?"

"He is so sorry that he couldn't make it but the jet lag and all the travel has gotten to him. Plus, he has a long day tomorrow."

"Oh, I'm so disappointed. But I'm glad you made it. A beautiful and accomplished woman always makes a perfect mix for my soirees."

"I hope you will make the concert. There will be tickets for you."

"Oh, darling, concerts aren't my scene, but my niece Latisha would be thrilled."

"I will make sure she gets as many as she wants."

"I'm having a few guests at our weekend retreat this week, and you and Naive must come. I won't accept any answer except yes. I will send a car to your hotel."

"We will leave for Paris on Sunday. So, I don't think we will make it."

"Nonsense. Paris is only a hop and skip away. After your show, there will be a car waiting to whisk you and Naive away to our retreat. You can have a day or two to relax before the next show. Like I said, I won't take no for an answer."

She turned away to greet another guest that entered the room. "Katherine is very persistent, but she gives great soirees. You definitely impressed her because she invited you to her weekend retreat," said Caruthers.

"I really don't think we can make it". Caruthers sipped his drink and used his glass as an indicator circling the room. "Look around. Do you see the mix of notable faces? These are people who feel comfortable only in this type of environment. This isn't really one of her most exclusive parties. She doesn't just invite anyone to her weekend home. The number of guests is small and the real cognoscenti of not just London but also from the continent."

Caruthers took another sip of his wine and stared at Johnny. "If I was someone who needed to find out specific information, Katherine's weekend retreat would be a place I wouldn't miss." He walked away and headed towards a woman, whom he gives a double French kiss on the cheek.

Johnny asked one of the waitstaff for the lady's room. A finger pointed in an ambiguous direction, which confused her. She walked towards double doors she believed was the correct direction. Johnny noticed the handles on the door are in the shape of golden pineapples. She entered the room and got the tingle feeling of déjà vu.

Johnny moved towards a side board which had several pictures of Katherine with various people. Some appeared to be family. She picked up one frame. Her eyes widened. She stared at the photo. The picture had Katherine with a gentleman she remembered seeing at Ashton's home in Barbados. The man in the picture arrived in the Ashton Martin. Johnny glimpsed briefly at him, but was certain it was the same man.

Chapter 22

21:00 Hyde Park London

E xcuse me, Miss, but can I help you?" asked a voice coming from behind her. When she turned around, the person addressing her didn't have the uniform of the waitstaff, but he didn't seem like a guest either. She quickly placed the picture down and said, "Oh, I was looking for the bathroom. I thought the waitstaff pointed in this direction."

"This is the first time most of them have entered the house, so I would be surprised if they knew where anything is besides the kitchen and wine cellar. This way, please," the man said as he escorted her out. He pointed Johnny to the restroom door, and she entered. She reapplied her lipstick. *I need to look at that picture again and check out that room.*

She peeked out the door and scurried back to check out the picture. Johnny moved closer to the door, observed her surroundings to be sure no one was coming, and turned the knob. But the door was locked. She turned the knob again to make sure, but the unyielding knob confirmed the door's status.

Johnny, disappointed, walked back to the ballroom.

"Oh, there you are," said Katherine as Johnny entered. "There is someone I want to introduce to you." She took Johnny's arm and pulled her toward a tall man with a haughty appearance. "Johnny, this is Harry Belacorte. He is a huge fan of Naive's music. I told him he had to meet you."

Belacorte bowed his head and said, "It's my pleasure." Johnny could detect a slight accent but knew it wasn't British.

"Will you be in London tomorrow? I can make sure you get tickets for the show."

"Unfortunately, I do not think I will make it. I have to leave the country for business tomorrow," Belacorte said, as he gave a perfunctory glance around the room.

"Maybe at his—" Belacorte cut Johnny off in the middle of her sentence as he said, "Please excuse me." He made a courtly bow, turned, and languorously walked away.

Caruthers sidled up to Johnny and whispered, "I see you met Belacorte."

"Yes."

"Some people find him to be cold and off-putting."

"I can understand that."

Caruthers sighed and said, "Belacorte doesn't take fools lightly."

"I guess that applies to me."

"Not just you, darling. That applies to everyone. Belacorte is supposedly part of European royalty. A Viscount or something from some European country—I'm not sure which country or which title. But if you see Belacorte somewhere, I can assure you, you're in exclusive company."

"I think I've had enough of this exclusivity for tonight. It's time for me to leave."

"You seem disappointed. Did you think you would solve your mystery in one night with one party?" Johnny felt herself getting irritated by Caruthers's comments and didn't want him to see her mood change.

"I'm just tired. I guess the jet lag is taking over." Johnny was aware that Caruthers was right on point. She was disappointed. Although she didn't really know what clues she was looking for, the way Caruthers talked about this party, she just felt she would find or see something. *The picture—if only I could get back in the room. But I'm too tired to even think about that now.*

"Can I get a cab from here?"

"No need. Katherine has drivers available for guests. I can walk you out."

"I want to say goodbye to Katherine," Johnny said as they walked out of the room.

"No need, you will see her this weekend." Caruthers signaled to a car that stopped next to them.

"Like I told her, that is not possible."

Caruthers smiled as he closed the cab door and said, "You're an enterprising woman. I'm sure you'll make it work."

As Johnny rode in the cab, she thought, Why do I always seem to end my visits with Caruthers not only leaving in a car but with a lingering question about his comments?

Johnny sat in the green room of ITV's Good Morning Britain with Naïve. He nursed a hangover, drinking what he described as his "medicine". Although she thought she left Naive in his room safe and sound and away from any trouble, she forgot about room service. He stayed at the hotel and ordered in his vices.

"Naive, you need to drink the coffee."

"Yeah, yeah. Let me just get this down." He took the final swig, made a grimace, and then drank the coffee. The sound of knock came from the door. A Production Assistant entered the room and asked, "Is Mr. Naive ready for the make-up chair?"

Television shows want the talent to have their make-up touched up right before they go on air. Johnny knew that if they asked him to get in the chair, he will be on air soon. She wanted to give him as much time as possible to get his act together before he has his interview. Especially since it was live television, he had to be on point.

"He'll be right there. Just two more minutes", said Johnny. The PA gave a sheepish smile and closed the door.

"Look Naive, you can't hold off any longer. You've got to get it together. You know this is live television."

"I'm going to need something." Johnny was trying to keep Naive off of his pills, but it had been getting harder. She would normally try to distract him from taking them, but this was different. Not only was he suffering from a hangover, the interviewer, Piers Morgan, terrified him. Piers goes for the jugular, and he can also smell out a weak prey.

At that moment, Naive was definitely weak prey. "Okay." Johnny went into her bag, took out two pills, and handed it to Naive with a bottle of water. He liked to drink it with vodka, but she won't let him take it that way.

Naive took the pills and said, "Don't worry, Shortie, it will be fine. You know I always nail it at the end."

He pulled himself off of the couch, treaded carefully to the door, and opened it. The PA that was waiting to take him to the makeup chair, escorted him down the hallway. Johnny shook her head and followed behind him. The Naive that was in the green room disappeared. The artist Johnny watched interviewed by Piers Morgan was the confident and charming Naive. The one the world sees.

The fabricated Naïve. Brought to them, courtesy of the amazing magic of prescription pills. Johnny watched from the sidelines of the stage. Her phone lit up. Although, she kept her phone on silent when they do interviews, it is always on vibrate mode to see important calls. She checked her phone and read the text.

> Henley: Just got in town. Ashton told me you are here. Can we meet?

> Johnny: Doing interviews all day with Naive. Maybe for a drink tonight.

Henley: Where r u staying?

Johnny: The Connaught.

Henley: Let me know when u r available.

Johnny: OK.

Johnny smiled while watching Naive wrap up the interview and thinking about meeting Henley. After Naive walked off the set and Johnny said her thanks to Piers and the crew, Naive turned to Johnny.

"Well?"

"Yes, it's good"

"I told you Shortie, it would be okay", said Naive with a self-satisfying smile. Johnny sighed. She thought this is just the beginning of a long day. Naive might need another set of pills before the day is over. She checked her bag for the extra set. With a resigned sigh, She is sure the last stop on the tour will probably be the Betty Ford Clinic.

As Johnny and Naive went through the grueling press day itinerary, she couldn't help but think about her upcoming meeting with Henley. During the last interview at BBC 1 Radio, Johnny listened to Naive's repetitive talking points promoting his upcoming concert and dodging salacious rumor questions as she texted Henley to let him know she would be at the hotel in an hour.

Naive seemed more energized than in the morning. The pills were doing their job, which was a problem. They will hype him up the entire day and he will need something to bring him down. She texted one of the roadies.

Johnny: Need you to help out Naive tonight.

Lou: I got ya.

Back in her room, Johnny returned the obligatory reassuring call to the promoter. This has now become a routine on Naive's tour since he passed out on stage two years ago and had to cancel the tour. "He's in the best shape that he has been in years, Bill" , said Johnny on her phone call.

"Didn't you see him this morning on Good Day Britain?"

"Well then, you saw for yourself. Yes, yes Bill. I know he has sold out the Odeon. He will deliver. I promise you." The sound of a text came through and she glanced down at her phone.

Henley: I'm in the lobby.

Johnny: Be there in 10 min

Henley: Ok

Bill continued to rattle on. Most of the time she had the patience to deal with him but not tonight. She didn't want to appear rude. Johnny understood he was taking a risk booking Naive's first European tour since the incident. But he was also going to make a lot of money.

"Bill, Bill." She rolled her eyes. "Don't worry. We got this. I've got to go but I 'll see you tomorrow. You can come to the soundcheck. Yes. Yes. See you then."

Johnny quickly changed out of her outfit that she wore for press day and touched up her make-up. She was about to run out the door when the hotel phone rang. She stopped and looked surprised since everyone called her on her cell phone. Johnny thought it had to be the front desk and now she wondered what problem has Naive caused. She picked up the phone.

"Hello"

"Johnny, Lockwood here" It totally surprised her to hear from him and especially on the hotel phone.

She placed her bag down and said, "Mr. Lockwood, this is a surprise. I didn't expect to hear from you so soon."

"Just checking in on you, my dear. Did you have time to meet Caruthers?"

"Yes, he is quite a character."

"Caruthers is a good man. He is a good person to know in London. Caruthers knows everyone and if he doesn't know them, he can find them."

"He has been keeping an eye on me as you have instructed. In fact, he encouraged me to go to a party given by the Hawthornes. I was tired, but I went."

"The Hawthornes? The townhouse in London?"

"Yes. There was an eclectic group of guests. In fact, I saw a picture in the house and I swear I saw a man in the picture that came out of Ashton's house when I was in Barbados."

"Ashton? Was he there?"

"No, but Caruthers showed up, and he introduced me to Katherine Hawthorne."

"Did you meet Henry Hawthorne?"

"No, who is that?"

"Her husband."

"Maybe he was there, but I didn't stay long."

"You would have known if he was there. That is surprising."

"They are always together at her London parties."

"Maybe he wasn't there because she is having people over this weekend at her weekend home"

"How do you know this?"

"She invited me, but I told her I don't think I will make it because of our schedule. But she is very persistent. Even said she will send a car to the venue." Lockwood's inquisitive tone suddenly turned cryptic.

"Listen Johnny. Buy a burner phone and call me tomorrow. Call my office." Johnny's usual response would be to ask why, but she felt not this time.

"Ok. But what time?" Before she finished the sentence, Lockwood hung up the phone.

She stood looking at the phone, perplexed for a moment, then realized that Henley was still waiting and dashed out the door.

Chapter 23

20:00 Marylebone London

As soon as Johnny reached the bottom of the stairs, she noticed Henley seated in one of the lobby's high-back chairs, talking on his cellphone. He spotted her walking toward him and quickly ended his call. Henley, still tanned and looking especially fit in his bespoke suit, stood up to greet her. This was a different Henley than the one she had met in Barbados. He hugged her warmly and gave her a light peck on the forehead.

"Are you hungry?" he asked.

"Yes," Johnny replied.

"Good. I just made us reservations."

They stepped outside and got into a black cab. Henley started with friendly chatter but seemed slightly more formal than Johnny expected. There was a subtle tension between them. She realized that Henley, being too polite to ask outright about her abrupt departure from Barbados, was likely waiting for her to offer an explanation.

The cab stopped in an area Johnny didn't recognize at first. As they approached the restaurant doorway, the name caught her eye.

"Good evening, Mr. Williams, so good to have you with us again," the maître d' greeted. "We just finished setting up your usual table."

"Thanks, Brad. I know I gave you short notice, so I really appreciate this."

"No problem. We can always accommodate you."

As the maître d' pulled out Johnny's chair, she took in her surroundings. *The famous Chiltern Firehouse.* Most of the time, her schedule hadn't allowed her to visit, and on the rare occasions she could, reservations were impossible to get.

"They have an impressive wine list here, and I love the sea bass," Henley said.

"I've heard so much about this place, but I've never been able to get a reservation while on tour," Johnny admitted.

"Just let me know anytime you want to come, and I'll call Brad to set up a table. I'm sure they'd love to have Naive as a customer."

Johnny realized it was time to address the elephant in the room. "I'm sorry I didn't respond to your calls when we were last in Barbados. A close friend of mine suddenly died, and I—"

Henley reached across the table, took her hand, and kissed it. "We're here now, in another country and a different time. Let's enjoy this moment together."

They spent the evening talking about London and the upcoming concert while enjoying their meal. Henley ordered several bottles of wine, and Johnny found herself not only enjoying the food but also his company. When she glanced at her phone, she realized how late it had gotten.

"It's really getting late. I need to look over some work before bed," she said.

"I'll have Brad call us a car."

Henley signed for the meal without using a credit card—likely an ongoing tab paid through the company's expense account. Suave, Johnny thought as they left the restaurant.

The cab ride back to The Connaught was quiet but pleasant. At the hotel, Johnny was surprised when Henley followed her to the door. He walked her into the lobby and stopped at the elevator.

"This was really nice, but I have to end the evening," Johnny said firmly.

"When can I have some more time with you?" Henley asked.

"I don't know. Between the show and the press days, things get really hectic," she replied.

Henley leaned in, kissed her cheek, and said, "I'll call you."

Johnny watched him leave through the lobby doors before taking the stairs to her room. Her thoughts were filled with the evening spent with Henley. Once inside, she collapsed onto her bed, exhausted from the busy press day and the evening's wine. Suddenly, she jolted upright, remembering the call she had with Lockwood.

Chapter 24

16:00 Odeon Milton Keynes Stadium London

The day of a show is like the calm before the storm. A quiet sea. Then the waves rush back, taking over the shore and the land, destroying everything in its path. This is what life is like when a tour comes into a city, and finally, it is opening night. Johnny entered the Hammersmith Odeon and passed the roadies setting up the equipment.

Although she had seen many venues during the day for soundcheck, there was a sadness in their appearance. It's like seeing an old whore in the daylight. You see all of her flaws behind the fading beauty, but at night, with makeup and the perfect lighting, she is an eternal beauty. She walked over to Lou as he began to set up the microphones and said, "Thanks, Lou, for taking care of the problem last night."

"No worries. Let me know if you need any more."

"Hopefully not."

Lou gave Johnny a sly grin with a chuckle and said, "Okay."

The backup singers had arrived and were going through their portion of the soundcheck. Johnny stood at the side of the road manager as he talked to the sound engineer.

126

"Check Ayesha's levels. I think they are off," said Bobby.

"I went through them twice already. Maybe it is her, not the equipment," said the sound engineer.

"Take off just a little of the treble, and let's see how that sounds." The engineer followed Bobby's instructions and nodded. Bobby smiled at him.

"Okay, okay, you're right."

"I'm always right, my man," said Bobby confidently as he stepped off the sound engineer's platform. Johnny respected Bobby's strive for perfection in every part of the tour, yet she was confounded by the disparities between his life on and off the road. Bobby could be so reckless in his personal life, which was full of women and booze. As soon as he hit the road, that all went away. He was as straight as an arrow, putting all his vices behind him.

"How's everything going?" asked Johnny.

"As well as it can get without Naive."

"He's not here yet?"

"You know how he gets. I just sent Freddy and Lou to get him over here."

"If I knew he wasn't here, I would've gone to his room."

"Hey, that's our job. You know we take care of that."

Johnny checked the time. There would be a few hours before the show and the opportunity to sneak away before Naive came.

"Bobby, I have to do some errands. I'll be back in a few."

"Go do you, babe. That light sequence is off. Try it again," Bobby yelled to the light technician as Johnny walked out the door. She jumped into a cab and directed the driver to take her to Hackney. The neighborhood started as a British working-class area and now is an immigrant working-class area.

Now that gentrification has taken over most places in London, Hackney is part of the trend. Johnny noticed the changes in the neighborhood as the cab drove through the narrow streets. The lonely Burberry outlet that was a fashionista's secret is now a more upscale satellite store than an outlet. It isn't so lonely anymore. It has neighbors such as Pringle, Aquascutum, Nike, Prada, and other designer boutiques.

These boutiques may have moved into the neighborhood, but there was still the greasy fish & chips shop and curry spot Johnny loved. The cab turned down a street that still had all the old Hackney shops and West Indian grocery markets with plantains, yams, and cassava displayed in their vegetable stands. The cab stopped in front of a tiny indistinguishable shop. It would not be easy to get a cab in this area, so she asked the driver to wait.

"I'll have to keep the meter on Miss" , the driver said with a cockney accent.

"No problem, I will be back in five."

Johnny entered the congested store that seemed to sell everything.

"I'm looking to purchase a phone with a sim card for international calls."

"Do you want data capability also, asked the salesperson."

"Yes, I feel so silly but I lost my phone on the plane." Johnny knows the owner can tell she has an American accent and wouldn't be suspicious why she wanted to buy a phone with international capability.

Unfazed, he brought out a couple of different phones for Johnny to choose. After purchasing the phone, she headed back into the cab.

"I think I'm going to try some shopping around here. Can you please drop me off at the corner?" Johnny paid the cab and walked toward Chatham Place. She passed the windows of the Burberry store and then strolled over to Aquascutum. After perusing some sweaters, she crossed the street for her favorite fish and chips shop.

Johnny placed her order and then sat at a small corner table. She surveyed her area. The shop is empty except for another customer eating alone at the opposite end of the shop. Johnny checked the time and then took out the phone she just purchased and placed a call.

"It's Johnny. I wasn't sure if I should let Ms. Braithwaite know who it is."

"Don't worry, there isn't anyone that I can trust more than Braithwaite" , said Lockwood. "Plus, she knew it was you. After all these years, she knows your voice. I instructed her to send your calls directly to me no matter what I'm doing."

"So, what is the big mystery? What is with me having to get this phone? Did you hear from Winslow?", Johnny asked excitedly.

"Where are you?" asked Lockwood.

"I'm in the Hackney area at a fish & chips shop."

"Is there anyone else around who can hear this conversation?"

Johnny took a furtive glance at the other customers. "No, just one customer at the other end of the shop. Why did you need me to buy a phone to call you?"

"I needed you to have a burner phone because after our conversation, you must destroy the sim card and the phone."

"What?" Johnny took a quick stare at the phone. "Ok. Tell me what this is all about."

"You need to accept the invitation to the Hawthorne's weekend retreat."

"It doesn't seem that she is going to let us refuse. She said that she will be sending a car to the venue to pick us up after the show."

"Good. Perfect. The Hawthornes are part of London's chic high society, but we believe they are involved or at least surround themselves with an international drug ring. There is a surveillance on them. Many of the people we believe are part of the ring have been tailed to the Hawthorne's weekend house.

But we haven't been able to get inside. You will be our first chance." Lockwood's revelations surprised Johnny. She thought she would hear a few things, maybe while backstage at a concert or at a party. It might just be gossip, but maybe it would be something that Lockwood could use. Now she is being asked to go to another level. Somehow it felt more real than she might be ready for.

"Wow. I really wasn't expecting to hear this."

"Look, Johnny, I'm just telling you this because I know you said you wanted to help with the investigation. You can back out anytime.

I was wary of you getting involved any way. I would understand if you don't feel comfortable."

"No no. I'm fine. I'm just shocked that now it seems so real now but I'm ready. Whatever you need.", said Johnny eagerly.

"If at any time, you feel uncomfortable, just leave wherever you are. Nothing is worth you getting hurt or worse."

"I'll be fine, remember I'll be with the Hawthornes and they are part of polite society. Johnny dipped one of her chips in ketchup before eating it. "They don't call it polite society for nothing."

"Just watch and listen carefully to happenings while you are in the house. If you can take pictures, that would also be good. But don't make them suspicious. Try to buy a couple of burner phones to use while you are out there."

"Burner phones?" Johnny continued to eat some of her chips.

"I hope no one can hear you."

"No, I told you there is just one customer across the room and he is all into scrolling through his phone."

"Yes, a burner phone. Like the one you are talking to me on right now. You should never call me on your own phone. I don't want your calls to be traced. And please don't ever say burner phone again where there is a possibility for someone to hear you." Lockwood shook his head and wondered whether he is making the right decision by letting Johnny get involved in this investigation.

"Ok. I get it."

"After you use this phone, I want you to destroy it. Do you know how?", asked Lockwood.

"I'll take out the sim card, cut it up and throw out the phone" , said Johnny confidently.

"That isn't good enough. You will need to destroy the actual phone as well." If you can't destroy the phone. Just destroy the sim card and keep the phone with you until you can destroy it."

"Okay. No problem. Have you heard anything from Winslow?"

"No, and I don't expect I will.

"I guess I'll call you when I get to the Hawthornes."

"No, don't call unless it is really important information that can't wait until you leave the house. And of course, if you need help."

"I'll be fine."

"Just be careful." Johnny called for an Uber and returned to the Odeon.

Chapter 25

19:00 Backstage Odeon Milton Keynes Stadium London

Johnny entered the backstage area, confronted by the sounds of a weary Naive going through his soundcheck. Bobby was in his usual stance at the back of the theater, arms crossed in front of him. He concentrated on every note that was sung and every move made by the background singers and dancers. While he was in this trancelike state, everyone knew not to interrupt him. Johnny walked toward him and stood quietly by his side. The music stopped, and the dancers weren't moving. The theater was quiet until Bobby spoke.

"Ava is a little off. Turn up her treble. Jada, you didn't hit your spot on time. Go over the steps again."

"I was on time; it's Jalen."

"Ava, I said you were off. Are you the road manager? Are you the choreographer?"

"No, but—"

"But nothing," Bobby said slowly and deliberately. "Until I change your position on this tour, you will go over your steps. Do we understand each other?" Ava knew by Bobby's tone that if she wanted to stay on this tour, the argument was now over. She rehearsed her steps again with the other girls.

"How is Naive?" asked Johnny.

Bobby kept looking at the stage.

"Like he usually is before the beginning of a tour. He'll be fine by tonight."

Johnny took out her work phone and checked the texts. She noticed one from Henley.

Henley: Hope to see you again soon

Johnny smirked as she read the text. She had almost forgotten about the evening she had with Henley after getting the call from Lockwood. There wasn't any possibility that she could meet Henley before she went to the Hawthornes.

Johnny: Me too.

Johnny searched in her bag and found the burner phones she purchased, separating them from her work phone. She removed the receipts from the different shops where she bought the phones and threw them away. Johnny listened to Bobby continue to give out directions, but her mind was thinking about her upcoming trip to the Hawthornes.

****

Johnny stood at her usual spot at the side of the stage as the first show of the tour ended. Naive finished his last step and jumped off the stage. They hyped him up as usual, and his eyes searched for Johnny to see her reaction. She smiled, gave him a nod, and a wink. He returned to the stage for a final encore and applause before he finally went backstage.

"Starting off good, right, Shortie?"

"Yep, great." She walked with him to the wardrobe room. He

dropped onto the couch, pulled a Heineken out of the cooler, and took a swig.

"Don't get too comfortable. We need to leave as soon as possible," said Johnny.

"Why? We don't have to leave for Paris yet, and I'm sure there's a party over at Annabelle's."

"They've invited us to the Hawthornes' weekend retreat, which is right outside of London."

"Why would I want to leave London? All the fun is here. Plus, there are a few people I need to look up." Johnny knew when Naive said he had a few "people" to look up, it meant checking out his London groupies.

"The Hawthornes invited us to their party, but you weren't really up to it that night, so they are expecting you to come to their weekend home."

"Am I supposed to be a show pony? Why should they expect me to come to them?" Naive asked as he guzzled his beer.

Johnny had to convince Naive to spend the weekend at the Hawthornes, or else he would blow everything for her.

"Okay, maybe I shouldn't say that they expect you to come but that they would be very disappointed if you are not there."

"Like I said, all the fun is in London. Why should I go the countryside?"

"You know, when I went to their party, it seemed like most of the social London set was there. She had quite a mix of people."

Naïve placed is feet on the table. "I don't give a shit about the London social set. They bore me."

Johnny stared at his dressing room mirror and fixed her hair in a desultory manner.

"Oh, I know that, but I thought you might be interested in Chloe Armand." Naive suddenly sat up and put his beer down.

"Chloe Armand. She was at the party?"

"Oh, yeah. I heard she is usually at all of their soirees. She's practically a part of their family." Johnny knew she would have to dangle this secret weapon to get Naive to change his mind. He had been trying to get close to Chloe for a few years, after she brushed him off at the Vanity Fair Oscars Party. She's an international movie star and even though he is an international music artist, she wouldn't give him the time of day. Chloe was usually in a scandalous relationship with a married billionaire and only billionaires. She doesn't even date multi-millionaires, she thinks they are a waste of her time.

"Is she going to be there for the weekend?" Johnny knew she had him on a hook and needed to keep him there.

"I would think so, since she was at their party." Now was the time to add the extra bait to assure his attention.

"You are not still interested in her, are you? You know you are not her type." That was the stab at his ego that he couldn't resist. Johnny just waved a red cloth in front of Naive like a bullfighter waving at a bull.

"What time are we leaving?"

Chapter 26

01:00 Blenhen Estate Herefordshire UK

After the congratulations from well-wishers, Johnny and Naive hurried out through the backstage door. Naive paused briefly to sign a few autographs before they jumped into the car. Despite the late hour, Naive wore his obligatory black sunglasses, not only to conceal his red eyes but also to shield himself from the relentless paparazzi flashes. He slumped into the car seat.

Johnny scrolled through her phone for messages as the bright lights of the city gradually receded into the distance. She skimmed through the texts but couldn't stop thinking about what she would do if Chloe wasn't at the Hawthornes. It had been a huge gamble to lie to Naive, but she'd had no other way to change his mind.

The driver veered off the highway, continuing along small country roads. Here and there, dim lights glowed from cottages and small manor houses. Soon, the car rolled onto dark, narrow roads illuminated only by the car's headlights. Finally, they turned onto a path leading to a massive estate house. The car stopped on the gravel driveway in front of the house.

The driver opened the door, and Johnny nudged Naive awake. As they stepped out, a butler greeted them warmly.

"Because of the late hour, the Hawthornes have retired, but anything you need will be provided. I can have the cook prepare something for you if you are hungry," the butler offered.

Johnny shook her head politely. She typically avoided eating this late, as they often snacked on the backstage food provided by the promoter.

"No, we're fine. Just tired," she replied.

"Of course. I'll show you to your rooms."

"I would really like a drink," Naive interjected.

"Of course. I can have it sent up to your room," the butler replied smoothly.

"Scotch and soda on ice," Naive specified.

"Certainly. If you'll follow me," the butler said, leading them up a winding staircase to the second floor and down a long hallway. He opened a door to reveal Naive's room, where his luggage had already been placed.

"By the way, could you bring a shaker with some ice to go with the bottle of scotch?" Naive added.

The butler smiled and nodded. "Of course."

"The Hawthornes will be in the breakfast room by 10:00 a.m.," the butler informed them.

"Naive won't be downstairs until 2:00 p.m.," Naive mockingly replied. Johnny shot him a scolding look before thanking the butler for the information.

After leaving Naive's room, they walked further down the hallway to Johnny's. Her room mirrored Naive's, with a massive wooden four-poster bed draped in fabric and topped with a canopy. An upholstered daybed occupied one corner, and a set of doors led to a balcony overlooking the sprawling grounds. Johnny moved the luggage placed in her room and took in her surroundings. If she'd been blindfolded and brought here, she would have assumed she was in a five-star hotel.

"Can I get you anything?" , the butler asked in his clip British accent.

"No, thank you", Johnny told him as he turned to leave. "But one more thing."

The butler turned around to face her as Johnny walked towards him.

"Please send just one glass of Scotch whiskey and water for Naive, and not the entire bottle. I'm sure the Hawthornes would like to see him during the day."

The butler nodded with a serious face and said, "Of course." Johnny opened the balcony door. She spotted another car approaching the estate and stepped onto the balcony. The car door opened and two men stepped out of the car and walked towards the house. She glanced at her watch.

It was 2:00am. Johnny thought they would be the last guests to arrive at the Hawthornes, but she was wrong. While Johnny was lying in the bed and about to close her eyes, she looked drowsily up at the canopy. The design of a pineapple is in the center of the canopy as she fell asleep.

*****

Johnny entered the breakfast room and the face the Hawthornes sitting at the head of the dining table that could seat at least 15 people. The room had wood panel walls with floor to ceiling windows and doors that faced out to a large patio. Katherine turned and smiled at Johnny.

"Good morning. So sorry that we weren't up to greet you but I hope you slept well."

"Yes, I did. It is a very comfortable room."

"Oh, good. Please come over and let me introduce you to my husband, Henry. Henry, this is Ms. Johnny Harrington that I spoke about to you." He rose out of his seat, smiled, and pulled out her seat.

"Welcome, my dear. We are so glad you can join us for the weekend." A waitstaff comes over to Johnny and asked if she would like some coffee or tea.

"Coffee please, black with no sugar."

"We have a buffet laid out for everyone, but if you want anything that isn't there, just let me know and I will have the cook make it for you."

"I'm sure this will be fine." She walked over to the sideboard, which was laid out with covered silver serving dishes over warming trays keeping the breakfast food warm. As Johnny picked out her food, Katherine said to her, "I guess Naive is just like some of our other guests who are sleeping in late."

"Naive rarely wakes up until after midday."

"Well, he will be in good company when he comes down to breakfast," said Henry.

"He never eats breakfast. Only drinks coffee in the morning.", said Johnny, after sipping her mimosa.

"We try to make the weekend as comfortable and relaxing for everyone. No schedules. It's really a laissez-faire attitude for the weekend. But for people who would like to take part in some activities, I have my yoga instructor coming over to do a session in the sunroom. It's quite a lovely place to practice yoga in the afternoon," said Katherine.

"For the outdoorsy type, we have skeet shooting which Williams sets up", said Henry. It surprised Johnny they didn't say there was going to be a hunt, since they seem like the quintessential British Lady and Lord of manor. Katherine appeared different in her tweed jacket and jodhpurs from the urban socialite that Johnny met a few nights ago in London.

"I would love to walk around the estate and take in some views of the area," said Johnny.

"We can have one of our staff give you a tour of Blenhen or if you ride, you can take one of the horses," said Henry. *This would be a good time to look around the estate.*

"I would love to just take some pictures, if you don't mind. We are thinking about shooting Naive's next video in a setting just like this estate. I think we could get some wonderful ideas." To Johnny,

Katherine was the typical society fame seeker. Although they have immense wealth, they crave fame also. Their estates are featured in different architectural magazines but most aren't in film. This is the apex for fame seekers.

"Of course, but I think you could get a better idea if I had our estate manager escort you around."

"I really would like to walk around by myself but if I find I need more information, I will definitely talk to him."

"If you are looking for a setting like this estate, why not use the real thing. You could shoot it right here," Katherine says gleefully as she waved her hand around the room.

"Well, that isn't up to me, but I will definitely bring up the idea if they like the photos." Johnny was getting deeper into the lie than she intended. She hoped Katherine will not bring up the subject with Naive because he wouldn't know what she was talking about. As Katherine was talking about the virtues of filming at Blenhen,

Johnny glanced out the window. Two men with guns slung across their shoulders for the skeet shoot were walking across the estate. *Maybe they are the men that arrived late last night.* As one of them turned to look back, Johnny caught a glimpse of his face. Her eyes opened wide as he walked with the other men. It was the man she saw leaving Ashton's house in Barbados.

"Oh, I see you like my ideas. I have plenty more that I can tell you", said Katherine as she noticed the expression on Johnny's face suddenly change.

Johnny started to put her jacket on. "I really would like to get out and start taking some pictures while I have good sunlight. You never know with the British weather, if there will be a sudden downpour."

"Please enjoy yourself." As Johnny was about to go out the patio doors, she turned back and asked," Which way is the skeet shooting?"

Henry entered the room. "It is on the other border of the estate. Near the lake. I was just on my way......."

"Thanks" She rushed out before Henry finished his sentence and closed the patio doors.

Johnny took some perfunctory pictures while the Hawthornes could see her. When she was out of their view, she rushed towards the skeet shoot. Heading towards the woods, the sounds of the clay pigeons exploding got louder the closer she came to the shoot. She got as near as she could without them having the ability to spot her and tried to get some pictures of the men.

Johnny searched for the man that she recognized. She spotted him but had to get closer to get a picture of his face. Johnny stepped lightly among the leaves in the woods as she moved as close as possible. She took two shots and was about to take a third when a twig snapped. Johnny jumped and spun around to see Henry Hawthorne facing her.

"My dear, why are you hiding behind these trees taking pictures?" Johnny couldn't believe she didn't hear him approaching. The noise of the guns from the skeet shooting camouflaged his steps.

"Trying not to disturb them and I wanted to get natural shots while they were shooting."

Hawthorne smiled and said, "Don't worry, nothing can disturb them when they are concentrating on their shots. You are welcome to join the shoot."

"I think I have enough. I'm going to walk to the creek." Johnny walked away as Hawthorne joined the skeet shoot. She turned around quickly. Hawthorne was talking to the other men while they stared in her direction. Hopefully, he believed her story. She made a note to be more aware of her surroundings while she walked around. Johnny walked on the separate side of the Blenhen to take photos.

She stopped and peeked through the pane glass door windows that opened into a large room. Through the window, the room appeared to be a study or a library. She turned the doorknob and it opened. Johnny surveyed the area before entering the room. There was a leather couch and two leather chairs on the side of the room. On the other end were shelves full of first edition classic books.

In front of the shelves was a large wooden desk that had the pineapple motifs carved in the front panel. She took a few pictures and then walked behind the desk. The top of the desk was empty. She peeked out the window to see if anyone is in her sight line. Johnny pulled the top draw of the desk and found pens, paperclips, and other stationery materials.

She searched through another drawer and came across stationary with the same pineapple motif. Johnny kept searching until voices of people talking in the hallway came towards the room. She quickly opened the glass door and went back out on the grounds, closing the door quietly behind her. Johnny walked back towards the front of the house when she was confronted by Katherine.

Chapter 27

11:00 Blenhen Estate Herefordshire UK

"Oh, I was just going to look for you." Katherine walked over to Johnny and linked their arms as they strolled the grounds together.

"I think that I have made a match." Katherine led Johnny to the other end of the estate. They walked outside of the breakfast room, where Katherine pointed to Chloe Armand and Naive sitting close, talking and laughing as they drank mimosas.

On one hand, Johnny smiled as she gave a sigh of relief that Chloe Armand was at Blenhen. She didn't know how she would have kept Naive there if Chloe hadn't shown up. However, the sight of mimosas flowing and animated conversation could only signal trouble Johnny would eventually have to clean up.

"They seem to get along so well," Katherine said gleefully.

"I know Naive will be grateful that you invited Chloe. They know each other, but their schedules never seem to coincide."

"Well, maybe the love gods—with a little help from mortal me— have made a love connection," Katherine quipped.

Johnny sighed. "Well, we'll see."

"Will you be joining us for afternoon tea?" Katherine asked.

Maybe the men at the shoot would be there, Johnny thought. It would give her a chance to get a closer look at them and get an idea of who they were. "Will I have to change?" she asked.

"Darling, it's a casual weekend. You can come as you are."

"What will most of your guests be wearing?" Johnny hoped for a more definitive answer to gauge how many people might be there.

"Most of them will come in from roaming around the estate. You'll be fine," Katherine said as she walked inside Blenhen.

Johnny went back inside to check on Naive's mood. She was glad that Lady Luck had given her a break, with Chloe actually spending the weekend at Blenhen. It was perfect. Naive would be busy with Chloe, leaving Johnny free to gather more information.

As Johnny entered the breakfast room, Naive and Chloe were so enthralled with each other that they didn't notice her. She approached the table, and Chloe turned toward her with a smile. Naive finally shifted his attention to her, a boyish grin spreading across his face.

"Johnny, come and meet Chloe. Chloe, this is my girl—I mean, you know, not my girlfriend, but you know..." Naive stammered.

Johnny felt sorry for him. Despite his public persona as a cool guy with plenty of swagger, he now seemed like a lost puppy meeting his new family for the first time. She decided to rescue him from his awkwardness.

"It's great to meet you," Johnny said to Chloe. "I work with Naive and make sure the trains run on time."

Chloe returned the smile but gave her a curious look.

"Don't worry, it's an inside joke," Johnny added quickly.

"They'll be serving afternoon tea in a few minutes. All the guests will probably be there," she informed them.

Naive gazed at Chloe. "We just finished breakfast not too long ago."

"I'm surprised you're up this early. So unlike you," Johnny teased.

"Yeah, I only got up to find out if I could get something for my headache—and bumped into Chloe."

"Oh, and how's the headache? Did you get something for it?"

"You know, it just went away," Naive said, smiling, his eyes fixed on Chloe, who giggled like an innocent schoolgirl.

Johnny couldn't take any more of their phony façade. After he sleeps with her a few times, the fascination will wear off. She smirked inwardly. And Chloe—using her acting skills to pull off this coy act? Everyone knows she's bedded some of the biggest stars in Hollywood, both men and women.

"I think we should go to tea. Katherine always has the most interesting people," Chloe purred.

"Whatever you want to do. I'm with it," Naive replied.

"Okay, I'll see you both in a bit."

As Johnny headed upstairs to her room, voices echoed through the grand entrance hallway. From the second-floor balcony, she saw the Barbadian man from Ashton's house entering the grand hallway. Her heart raced. Johnny rushed to her room, fixed her makeup and hair, and then made her way to the tea room.

The large room, which has ceiling to floor windows that open out to the grounds, had several seating areas. Each area had a tea service complete with typical British tea sandwiches, scones, and pastries for six people.

Right across the room from Johnny was Naive, in one corner, cozying up with Chloe. Across the room were the men from the shoot sitting having whiskey along with their tea, but the man from Barbados wasn't with them. She glanced around the room but didn't find him. Johnny moved towards Naive's table.

"I see you are still with us," Johnny said to Naive as she sat and the butler asked her to choose her tea.

"I'll take Darjeeling." Johnny turned to Chloe and said, "You seem to be an excellent influence on him. We need you to be on tour with us."

"That's what I told her," said Naive. Johnny was joking and definitely doesn't want Chloe to take up on the offer. She imagined the full-blown headache with Chloe on the road. The fights she would referee between Naive, Chloe, groupies, and the press. She signaled the butler.

"Can I get a French 45?" The butler nodded in acknowledgement before he walked away.

"You rarely drink," said Naive slightly surprised. "I'm glad to see you loosen up a little."

"Somebody needs to be sober during the tours."

"Yeah, and I'm glad that's your job. Don't know how you do it."

After the butler brought her drink, Johnny roamed the room to get closer to where Henry was sitting with the men from the skeet shoot. She walked by the window near their sitting area. Gazed out towards the grounds as she sipped her drink. Johnny tried to pick up some tidbits from their conversation, but she wasn't close enough to hear them.

She was as close as she could get without them thinking she was eavesdropping on their conversation. Before she turned away, Henry waved for her to come over. One of the gentlemen rose and pulled out a chair for her to sit at their table. Trepidation flew over her. She hoped Henry would not talk about meeting at the skeet shoot. "I don't want to interrupt your conversation."

"Please sit with us," said Henry, gesturing towards the chair. "Let me introduce you. This is Babbs, Pinky, and Shelby. Each person stood and extended a handshake. *So British.* "Gentlemen, this is Johnny Harrington, the formidable publicist working with Naive. They have been gracious enough to join us this weekend before continuing their tour."

"No, you and Ms. Hawthorne are the gracious ones to extend your invitation to us."

"We hope that you and Naive are enjoying the weekend."

"Yes, very much so. As you can see, Naive is especially enjoying himself." She nodded over at them canoodling.

"Chloe can be quite enchanting. I hope you got all the pictures that you needed."

"The grounds are beautiful," Johnny said nonchalantly while sipping her drink.

"I hope you got enough pictures to consider the estate for your video. Do you really think it will be filmed here" Did he tell Katherine how he caught her taking pictures by the shoot or did she excitedly tell him what she hopes will happen?

"It's possible. That's why I wanted the pictures to take back when we discuss plans for the next video."

"When will you shoot the next video?" asked Babbs. Suddenly, this casual conversation felt like an interrogation.

"I'm not sure of the exact date. In fact, I don't think they have confirmed a date yet." Johnny wanted to end the conversation. She got up and checked her phone.

"Excuse me, I just realized I have to return a missed call." The pictures needed to be sent to Lockwood as soon as possible. She quickly checked her surroundings before she sent the pictures. In order to give Lockwood time to look them over, she decided to take a leisurely stroll.

Hopefully, he would call her before she had to go back inside. If not, the phone would have to be destroyed before he talked to her. She walked in the garden. The man from Barbados trekked across the path and towards the woods. Johnny's heart began racing. She sprinted after him. This is the picture that she needed to send to Lockwood.

Chapter 28

13:00 Blenhen Estate Herefordshire UK

Johnny treaded lightly, trying not to make the sounds of extra footsteps. She stopped, hiding behind a tree to put some distance between her and the Barbados man. He made a sharp right, and she lost sight of him. Johnny scurried to catch up, where the trees were now closer, denser, making the area foreboding.

Now, she was too far to go back but apprehensive about moving ahead. The Barbados man was in her sight. He walked toward a clearing in the woods. She got to the edge of the clearing and jumped behind a tree before the Barbados man turned his head in her direction.

He walked a few feet and entered a cabin. Johnny dashed out of the woods and raced to the tail of the building. Crouching down, she crept under the windows and got next to a side door. Edging up and peeking through the door window, she got a close view of the Barbados man. Johnny took out the phone to take a picture. The phone rang. Oh shit. Her body froze along with her heart and breath. Panic slowly enveloped her body. Her shaking hands tried to find the ring button she had forgotten to turn off.

Click. The latch pulled open. Johnny didn't have time to run. She used cat-like steps to move her body toward the end of the cabin and lie against the wall, hoping he wouldn't turn in that direction. The Barbados man's back was visible to Johnny as he faced the woods.

He turned, glanced around, and walked toward her side of the cabin. She got a glimpse of his leg. A bead of sweat slowly ran down her face. A loud sound of a phone ringing made the leg move in the opposite direction. The slam of the door closing allowed Johnny to stop holding her breath.

She peeked around the cabin before running into the woods, hoping it was the right direction to get out of the dense area. The trees began thinning out, and in her view was Blenhen. Traversing back to the house, she spotted the groundskeeper by a barn-like structure putting wood in a compactor. Johnny brushed herself off, strolled over, and smiled.

"Hi, while you have been working here, did you see a set of keys?"

"No, Miss," said the groundskeeper. He placed wood in the compactor.

"If my head wasn't attached to my body, I'd probably lose that, too. Do you mind if I look around?" Johnny kicked the leaves around the compactor.

"Please, Miss, be careful. Don't want ya to get too close to the machine." A thick Scottish accent accompanied his words.

Johnny bent down, scanning the ground. The groundskeeper came by her side. She threw the phone into the compactor, and the sounds of the phone being crushed along with the wood were music to her ears.

"Please, Miss. I don't want any troubles. You can get hurt near this machine. I'll look for your keys when I finish with this set of wood."

"It's okay. I'll just have to get another set made." Johnny closed her eyes and sighed deeply as she made her way back to the house.

. . .

The sun disappeared quickly in the British countryside as the evening lights illuminated Blenhen. Johnny was in her room, getting ready for dinner. She would really like to hear from Lockwood, but since she had to destroy the phone with the pictures, it wasn't possible.

She stared into her bag at the hidden burner phones. They tempted her to call him. Johnny pulled out one phone. The sudden sounds of knocking made her drop it on the bed. She opened the door. Naive rushed in. Right away, Johnny could see he was in one of his manic moods.

"Johnny, Chloe is the best thing to happen to me. She's given me such inspiration that I'm writing again! Look!" He held up a paper. "We've got to convince her to come on tour." Johnny walked to the bed, sat, and pushed the phone behind her. She leaned back and continued to push it under the pillow while Naive talked.

"Good, that you are writing again. Maybe it is the change of scenery and the fresh country air that is giving you the inspiration."

"Yeah, yeah, but I know it is Chloe. I can hear the music again. You've got to talk to her about coming with us."

"Have you asked her?"

"Yeah, kind of. I've been throwing out, you know, hints."

"And?"

"She hasn't said yes, but she hasn't said no either," Naive said as he walked frantically around the room. He stopped and held Johnny by the shoulders. "I need her on this tour."

"Naive, she is a big star. She probably has a schedule that is already planned. She could have a movie shoot to go to."

"If she did, why didn't she say so?"

"I don't know."

"Just try Johnny. I know you can get it done." He abruptly left the room. *Chloe on tour. Just what I need.* She was sure that Chloe was just trying to be nice but probably has a movie set she needs to be on or a modeling gig in some exotic place. Unlike some groupie, Johnny was sure that Chloe won't be following them on tour.

By the time that Johnny arrived at the ante dinner sitting room, cocktails have been flowing for quite a while. The conversations are much louder and more animated than at tea time. There were also more guests than were at the afternoon tea. A few are fresh faces, plus Babbs, Pinky, and Shelby huddled together in the corner across the room. *No Barbados man.*

Johnny took a glass of wine from the roaming waitstaff and tried to keep a distance from the skeet shoot group. Shelby noticed her and tried to get her attention. She quickly turned in the opposite direction when she bumped into Caruthers. Relieved to see a friendly face, she lit up with a grin.

"Didn't expect to see you here."

Caruthers sipped from his highball glass.

"Haven't you learned yet that you never know where I will show up my dear."

"Are you here for the weekend?"

"No, my plans didn't allow me to spend the entire weekend but Katherine wouldn't forgive me if I didn't at least show up for dinner." *That's a long journey just for a meal. Probably came to check up on me.*

"That's a long ride to just show up"

"I have a little country cottage not far from here." A small cottage? Didn't see any cottages on the way here. It's probably one of the smaller mansions. He gets more interesting every time we meet. She watched him survey the room. He caught the attention of Babbs and Shelby as they walked towards them.

Babbs gave Caruthers a friendly slap on his shoulder. "It's good to see you old boy."

"I see that you've met the enchanting Ms. Harrington."

"Johnny and I are practically old friends at this point." Shelby raised his eyebrows. "At this point?" Caruthers glanced around and said, "Where is Pinky?"

"He was with us a minute ago. He might have gone to the loo." The head butler announced that dinner was being served. Everyone queued up, orderly like sheep being herded into a pen as they head into the dining room. They lined the long dining room table with place cards that has each guest's name.

Two stately gentlemen whose place cards have titled names on them sat on each side of Johnny. One seemed to be a Lord, and another one is a knight with Sir in front of his name. Caruthers sat directly across from her, and on the other end is Naive, seated next to Chloe.

There were quiet conversations among the diners, and Johnny found Lord Huntley and Sir Benjamin humble even with their titles. They are more fascinated with what she does for a living.

The skeet shoot crew has reemerged to join the group and sat on the same side as Caruthers and Pinky. The dinner was served in courses. As they served the food with the drinks flowing, the conversations grew from quiet, polite buzz to boisterous and sometimes noxious dialogues.

Pinky seemed to more inebriated than most of the guests and the waitstaff had to clean up his tipped over glass several times. At one point, Johnny observed Shelby signaling to the waitstaff not to serve Pinky anymore liquor. But that only made Pinky get louder, so waitstaff refilled his glass. Again, Pinky nearly tipped a water glass on the woman sitting to his right.

"Now, don't you think that is enough Pinky," said Babbs

"Pinky, Pinky, don't you think it is enough? Enough of what?" Pinky's flushed face became redder. "You of all people shouldn't be chastising me about a few drinks. Didn't I help you at the last meet with them? Remember, it was in where?" He is now slurring his words. "Barbados. Yes. I came to your aid. They wanted you out of the firm, wanted you out."

"That's enough, Pinky. Maybe you need to walk it off," said Shelby as he tried to help Pinky out of his seat.

"Yes, Pinky. Some fresh air will help," said Katherine.

"Babbs help Shelby with Pinky," said Henry Hawthorne as Pinky tried to get up, he stumbled and Shelby retrieved him. Pinky brushed him away.

"I'm fine. I can get up without your assistance. Ladies. Lords, and gents, please forgive me but I must depart." He straightened up, buttoned his jacket, and stood erect as he walked out of the dining room with Shelby and Babbs on either side of him. The room turned silent as Pinky left When he was out of sight the conversations continued as though nothing happened.

"That Pinky is a lively one, isn't he," said Lord Huntley to Johnny.

"I hope he will be okay."

"He will be fine. Katherine's dinners would not be the same if Pinky didn't make a spectacle of himself. He is practically a part of the dinner ritual." Johnny turned to look at Caruthers, who was chatting with one of the other dinner guests, and caught Johnny's glance. He winked at her and smiled as he continued his conversation.

Chapter 29

10:30 Herefordshire UK

Caruthers squinted at the slivers of light peeking through the heavy tapestry drapes in his bedroom. He rolled over, picked up the clock on his bedside table, and sat up in his draped four-poster mahogany bed. He checked the clock again before deciding to get dressed. After putting on his usual casual country attire—a tweed sports jacket, jodhpurs, and wading boots—he drove his Jaguar to the local teahouse. He didn't frequent it often enough for the staff to know his usual order, unlike most regular customers.

The server greeted him cautiously, trying to recall his face without success, and seated him. He ordered breakfast scones with Darjeeling tea and scrolled through emails on his phone. After paying the bill, he headed toward Blenhen. He hoped to catch Johnny before she left for Paris.

As he entered Blenhen's driveway, he saw Johnny and Naive stepping out of the house and walking toward the waiting SUV. Caruthers walked toward Johnny as she spoke to Naive.

"I'm glad I caught you before you left," Caruthers said, smiling at Johnny.

"Please excuse me if I'm interrupting."

"No, I'm glad you came back," replied Johnny as she took Caruthers' arm and walked away, leaving Naive looking perplexed.

"You just saved me from an uncomfortable conversation."

"Glad to be of service." As Caruthers walked with Johnny, he enjoyed the feeling of her body close to his.

"I just wanted to say goodbye before you left since I know you're heading to Paris."

"Yes, we're going straight to Heathrow from here."

"I hope your quest wasn't too disappointing."

"Not at all. Did you see what happened with Pinky last night?"

Caruthers chuckled. "Oh yes, Pinky. He did his usual drunken debacle for the guests."

"Yeah, I know. Lord Huntley told me it's almost a ritual at Katherine's dinner parties, but there was something unusual about it. Don't you think?"

"Like what?"

"It's what he said—something about sticking up for Babbs."

"Babbs and Pinky are always arguing, especially when they get drunk."

They stopped walking, and Caruthers pulled a twig from the hedge beside them.

"The firm? I don't remember hearing that."

"Yes, he definitely mentioned the firm. There's something fishy about Shelby and Babbs. I'm sure I saw another man with them, but he wasn't at the dinner."

He smiled at Johnny. "I'll ask Katherine about the other man who was with Shelby and Babbs, but she always has so many guests coming and going. Look, I was at the dinner, not at afternoon tea, and I didn't stay for the weekend."

"But I think I saw that man in Barbados."

"Many people who socialize with Katherine travel all over the world. You might even see some in Paris. It really is a small social circle when you think about it. But your sleuthing skills are getting better. You remember and recognize people you've seen before. I believe that would be part of the course for *Sleuthing 101*."

"Okay, now you're making fun of me."

"Not at all, my dear. I just think you're quite charming. I'll be sorry to see you go."

"You could always skip the pond."

"No, the pond is what we call the Atlantic when we refer to the States."

"Oh, yeah, right. Well, if you change your mind, text me and I'll leave a ticket for you."

"If I text you, it won't be for a ticket but for a dinner date. Paris is lovely this time of year."

Johnny waved goodbye before she returned to Naive. Is there something going on with Shelby and Babbs? Pinky was definitely over the top last night. She might be getting in over her head. I promised my old friend to keep an eye on her. There might really have to be a trip to Paris, after all. It is a lovely time of year to visit the City of Lights. Caruthers smiled as he sped off in his jaguar.

Chapter 30

13:00 Paris France

As soon as Johnny and Naive cleared passport control at Orly Airport, she noticed a driver holding up a sign with her name. Although Naive wore his usual dark glasses and baseball hat to disguise his appearance, fans still recognized him. He stopped to take a few selfies and sign autographs before they got into the SUV.

"I wish we could find another exit. If we had a private plane, we could have a car pull up right by it," Naive grumbled irritably.

Johnny scrolled through her messages, trying to ignore him. She held her breath for a moment, sensing that he was slipping into one of his awful moods.

"We're making two stops. The first is The Ritz, and the second is the Hotel Regina by Place Pyramides," Johnny instructed the driver.

Naive scowled. "Why aren't you staying at The Ritz?"

"The hotel is full. The only room left was the Presidential suite, which they booked for you. Plus, Hotel Regina is just down the street from The Ritz."

"I can't believe this. No private plane, and now I'm alone in the hotel," Naive slumped in his seat.

As they rode to the hotel, Johnny gazed out the window at the obelisk in the center of Place de la Concorde. The carousel at the Tuileries Garden flashed by as the car headed toward Place Vendôme. They arrived at The Ritz, and the doorman opened the car door. Naive jumped out and went straight to the bar. Johnny followed him until the concierge greeted her.

"Bienvenue, Ms. Harrington. So nice to have you and Mr. Naive stay with us again. His suite is ready. The luggage will be brought up right away."

"Thank you, Jacques."

"We're so sorry we couldn't accommodate you this time. However, a complimentary room will be waiting for you on your next visit."

"No worries. I don't mind a little distance from Naive." She winked at Jacques and then headed to the bar.

As she got closer, she saw Naive sitting in a banquette, snuggled up with Chloe. Johnny stood at the table before Naive even noticed her.

"Look who's here! Isn't this wonderful?" Naive said as he kissed Chloe.

"Couldn't be any better." Johnny's voice strained as she fought to hide her incredulity. "We didn't know you were going to be in Paris. I would've made arrangements to get you VIP tickets. I thought you had a movie to shoot in L.A."

"No, they postponed it, so I came to Paris for a few days before heading back to L.A."

"It's unfortunate Naive won't be able to spend as much time with you as in England. His schedule is jam-packed before the show."

"She'll be with me on the press junket."

Johnny shook her head while forcing a smile. "Well, welcome aboard our crazy road trip. Naive, don't forget you have a sound check tomorrow afternoon. You can't miss it."

"Oh, don't worry, we'll be there," Naive said as he stared lovingly into Chloe's eyes.

Great. Just perfect. I thought Blenhen would be the end of her. A star of her caliber should have an itinerary planned months, even years, in advance with movie shoots, press junkets, and photo shoots. How does she suddenly have time to follow Naive on tour? Something isn't right. If anyone knows what is really going on, it would be Jerry. Johnny knew he kept up with all the latest gossip. She intended to make him her next call.

"I have the card key, so we can head to the suite," Johnny said.

Naive and Chloe followed her to the special elevator that went straight up to the Presidential suite. The door opened, and as Naive and Chloe entered, Naive snatched the card key from Johnny before she could step inside the elevator.

"We'll take it from here, Shortie. See you at the soundcheck." Johnny watched Naïve's Cheshire cat grin as the elevator door closed. She decided not to intervene with Naive, check into her hotel, and try to get some pre-concert work done before the soundcheck.

But the first pre-caution was to instruct Jacques to direct any calls coming to Naive's room to her phone as usual. Jacques greeted her with his usual obeisant smile.

"I'm heading to my hotel. Please direct all Naive's calls to my phone. Do you have the correct number in your files?"

"Bien Sur, Ms. Harrington." He found the phone number and repeated it to her.

"That's it." The doorman attempted to get a car for Johnny, but she stopped him. It was a crisp winter day, and she rarely had time to herself, so she took a leisurely stroll to Hotel Regina. She reached in her bag to take out her phone, but accidentally pulled out the extra burner phone.

It reminded her she hadn't heard from Lockwood. *Did he get the pictures? There is a time difference, but he works late.* The phone rang a few more times than usual and her finger hoovered over the end call bar when he finally answered.

"Hello. Where are you?" Lockwood asked as he tried to catch his breath.

"Are you okay? You sound out of breath."

"Yes, I was leaving when I heard the phone and ran back to catch it. I knew it had to be you calling."

"I'm in Paris. You didn't call me about the pictures so I'm reaching out."

"Johnny, how could I call you when you get rid of the burner phones."

"I was waiting to hear from you before I got rid of the phone at Blenhen but you didn't call."

"I needed time to confirm the identification of the men in the picture."

"Confirm with who? You know who they are?"

"As soon as I saw the pictures, I recognized two of the men, but I needed a confirmation with Interpol."

"You need Interpol to recognize the man from Barbados?"

"Barbados? I didn't see anyone that I recognized from Barbados. I saw two men, one with a brown tweed jacket, and one with a quilted jacket."

Before Lockwood finished his sentence, the words rushed out of her mouth. "What about the guy in the black jacket with the hood?"

"Something blurred his face out, the face recognition technology couldn't identify him."

Johnny stopped took a deep breath as she closed her eyes. "But he was the man I told you that I saw leaving Ashton's house in Barbados. He was also the man in the picture in the Hawthorne's study."

"I'm sorry, Johnny, but his face wasn't clear enough. It seems like you caught him as he was turning. But the other two men were definitely people that have been on our radar. Were they there all weekend.?" Johnny's disappointment about the guy in the black jacket turned into intrigue after Lockwood's interest in the other men.

She scoped out some of the shop windows as she continued her journey. "I'm not sure but they were at the afternoon tea. They were sitting with Henry when he called me over to meet them."

"Did you have time to sit with them?"

"Yes. But not too long. I made an excuse to leave. I wanted to avoid Henry asking me more questions about the pictures."

"Henry saw you taking the pictures?"

"Yes, but I made an excuse for taking pictures of the grounds for a video shoot with Naive. "

"You think he bought it?"

"Yeah, he asked me about the video shoot that I discussed with Katherine."

"I don't know Johnny. You have to be more careful. Maybe you're not ready for this."

"I'm fine."

Lockwood began to fidget with the paperweight on his desk. "Some of these people may be dangerous. I can't let you put yourself in a precarious situation."

"Look, I got pictures you wouldn't have been able to get. In fact, who are those men?"

"Shelby Livingston has an import/export business that has ties in Cartagena. Robert "Babbs" Goodwich also has a coffee trading business in South America and throughout the Caribbean. We have been surveilling them for a while but got nothing concrete."

"What about Pinky?"

"Although all of them are from British aristocracy, John "Pinky" Hollingston is the wealthiest of them all. His family has ties with the royal family.

"What is Pinky's business?"

"Debauchery."

"What?"

"He is a lay about. His wealth allows him to do nothing and have no responsibilities. He can't keep a wife or girlfriend and is an only child."

"Well, that explains a lot about his drunken behavior at Katherine's dinner that made them remove him. But before he left, he said something interesting."

"What?"

"Something about saving Babbs because they wanted him out of the firm. They quickly tried to shut him up and took him out of the room. He was pretty sloshed, slurring and everything."

"He said the firm?"

"Yes."

Lockwood straightened up. "Are you sure?"

"Yeah, I'm sure, because I thought he didn't look like anyone who would work at a firm. He seems the least corporate."

"The Firm is a term heard among the chatter that Interpol has collected. Did he say anything else?"

"No, like I said, they said he needed some air and Shelby and Babbs escorted him out."

"We didn't know for sure if Pinky was part of the organization, but from what you heard, it seems like he is. "

"If he is, he is definitely the weak link."

"Well, you got us some information. I'm glad you are out of that house."

"There has to be something else I can do. "

"I don't think so, Johnny. You are in Paris and I don't have a contact there."

"I know you will think of something." Johnny's absorption in the conversation with Lockwood made her almost pass Hotel Regina.

"I just got to my hotel. Call me with my new assignment." Before Lockwood could argue with her. She ended the call.

Chapter 31

15:00 Hotel Regina Paris France

"Bienvenu, Ms. Harrington. Your regular room is ready, and your luggage arrived early, so we've placed it in your room," Yves said warmly.

"Thanks so much, Yves." She took the key and started toward the stairs, but Yves stopped her.

"Ms. Harrington, this envelope is for you." Johnny took it and skipped up the stairs, eager to rest in her room.

Once inside, she opened the balcony door and took a deep breath, gazing at the Eiffel Tower to her right and the Louvre directly across from her. Johnny watched the fashionable Parisians walking past the Louvre, admiring their chicness, when her eyes widened. Among the throng of pedestrians, one figure stood out.

Her eyes followed a familiar face—clothes well-tailored but slightly ruffled—plodding along toward the entrance of the Louvre. Johnny grabbed her bag and dashed out of the room. She hurried down the stairs and scampered out the door, hoping not to raise suspicion with Yves. Her brisk walk turned into a run as she tried to catch up. Luckily, he moved at a leisurely pace, allowing her to follow him unnoticed. She slowed down to catch her breath, then sidled up next to him as he approached the Louvre's grounds.

"Hello, Pinky." He turned and squinted at her, and then his flushed face beamed.

"Well, hello, the formidable publicist, as Henley called you."

"So, you remember me."

"Well, of course." He moved close to her face and whispered, "You are an unforgettable young lady." The stench of alcohol wafted off his breath.

"What a surprise to run into you in Paris. Are you here with Shelby and Babbs?"

His posture stiffened as he sneered. "Definitely not. Why would I be here with them?"

"You seemed to be all buddies at the Hawthornes'."

"People aren't always as they appear, my dear. Let's not discuss them. What brings you to the City of Lights?"

"Work. I'm on tour with Naive."

"Oh, yes. He was all over that actress, Chloe. Do you have time in your busy schedule for dinner?"

"In fact, I do."

"Wonderful. I'm on my way to meet my art curator. Where are you staying?"

"Across the street. Hotel Regina."

"Lovely. I'm not too far away at Hôtel Dodun. Let's meet at 8?"

"Perfect."

Johnny headed back to Hotel Regina, excited about her serendipitous meeting. Back in her room, she checked her phone messages and opened the envelope Yves had given her. Inside was an invitation to an evening event at Château de Calluau in Palluau-sur-Indre, located in the Loire Valley.

Should I tell Naive? she thought. The event could conflict with her dinner plans with Pinky. But she reasoned that Naive probably wouldn't be interested since he was totally captivated by Chloe. *Let sleeping dogs lie*, she decided. Her thoughts were interrupted by her ringing phone.

"Naive, what's up?"

"Hey, Shortie," Naive slurred. His tone gave away that he was likely lying in bed after sex. "Did you get an invitation for us?"

Johnny's eyes widened. "Why?"

"Chloe told me there's some kind of performance event at a château this evening."

"Yes, I just opened it and was about to call you," Johnny replied, rolling her eyes. "I didn't think this would be your kind of thing."

"Chloe says it's the hottest event in Paris and I should be there. I'm thinking about getting into art more."

"So you want to go?"

"Yeah. Set it up."

Chloe again, messing everything up, Johnny mumbled to herself as she called to arrange for a car to pick up Naive.

It'll have to be a quick dinner with Pinky—maybe just drinks. Remembering the stench of alcohol on his breath, she was sure he wouldn't have a problem with the change of plans. Fatigue was running a close race with Johnny, and she didn't have the luxury of letting it catch her.

She laid down on the bed for a quick nap to revive her before the upcoming long night. Johnny's body sunk into the soft European down comforter and the floating sensation moved her into a deep sleep. She was far away floating on a cloud and the sound of bells ringing surrounded her. At first the bells were far away, but now they are getting closer and louder. Johnny sprung up and picked up the hotel room phone.

"Ms. Harrington. There is a Mr. Pinky here for you." Johnny checked her watch. It was eight o'clock.

"Tell him I will be down in ten minutes."

"Bien Sûr Ms. Harrington."

Johnny jumped out of the bed. Rushed around to change her

clothes, fix her hair and make-up, while she wondered how the sleep won her over. *How isn't only 15 minutes, instead of two hours. I can't afford to be late for this date.* She ran out of the room, electing to pass the elevator although she was late, and took the steps to the lobby. Johnny spotted Pinky sitting in the hotel's armchair in his usual blue blazer with the pocket square and grey pants. He stood as she approached him.

"So sorry for the delay, I didn't realize the time."

"No worries. It's just across the street. Café Marly. They always have a table for me."

"About dinner. It may have to be just drinks. Naive got an invitation to an event at Château de Palluau. Just found out when I went back to my room. I'm sorry about this." He placed his hand on the small of her back to guide her towards the door.

"You say sorry too much. We can have hors d'oeuvues and a few cocktails." They crossed the street to the same entrance of the Louvre's courtyard where they met earlier.

"Bon soir Monsieur Hollingston, your usual table?"

"Yes." The maître d' led them to a table, next to the window, that has a direct view of the Louvre's lit up pyramid, a sparkling diamond in the midst of the courtyard.

"What are you drinking, my dear?"

"Club soda with lime." Pinky cocked his head and squinted his eyes.

"I'm still working this evening, so I can't indulge like I would like to."

"Nonsense. Some champagne will help you to get ready for your evening. Plus, you owe me a drink for cancelling our dinner. Club soda isn't a drink."

He waved over a server. "A bottle of Veuve Clicquot. You obviously like carbonated drinks, so champagne is perfect. Plus, I'm celebrating"

"Oh, really?"

"Yes. My curator found the perfect piece of art for my boat. I didn't even let them ship it. I took it right away. They had a fit." The server poured the champagne into the crystal flutes.

"A toast for your good fortune," Johnny said as they clicked their flutes.

"Too bad Shelby and Babbs aren't here to share the celebration."

Pinky's cheeks became flushed as he pinched his downturned mouth. "I wish you would stop mentioning those two." He gulped the rest of his champagne and the server quickly refilled his flute.

"I'm sorry, but at Blenhen, the three of you seem to be having a wonderful time. You were together at the shoot, at afternoon tea, at dinner. The entire weekend."

"I don't remember you being at the shoot."

"I wasn't, but I heard you all talking about it during the afternoon tea. Henry mentioned it."

"Henry is full of shite. They all are."

"Why?" Johnny coyly asked as Pinky gulped down more champagne.

"Did you see how they treated me at dinner? After all, I did for them." He began to slur his words.

"I'm sure they did a lot for you too."

"They've done nothing, nothing for me. Never did." Johnny signaled for the server to pour more champagne in Pinky's glass, hoping to speed up his inebriated state.

Pinky bent his head close to her. "If it wasn't for me, they all would have gone down. The whole lot." *The weakest link.* Johnny observed Pinky's slurred speech is now almost incoherent. The time flashed on her phone. If she could get into Pinky's room, there may be some information that would be useful to Lockwood.

"Pinky, I think you hit your limit. Let me get a car to take you back to your hotel."

"Limit, the night is young. Server another bottle."

"No, Pinky, I can't stay, I have to work, remember."

"Work, work., work, work. Such a boring concept."

"Please let me drop you off."

"Okay, okay." He gulped down the rest of his champagne after settling the bill. He struggled to stand up, stumbled, and almost fell on top of the empty table next to him. The waitstaff ran over to help and he waved them off as the patrons in the surrounding table gaped at him.

"I'm fine. I don't know why they put the tables so close."

"Let's get a car." Johnny took his arm and led him out the restaurant. They entered into one of the waiting taxis outside of the Louvre's courtyard.

"Where are you staying?"

"Hôtel Dodun." Pinky nodded off as the car went through the Paris streets. Johnny hoped he would fall out by the time they get to his room. The taxi stopped by a limestone building with a large green door. Pinky's head has fallen on her shoulder. The sounds of a drunk's snore emitted out of his mouth.

"This is Hôtel Dodun?"

"Oui, madame." She paid the driver and tried her best to wake up Pinky. Barely awake but he managed to put in the code to unlock the gate. Johnny made note of the code, hoping it will be the same one to exit. The gate opened up to a courtyard that led to the door of the building. She held his arm to steady him as they walked to the next door. *This is a hôtel particulier.*

Chapter 32

19:00 Hôtel Dodun Paris France

They entered a marble entrance way with a winding staircase. She remembered when the movie studio put Naive in a hôtel particulier while he was in Paris shooting a scene. Private residences which are usually updated ancient mansions. They give celebrities all the amenities with the utmost privacy.

The staircase. *How is he going to get up that winding staircase? He will probably take the elevator.* But to her surprise, he moved to the staircase. Stumbling up the stairs, he almost fell backwards when he exited onto the second floor. Johnny followed him into his suite of rooms, where Pinky went straight to the bar and filled a tumbler with whiskey on the rocks.

"What are you having?"

"Nothing, I just want to make sure you got back to your hotel." Johnny quickly scanned the room capturing every detail with her didactic memory. She veered to the door when Pinky stumbled towards her and pulled her arm.

"Don't leave yet, don't you want to see the prize I acquired?"

"It's getting late, I need to go back to my hotel." She placed her hand to open the door. Pinky leaned his body against it and tried to kiss her.

"What are you doing?" She pushed him away.

"Come on. I heard you Black girls know how to have fun."

Johnny squinted her eyes and sneered at him. "That's really crass, even for you Pinky." He moved away, poured himself another drink, and slumped down in the high back leather armchair.

"So that's what you think of me? Just like the others?" Although disgusted by Pinky, she felt sorry for him.

"You think those people are so much better? With their quasi manners and nouveau riche accoutrements. The Hawthornes. You think they are so respectful and Shelby, and Babbs? Well, they are not. They are just as dirty as they come."

"I don't know why you would say that, especially about Katherine and Henry. They are so generous with their homes."

"For a price, my dear, for a price." He gulped the rest of his drink, stumbled to the bar, and pours himself another drink.

Pinky started crying as his fully flushed face lived up to his name.

""If it wasn't for me, where would they be?" Pinky mumbled before falling back into the armchair. He placed his drink on the side table and continued mumbling until he passed out.

Johnny called across the room, "Pinky, I'm leaving." He didn't move. She walked closer and touched his shoulder. His head slumped to the side, and he began to snore. Johnny quickly moved around the room, her mind acting as a camera, filing away every detail. The ashtray was slightly off-center on the side table opposite Pinky.

She noticed a door ajar, opened it, and took a quick scan of the room. Darting to the desk, she began rifling through the papers. She lifted a paperweight pinning two papers. One was a receipt for artwork; the other bore the same pineapple logo she had seen at the Hawthornes'. She squinted at the handwriting: "Berlin" followed by numbers and a name scrawled beside them. She studied it carefully, committing it to memory.

The sound of Pinky groaning in the other room startled her. She quickly replaced everything exactly as she had found it and left the door ajar. Returning to the room, she found Pinky struggling to pull himself out of the chair, squinting at her.

"What were you doing?"

"I was trying to find the bathroom before I left," Johnny said casually.

"There's no bathroom over there."

Johnny rolled her eyes. "Obviously. But I couldn't ask you since you passed out. I really must go."

"Maybe we could have dinner tomorrow," Pinky said, attempting to rise before collapsing back into the chair.

"I have to work tomorrow. I'll call you." She raced out the door, and as it closed behind her, Pinky muttered, "But you don't have my number."

Johnny hurried down the stairs, calling an Uber as she checked the time. She could still make it to the Ritz to meet Naive, but it would be close. Her heels clacked against the cobblestones in the courtyard as she reached the exit gate. She pushed it, but it wouldn't budge. The exit code.

Closing her eyes, she tapped the numbers on the keypad, and the door swung open. She jumped into the waiting Uber.

"Au Ritz, s'il vous plaît."

****

Checking her compact mirror, Johnny ensured she didn't look disheveled. The Uber pulled up to the entrance. Naive, in a Gucci sweatsuit, and Chloe, wearing a black leather micro-mini dress with pleats that accentuated her colt-like legs, appeared in the doorway as paparazzi flashbulbs lit up the entrance. Security led them into their car.

Johnny approached the car, but security automatically pushed her away.

"It's me, Jimmy."

The guard turned, recognizing her. "So sorry, Johnny. I expected you to come out the door with Naive."

"It's okay. I got here later than I expected," she said as he opened the door.

Naive and Chloe were already kissing in the back seat and didn't notice Johnny enter the car.

The bright lights of the Paris streets quickly gave way to dark countryside roads. The car sped along the highway, illuminated only by the beams of passing cars. It exited onto a narrow, dark road, plunging them into near-total darkness until a towering structure appeared ahead, faintly glowing. Tiki torches lined the path to the Château entrance.

Even in the countryside, paparazzi snapped pictures as guests exited their cars. Male and female models, barely clothed and covered in colorful body paint, greeted them with trays of champagne. As they moved further into the Château, nymph-like models pranced through the crowd. Above them, dancers gyrated in cages, their bodies painted in bold, vivid designs.

"Who's hosting this party?" Johnny asked Chloe.

"No one really knows."

"Who owns the Château?"

"It belongs to the Reveille family, but they're never here."

The half-clothed nymphs danced around the guests, leading them into another room. Two enormous doors opened to reveal a cavernous chamber. In the center stood a glass encasement holding a woman lying on a platform, dressed in white, with her arms folded. A dagger above her dripped red liquid onto the floor.

The crowd gathered around the encasement, staring at the woman. Johnny couldn't understand what the spectacle was about and began thinking about how she could contact Lockwood with her new information. Suddenly, the woman sat up and began to scream. No one moved. The crowd simply stood there, watching her.

Johnny tugged on Naive's arm. "How long do you plan to stay for this?"

"I don't know. Chloe said it's the place to be tonight," he replied.

Chloe shot Johnny a derisive glance.

"I don't see anyone else here I recognize, do you?"

"These people aren't celebrities, they are the elite and aristocrats of France and Europe," sniffed Chloe. "See the man surrounded by that group? He's the Marquis d'Angély and next to him his Vicomte Épée. They are from some of the oldest royal families in France. And over there is Viscount Belacorte." Belacorte surveyed the room, like he did when Johnny met him, as he talked to an admiring young woman. He caught Johnny's eye but didn't acknowledge her as he kept scanning the room. What a prick.

"Why are the paparazzi here if no celebrities are at the event?" Johnny asked Chloe.

"Those aren't paparazzi. They are photographers the host hired for these events. No paparazzi are on the premises." So why the hell is Naive here. He isn't an elite and definitely not the cognoscenti. He probably can't even spell cognoscenti.

"Oh Naive, there is someone you have to meet. Johnny, can you excuse us for a minute?" Chloe dragged Naive with her. Johnny took another glass of champagne from one nymph and moved around the room.

She entered another dark hallway where half-clad nymphs started prancing around Johnny and few other people, leading them towards a huge bronze door. After a small group gathered by the bronze door, the nymphs opened it onto a large ballroom where a crowd was gathered.

People are standing around and it was quiet except for the sounds of soft groans, the sounds of sexual ecstasy. Johnny got closer and tried to find a space to see what was mesmerizing this crowd. She walked to a small corner and spied over a short man's shoulder.

Johnny's eyes opened wide and she stopped herself from gasping as she watched a naked Black woman and Black man lying on an elevated bed in full coital activity. Her stomach began churning from the bile forming inside of her.

The voyeurism and exploitation on display was too much for her to take. She swiveled around, pushing people aside to escape the crowd. Johnny felt a shortness of breath while her heart began palpitating. Finally finding her way out, she kept her head down. She closed her eyes to focus on slowing her breathing. Johnny pulled her head up, opened her eyes onto Belacorte, looking directly in her face.

Chapter 33

23:00 Château de Calluau Loire Valley France

I see the performance is not to your liking, Ms. Harrington," Belacorte said in a smug tone.

"No, it isn't."

"I don't care for it myself. Too carnal for my taste. You look like you could use a drink. Let's go."

Johnny didn't know if she was more surprised by Belacorte remembering her name or by his sudden kindness. Right now, it didn't matter. She wouldn't care if he turned up as the Wicked Witch of the West, as long as he could lead her out of the room. Belacorte moved in the opposite direction from where they had entered. She followed quietly beside him as he navigated the hallways with the ease of someone who had traveled them many times before.

He opened a door, and they stepped into a quieter room where small groups of people sat with drinks at intimate tables. Johnny took a seat, her eyes darting around the room, gathering details. A large window lined the left wall. There was a side door in the far corner and a marble fireplace adorned with pineapples carved into its mantle. A waitstaff approached their table.

"Glenfiddich on the rocks. What are you having?" Belacorte asked.

"A French 75."

"Ms. Harrington, you seem to turn up in the most interesting places."

"I'm here with Naive and Chloe. He received an invitation."

"Oh yes, of course. I wouldn't have guessed him to be someone interested in the arts."

"He isn't, but I don't think what we witnessed qualifies as art."

"The human body is one of the highest art forms. What was on display was performance art."

The server brought their drinks before Johnny could say something she might regret.

"Do you come to the Château's events often?" she asked.

"They're usually worth the trip. Since I have a home nearby, it's a good excuse to see some of my French amis."

As Belacorte talked, Johnny's eye caught a waitstaff member without a tray. He walked to different tables, whispered something into the ear of a guest, and led them to the side door. The waitstaff knocked, the door opened, and the guest entered. Strangely, none of these guests returned to their seats; someone new always replaced them.

"This room is so different from the main event. Like a gentlemen's club or smoking room," Johnny observed.

"To me, it's only a room—a respite from whatever spectacle is going on outside."

"What about that door?" she asked, nodding toward the side door.

"Which door?"

"The one people enter but don't return from."

"It leads to the loos," Belacorte said dismissively.

Why would waitstaff whisper to someone that it's time to use the loo? Johnny thought, skeptical of his explanation.

"Most people here seem to know each other well," she commented.

"The people at this event are mostly European society. It's a small circle."

A short, stout man approached their table.

"Belacorte, so you are here with your lovely companion."

"Ms. Harrington, this is Vicomte Boisenne. She's a friend of the Hawthornes."

"Enchanté." He took her outstretched hand and kissed it lightly.

"Is Henri here?" Boisenne asked as he glanced around the room.

"I don't believe so."

"Andrew was asking about you. I think you should talk to him."

Belacorte turned and nodded at a man who raised his glass from across the room. "Please excuse us," he said to Johnny as he stood and accompanied Boisenne to Andrew.

Johnny watched Belacorte as he spoke with Andrew. His body language shifted from stoic to agitated as he glanced in her direction. Then, a waitstaff member whispered in Belacorte's ear. Without hesitation, he followed the same routine as the others, disappearing behind the mysterious side door.

Johnny called over a waitstaff member and asked for directions to the ladies' room.

"It's right outside the main entrance."

Why would the ladies' and men's bathrooms be so far from each other? she wondered.

There had to be another way to access that side door, or at least a way to see inside from the outside. Johnny rose, pretending to amble toward the entrance, then pivoted and moved closer to the side door. She stood against the wall, sipping her drink, hoping to see the waitstaff bring another person.

Discomfort crept over her. She scanned the room. Fleeting glances darting in her direction.

The head butler approached her. "Can we help you?"

"I'm waiting for a friend of mine. He went behind this door. Is this the men's bathroom?" The butler gave her a condescending smile. "Who, may I ask, is your friend?"

"Belacorte"

"Lord Belacorte would like for you to meet him outside of the room."

"I'm okay. I can wait here."

"That is not possible." The butler led her away from the door. All the eyes focused on her as she exited, and the waitstaff passed by the door. Johnny snapped opened her purse and let her phone and other items fall out.

"Oh no." She stopped and bent down to pick up the items, while pushing some away to give herself a chance to view the door as it opened. The waitstaff knocked, the door opened out into a room with people sitting around a large round table.

They are all men except what seemed like the back of a woman's head. The person is about to face towards the open door when the butler stepped in front of Johnny and picked up the rest of her items. Her view was blocked and the door closed.

"I have to wait for Belacorte," Johnny said as the butler gave her the lipstick and compact which fell out of her bag.

The butler led her out the door. "Follow me please."

"Lord Belacorte will meet you here." There has to be another way to discover what is happening in that room. Johnny ruminated as she went to a door which led to an outside terrace.

She roamed the length of the terrace around the château looking out onto the grounds when the muffled sounds of voices emanated from a dimly lit window. Johnny took off her Jimmy Choos and scampered her bare feet along the cold stone walkway towards the voices.

She stepped by the curtain covered window and tried to peer through the small gap between the two panels. The men surrounded a round table. Johnny could identify some faces. They were the same people at Blenhen. She noticed the woman, the only woman in the room. Johnny moved her head, trying to see if she could catch her face. The woman stood up and began marching towards the window.

Johnny turned to go back. The sounds of footsteps heading in her direction stopped her. She ran in the other direction, but found a dead end. Trapped with no other route. She located another window.

The room was dark, and the curtain ajar. She tried to lift the window open, but it seemed stuck. If she broke it with her shoe, they could catch her. The sounds of footsteps were now accompanied by voices getting closer to the window. Johnny used more muscle and pulled the window open.

She quickly glanced around, threw her bag and shoes inside. She followed right behind them when she became aware one shoe dropped on the ledge. The voices turned the corner. She couldn't put her hand out to pick up the shoe. Johnny held her breath. The voices became so clear, as though they were right next to the window.

"Are you sure she came out here?" Johnny identified the voice as Belacorte's.

"Yes, sir."

"Well, I don't see her. Maybe she walked further down the walkway." Footsteps struck the pavers. They got closer to the window when the second voice said, "No sir. This walkway ends here." The footsteps stopped.

"Well, you must be wrong," Belacorte said as the footsteps moved away from the window. Johnny took a deep sigh of relief, peeked out before she took her shoe off of the ledge, and closed the window. She put on her shoes and scanned the room for a door to leave. After hearing Belacorte, it wouldn't be a good idea to be seen coming into the Château the same way she left.

Johnny quickly left the room, hoping she would find her way back to the main area. She wandered and came across a tall man in a suit with an earpiece. His back was in front of her. Johnny glanced behind, but couldn't find another way to go. She made her hair messy, took off one shoe, and stumbled towards the man.

Chapter 34

24:00 Château de Calluau Loire Valley France

"Oh, excuse me." She stumbled into him. He caught her, immediately launching into French.

Johnny giggled, giving him a drunken smile. "Oh darling, I can barely understand English right now, let alone French."

"This is a restricted area. You are not supposed to be here," he said firmly.

"I don't know how I got here. I needed some fresh air, and I guess I got lost. Can you tell me where the main room is?" Johnny slipped on her other shoe and adjusted her hair.

"I need to find out how you got here."

"Now why do that? You're only going to give yourself trouble for not doing your job, and I might not be invited to another one of these events." She leaned in close, her voice dropping to a coaxing tone. "Let's keep it our little secret."

The man shook his head reluctantly and led her toward the main room, pointing to its entrance before returning to his post. Johnny smoothed her dress and reentered, immediately spotting Chloe and Naive. As she moved toward them, Belacorte intercepted her.

"I was looking for you," he said coolly.

"I couldn't find you after you went through the door."

"I told the butler to inform you to meet me outside."

"I know, but I started wandering around and kind of got lost."

Belacorte raised an eyebrow. "It's never a good idea to wander in the Château. You must have dropped this." He opened his hand, revealing a key card with Hôtel Regina printed on it.

"Oh, thank you. Yes, when I dropped my bag in the other room, the butler must have missed it."

"I found this on the opposite side of the Château."

"Like I said, I got lost wandering around. I stopped to look into my bag, and it probably fell out."

"Snooping isn't a good trait, Ms. Harrington. It can put you in situations that won't be pleasant." Belacorte's usual condescending tone carried a sharp, ominous edge.

Johnny took the card from him and said evenly, "Well, then it's a good thing I wasn't snooping and only got lost. But I'll take your advice—not wandering in a Château again." She forced a smile. "Please excuse me, but duty calls."

Belacorte bowed slightly before she turned and walked confidently across the room toward Naive, remembering her uncle's old mantra: People are animals and can smell fear. Never let them smell fear.

"Hey Shortie, having a good time? Chloe knows all the right people here. You need to meet them."

Johnny's only thought was to get Naive out before Belacorte stirred any suspicion.

"We need to call it a night. You have a long day tomorrow," she said firmly.

"Chloe says the party doesn't really start until around 3 a.m."

"Chloe doesn't have a show tomorrow night with promoters breathing down her neck. We need to leave."

"Okay, but you've got to meet one person before we go." Naive grabbed her hand and dragged her across the room, stopping in front of an older man in a maroon velvet jacket with a young blonde woman draped around him.

"Johnny, this is Wolf Von Bulow and Eva Von Bulow," Naive said proudly.

Von Bulow bowed his head and said in a thick German accent, "You can call me Wolfie."

"Wolfie and Eva are having an anniversary party and want me to perform for their guests. I told them they'd have to arrange it with you." Naive grinned, oblivious to Johnny's disbelief.

Johnny gaped at him. Naive always dismissed private performances as beneath him. He had been crushed when he learned one of his idols, a legendary female singer, had performed at a private event in Russia.

"We're in the middle of a tour," Johnny said to Wolfie, trying to control her irritation.

"The three days we have off coincide perfectly with his party. Isn't that serendipitous?" Naive chimed in with a smug grin.

Serendipitous? What the hell! Where did he get that word?

"That's what Chloe calls it—serendipitous," Naive added cheerfully.

It figures. That damn Chloe again!

Wolfie smiled indulgently. "Of course, I'll cover all expenses. Cost is no issue. Eva is a big fan, and she always gets what she wants."

"Can I call you tomorrow about this?" Johnny asked, her voice tight.

"Chloe has all my information," Wolfie replied, his tone dismissive.

Johnny smiled tersely, leading Naive toward the exit. Naive turned to Chloe, who had rejoined Wolfie and Eva.

"I'm going to stay a little longer. I'll meet you back at the hotel, chéri," Chloe said, giving Naive a quick kiss before turning back to her conversation.

As Johnny and Naive got into the car, she felt a wave of relief at finally having him to herself without Chloe.

"You can't be serious about performing in Berlin".

"Yes, why not?" Naïve slumped in the back of the car.

"Why not, you are the one who was crushed when you heard your idol performed in Russia. You went on for days about it."

"Yeah, well I've changed my mind. A person can evolve, can't they?"

"Is Chloe the person who helped you change your mind?"

"What difference does it make?" Naive sneered. "You don't like her. I can tell. Every time she makes a suggestion, you have a problem."

"I have no problem with her. But it seems you indulge her every whim."

"What?" Naive gave her a blank look.

"Forget it. If you want to play Berlin, I will have to tell Bobby so he can put a small crew together."

Naive bent towards her and said "Look Johnny, the gig is good money."

"I'll talk to Bobby tomorrow." Johnny pondered how Bobby isn't going to be happy about this extra gig as she rode in the car. He will complain about the work he will have to do keep the tour on track, but he is the best and will do it. Johnny fell on the bed as soon as she got back in the room. Exhausted from not only the long day with Naive but the close call with Belacorte at the Château.

She lied on the bed, thinking about the events of the night. The nervous moments climbing through the window. Getting past the security. She smiled. The thought of her heart racing as her breathing got faster, was a thrill which moved all over her body. It was almost sensual. Before she talked to Bobby, Johnny would have to buy another burner phone. She must contact Lockwood.

Chapter 35

15:00 Le Zenith Paris France

Johnny decided to talk to Bobby at the venue. It's better to discuss Berlin while he is busy working with the crew. Walking through the loading dock area of the Zenith, her face lit up at the sight ahead of her.

"You are the person I want to see." Johnny grabbed Jerry's arm. What time did you get in?"

He gave her a European kiss and said "Late, last night. I called your phone but just got your voicemail." Johnny put her phone on vibrate since the incident at the Hawthorne's estate.

"It's on vibrate. I forgot to take it off."

"You have a lot to catch up on."

Jerry tilted his head towards Naive. "I see Naive's got a new piece."

"News travels fast. Even across the pond," said Johnny.

"Their pictures have been all over the gossip pages in New York and L.A."

"She's becoming an issue." Johnny rolled her eyes. "I thought she would have a movie set to go to by now. I'm sure you got the tea, so spill it." Jerry scanned the room before he moved closer to Johnny.

"Well, the official word is she is suffering from exhaustion and had to stop shooting the movie. But the real tea, is they kicked her off the set. Supposedly she and the director were smashing and the wife found out. Then came the ultimatum. Wifey or Chloe. This is his third wife, so it's cheaper to keep her."

"So she has nothing to do but help make my life harder. The only thing good about her is she has him on this holistic kick, so he's been sober."

"Well that's good news."

"Yeah, but the bad news is her influence is also sidelining the tour. Naive has decided to do a one-off performance in Berlin."

Jerry stepped back and blinked his eyes. "Naive? Are you sure it's him and not an alien taken over his body?"

Johnny sighed. "I wish it was that simple. Chloe introduced him to some German aristocrat, a Von Bulow whose wife is a big fan. They must have thrown some big cash at him because he said the money is good."

"You're talking about Wolfie?"

"Yes." This is what she loved about Jerry, he seemed to have information about everybody.

"Wolfie and Eva. They are known to give some of the most notorious parties in Berlin and that is saying a lot for Berlin."

"Well now I have to tell Bobby. Have you seen him yet?"

"Yeah, he is checking the equipment."

"How's his mood."

"Bobby is being Bobby."

Johnny went to the dock and found him checking the crew as they brought in the equipment.

"Hey. Everything is looking good."

"Okay, Johnny out with it. What do you want?"

"Can't I comment on how things are looking good?"

"No, number one, it's early in the morning. You don't come to the venue until the afternoon. Number two, you are too chippy this early." Nothing gets pass Bobby. The reason he is the best in the business.

"Naive wants to do a one off in Berlin." Bobby snapped his head up from his paperwork and stared at Johnny with disbelief. After a minute he took up his IPad and started scrolling through it.

"What day, which sets, how many sets? You can't come to me without all of the information."

"I know. Just want to give you a heads up." Bobby kept looking at his IPad and began yelling instructions to some of the crew. Johnny was aware this meant the conversation was over and time for her to leave. It went better than she expected but he may make her pay a price later. She stepped out the equipment area to find Jerry waiting for her.

"How did it go?"

"Better than I expected."

"Uhmm. It doesn't sound good."

She shrugged. "Anyway, I'm going to head over to Château D'eau. I'm running out of product for my hair."

"C'est caustrophe. Hurry. Vite," Jerry said as he waved her away.
****

The Uber sped along the highway and, in a flash, Johnny was back in central Paris, riding past Sacré-Coeur. She stepped out of the Uber in the heart of Château D'Eau, an area known as the center for Black hair supplies and beauty products. She strolled past shops selling native food from Africa and the Caribbean, passed Black hair salons and beauty stores, and entered a small shop called Afri Phone. Johnny purchased four phones.

When the salesman asked if she wanted extra SIM cards, she declined. Afterward, she made her way to her favorite hair supply shop, Prestige 55, where she bought curl-defining cream and sham-poo, completing her errands. The bright sunshine and warm winter weather made her walk back to the hotel feel effortless. On her way, she unwrapped one of the burner phones and called Lockwood.

Lockwood was in the middle of a meeting with his officers when he noticed an unknown number on his cellphone. He abruptly ended the meeting, waiting until the last officer closed the door before answering the call.

"Hello."

"Mr. Lockwood, it's Johnny."

"Are you still in Paris?"

"Yes."

"Did you hear—?" The call began to break up. "I didn't catch that," Johnny said.

"Did you hear—?" Lockwood repeated, but the poor signal interrupted him again. The line dropped entirely as Johnny meandered through the streets of Montmartre.

Johnny took in the unusually warm winter day as she strolled to Les Deux Magots. It was one of her favorite spots to enjoy a café au lait whenever she visited Paris, and she hoped the location would provide a better phone signal. She ordered her obligatory croissant to go with her coffee and tried calling Lockwood again.

The signal failed again. Frustration mounted. Why can't I get a signal here? Normally, she would people-watch while sitting under the bistro's awning, but her mood was too distracted. After paying her tab, she continued her walk, heading toward the bridge that crossed to the Right Bank. I need to talk to Lockwood before I get back to the hotel.

Finally, as Hotel Regina came into view, Johnny tried one last time to call him. This time, the phone rang.

"Johnny," Lockwood answered.

"Yes, you kept cutting off," Johnny replied.

Lockwood's words came quickly. "Did you hear about Pinky?"

"You knew about my meeting with Pinky?" she asked, surprised.

"You met with Pinky?" he replied, his tone sharp.

"Isn't that what you're talking about?" Johnny asked, confused.

"No, Pinky is dead. He was found in his hotel room."

Johnny froze in front of Hotel Regina. "What?"

Before she could process the shock, two men emerged from a dark vehicle and approached her.

"Ms. Harrington?" one of them said as he displayed an identification badge.

"Yes?" Johnny replied, still holding the phone to her ear.

"We are with the Paris Police," the man said. "We need to ask you some questions."

Chapter 36

16:00 Place des Pyramides Paris France

"Questions? About what?"

"Mr. Hollingston."

"Who?"

"The gentleman you met with last night."

"Oh, you mean Pinky. I was told he is dead. Is that true?"

"Yes, and we would like to talk to you about this."

"Why me?"

"You were the last person he was with before he died."

"Why would you think that?"

"We have camera footage of you leaving the hotel before he died."

"Pinky always drank too much. It finally caught up with him." She shook her head. "There isn't anything else I can tell you."

"Mademoiselle Harrington, Mr. Hollingston didn't die from drinking. He was strangulated." Johnny disconnected the call.

"Strangulated?"

"We would like you to answer some questions, if you would come with us."

"Am I under arrest? I didn't do anything. Do I need to contact someone?" Someone, who would I call?

"No, you are not under arrest. We only need to ask you some questions." Do I need to call a lawyer? What are the laws in France? A thousand questions were racing through her mind but she was aware she had to come up with one answer.

"Can I call someone before I go?"

"Mais oui, mademoiselle." She made a call and hoped it is the right one before the car took her to the police station.

Johnny sat in the detective's office while they are offered her water and coffee, trying to make her comfortable. But she was anything but comfortable. The more questions they asked, the room appeared to get smaller and it became harder to breathe. If she seemed scared, they might think she was guilty, so she smiled and sat back casually in the chair.

" Ms. Harrington. You said when you left Mr. Hollingston was asleep."

"Yes."

"And it was the first time you went to his hotel room."

"Yes."

"How did you find your way out? You have to know the code for the exit."

"I saw the code he put in when we entered."

"You remembered the code? Why? Did you plan to leave without Mr. Hollingston letting you out?"

"No. I just remembered. I have a knack for remembering things." Johnny's heart began to beat faster. Can they see it beating through my shirt? She knew it wasn't possible although her heart felt like it was coming out of her blouse.

"Okay, Ms. Harrington. Let's go over this again." A man rushed through the door.

"No, Ms. Harrington will not be going over anything. I am her representative. Do you have any other evidence besides the footage? Any forensic evidence?"

"No. Not yet."

"Well, you have no cause to keep her. Ms. Harrington will need to go." The man took Johnny's hand and led her out the room. The police detective followed them out.

"We might need to ask her more questions. We hope she will not be leaving Paris too soon." The man grinned at the detective and gave him his card.

"Ms. Harrington will be in Paris but if you have more questions, contact me first. She is a very busy person. She is working with Naive. You know who he is?"

"Mais oui."

"We wouldn't want to seem like Paris isn't hospitable to international artists and their entourage. Especially if false charges are being thrown around. Would we?"

"Mais non,"said the detective as he took the card.

"Come Ms. Harrington." Johnny followed him out of the police station.

"Thank you so much, whoever you are."

" Call me Cesar. Don't worry everything will be fine."

"But how did you — before she could finished her sentence, he opened a car door and Johnny entered. As she sat down, it was clear to her she made the right call.

"Thank you. I owe you." Thank God I made the right decision.

"It was nothing. Only a phone call," said Chloe as the car drove off.

"I didn't have anyone else to call and Naive wouldn't be any help"

"You mean you didn't want anyone else to know. N'est-ce pas ça? Don't worry, it will be our secret. Like Pinky was your secret," Chloe said with a Cheshire cat grin.

"Oh, no. Nothing was going on between Pinky and me. I bumped into him while I was walking by the Louvre. We met for drinks and he got so drunk I wanted to make sure he got to his hotel. I left him drunk and asleep in a chair."

"Chérie, it doesn't matter to me. It's only I didn't think Pinky was your type."

"He isn't, I mean he wasn't. Poor Pinky, who would want to kill him?"

"Je ne sais pas." Chloe shrugged her shoulders. "But isn't your problem now." The car pulled up to Hotel Regina and Johnny got out. She called Lockwood as soon as she entered her room.

"Johnny. What's going on?" Lockwood stumbled over his words.

"Pinky is dead."

"Yes, I was trying to tell you. I heard you talking to someone before you hung up. Was it the police?"

"Yes. They wanted to ask me some questions, since they claim I was the last individual to be with Pinky before he was killed."

Lockwood flopped into his chair. He couldn't believe what he heard. "What? Are you okay? You were with Pinky?"

"After we talked, I saw Pinky walking by the Louvre. Right after I talked to you, it seemed like a serendipitous moment I had to take advantage of. We met for drinks and as usual he got very drunk. He was stumbling, so I wanted to make sure he got back to his hotel room. He passed out in the chair after drinking again, so I decided to do some searching."

"Johnny you are taking too many risks."

"He was completely out. I did find out something. Before he passed out, he began talking again about Babbs and Shelby and the Hawthornes how they are as dirty, not as respectable as you would think. I also got a chance to look at some papers he had on a desk. There was a paper with the same pineapple seal and it had Berlin on it with some numbers.

"It could mean anything."

"What about how he talked about the Hawthornes and the others? Not only that. I went to a private party at a château last night and met Lord Belacorte. I saw some of the same people who were at the Hawthornes."

"They are an international crowd. They socialize together."

"Sitting in a separate room around a table with a woman at the head of the table."

Lockwood sat up as his brows furrowed. "You saw this?"

"Yes. There is a connection and I'm getting close."

"What was the name of the Château?"

"Château Palluau, it is in the Loire Valley. It was some type of big event last night."

"I will look into it. But Johnny it is getting too dangerous. I have to insist you stop. Pinky is dead. Murdered. Probably because he was the weakest link and was talking too much. If the police found out you were with Pinky, so will the people who killed him. They probably waited until you left before they entered."

"Why didn't the cameras have any footage of them?"

"They are definitely professionals. They knew exactly where the cameras were and how to avoid them. This has become way above your pay grade. Leave it alone."

"What about Winslow? We still haven't found out anything."

"This isn't going to get you any closer to finding out about Winslow. Johnny, I think you have to give up on him." She kept silent. This isn't what she wanted to hear. She could take Lockwood telling her it is too dangerous and to back off but not about Winslow. Not about giving up on him. She didn't want to hear this because as she got deeper into putting pieces together, Winslow was moving farther from her thoughts.

"I have to go." Johnny ended the call abruptly. Lockwood stared at the phone. He sat back in his chair and drew a deep breathe before he made a call.

"Ms. Braithwaite, can you connect me with Mr. Bénard , Yes Bénard at Interpol."

Chapter 37

10:00 Bridgetown Barbados

Lockwood finally received a call back from Etienne Bénard who he met at Interpol during one of their international conferences. They have kept in touch as friends and advisors on different cases over the years. The one constant between them is the drug trade which has kept them busy.

"Bérnard, Lockwood here."

"Ah, Lockwood. How are you?"

"Good, Good. I have some information you might be able to use."

"Yes? Is it from the same asset? The pictures were valuable ."

"I'm sure you know Hollingston is dead."

"Yes, murdered. We are trying to work with the Paris police on that one. Their only lead is an American woman was with him."

"That is my asset and she got some other information." As soon as Lockwood said the word "asset" to describe Johnny, he felt bile coming up towards his throat. He never used this term with her before. Lockwood walked over to his credenza and poured himself a tumbler with rum.

"Did she kill him?"

"No, I'm sure the murderer came in after she left. They were professionals. But she went to an event at Château Palluau the same night and saw the same crowd that was at the Hawthornes."

"Château Palluau in the Loire Valley?"

"Yes."

"It hasn't been occupied recently."

"Maybe it was open for the event."

"No, the Reveille family owned it but they had some money problems and moved. It was another site which was part of our surveillance. The estate has been shut for over a year now."

"My asset attended an event at the estate last night with some of the same crowd."

"Interesting. I will check on it."

"Let me know what you find out. She is an amateur and I need to bring her in."

"Pretty good for an amateur. You should think twice about that." Right before he hung up with Etienne, Lockwood said, "By the way, do me a favor can you make sure she leaves Paris with no problems?"

"No worries mon ami." Easy for him to say. Lockwood shook his head as he ended the call.

Chapter 38

19:30 Backstage Le Zenith Paris France

The clear night had a chill in the air, but the expected snow for the evening didn't appear. A line of people waited to get into Le Zenith as Johnny's car parked by the back entrance. Johnny walked into the main arena and stood next to Jerry, who looked her over.

"You seem a little stressed. Did they run out of your hair products?"

"No. It's the least of my problems."

"Chloe problems again?"

"No, in fact, she has really helped out."

Naive, with his hood over his head, went straight to his room backstage. Johnny headed to the box office to make sure the complimentary tickets for the press and guests were in place. As she strolled to the dressing room, she noticed Bobby in combat mode.

He was the general overseeing his troops before the final landing —the show. She walked past Bobby, who was yelling instructions to the roadies, and entered the backstage area. As soon as the door opened, the strong scent of weed permeating the room assaulted her.

Naive was lying on the couch with his headphones on, staring into space. It was his usual ritual before a performance—weed but no women or sex before the show.

"I thought you were on some kind of vegan health trip with Chloe."

"Weed is vegan, and I was able to find some organic stuff."

Johnny moved to the window and opened it. "This isn't Amsterdam. It isn't legal here."

"Don't worry. No police are coming to my dressing room."

Johnny stared at him, the memories of her recent interrogation racing through her mind. "Let's not take any chances."

The dressing room, now filled with the usual sycophants, made her stifle a grimace. Ugh! All the suits are here. The only time management appears is for the big shows or events. They don't care about the day-to-day problems; they think Johnny can deal with all of that. But they make sure not to miss the parties and press opps. She sidled to a corner, sat down, and observed the circus surrounding Naive.

Right before he went on stage, the room was cleared, and Johnny braced herself to deal with the nervousness and insecurities Naive went through before every show. Bobby cleared the room, then told Naive, "Ten minutes till you hit the stage." Management left, and Johnny was right behind them when Naive stopped her and asked her to stay.

"How are you feeling?" she asked.

"You know how it is. They're looking for me to fail—even management. Did you see how they looked at me before they left?"

"They said it's going to be a good show."

"Yeah, it was a pity 'good show.'"

"Look, Naive, the house is full. It's a good crowd. They're here to see you. They already love you. You got this."

They walked out the door, his head down, passing the industry people and sycophants lined against the wall. Right before the stage steps, the dancers and background singers waited for their ritual prayer, which they said together before every show.

While they prayed, the band began warming up the crowd. After the prayer, the background singers jumped on stage and started their vocals. The dancers followed, performing their routine. Naive gave Johnny a blank stare, and she winked at him. He joined the dancers, and the audience went wild. The sounds of the crowd's adulation instantly melted away all his nerves and insecurities.

Johnny stood in her usual spot at the side of the stage when she spotted two men in plain suits on the opposite side. They were talking to a stagehand wearing a headset. Their conversation became animated, and the stagehand began shaking his head no. This doesn't look good.

She was certain the stage hand would not let anyone come to her spot while Naive is performing. But as soon as the show was over, they would be free to come to her side. Panic started to come over Johnny. She was sure they are looking for her.

Did they find something else about Pinky? Lockwood said the murderer was a professional, so they could have tried to link something back to me. If they want to interrogate her again, she knew she might not be able to leave Paris with Naive. She didn't want Naive to know about Pinky.

Johnny began pacing up and down by the stage while she contemplated her next move. She stopped and peeked across the stage and the two men were still waiting. Only one thing she could do. Johnny hurried to Bobby's secret spot where he watched the performance. He was leaning on top of one of the speakers facing the house.

"Bobby, I need you to do something for me."

"Please don't tell me it is another private performance."

"No, I have to leave."

"Okay, see you tomorrow morning."

"No, I'm leaving Paris." Bobby turned and observed a strange look in Johnny's face. He noticed a nervousness in her eyes which was betraying her otherwise professional tone.

"Where are you going?"

"I'm going to Berlin early. I think I will need to make sure about some arrangements with Wolfie."

"I already talked to their people."

"No, it's not performance arrangements. Can you please cover for me?" Bobby could tell from the pleading in her voice she didn't want him to ask any other questions.

"Yeah okay. Are you alright?'

"Yes, I will be. I owe you." Johnny turned to leave and Bobby took her hand.

"Be careful, if you need something, l got you." Johnny squeezed his hand.

"Thanks Bobby." She pulled away and rushed out the side door. With quick steps while she looked over her shoulder, Johnny pulled up her coat collar. She turned the corner. A car pulled up beside her.

"Someone is in a rush?" Johnny bent her head to look in the car and her eyes opened wide. It was Caruthers.

"What are you doing here?"

"You did invite me to the show, didn't you?"

"Yes, but this isn't the entrance".

"Do you want to get in?" Johnny. elated to see him, jumped into the car.

"I was about to park the car but it looks like you are leaving."

"Yes."

"It wouldn't have anything to do with those two gentlemen?" Caruthers nodded his head towards the plainclothes officers who were standing by a side entrance.

"Yes. They think I have something to do with Pinky's death."

"Oh, yes poor Pinky."

"I was the last person with him. I already answered their questions but I'm sure they are here to ask some more. I can't be detained in Paris and then the tour finds out about Pinky."

"You mean Naive."

"Yes. He's going to Berlin to do a private show tomorrow. I want to leave tonight before the police find out."

"Well I guess I'm in time to see you off. Where to now Ms. Harrington?"

"I need to check out of my hotel and get to the airport, the last flight to Berlin leaves in about two hours."

"Well, let's make sure you make it" said Caruthers as he sped off towards the hotel. Johnny has a habit of never fully unpacking, so it was easy for her to get her things together and check out. As she went towards the front entrance, Yves stopped her.

"I think you may want to leave from the back exit". Yves shifted his eyes to the entrance where Johnny could see two black cars with plainclothes policeman waiting outside.

"Thanks Yves." He nodded before she pivoted towards the kitchen. This was the exit. she used with Naive when they wanted to avoid the paparazzi. Johnny smiled. She opened the exit door and is greeted by the sound of Caruther's car engine running.

"Your chariot awaits my dear. Órly or CDG?"

"CDG. How did you know to come to the back entrance?"

"I saw the two black cars pull up front after you went inside." During the ride, Johnny and Caruthers talked to each other sporadically. Her eyes shot glances at the passenger side mirrors.

"We are not being followed."

"What?" Johnny came out of her fog.

"I see you looking at the side mirror. Don't worry, even if we were, I would be able to lose them", Caruthers said with a confident smile. Johnny was grateful Caruthers didn't ask her anything else about Pinky. She sat back and tried to make use of this time to relax. The speed and smooth movement of the BMW sports car hypnotized and lulled Johnny towards sleep. She opened her window so the cold air would keep the sleep from overtaking her.

"Is it too hot, I can lower the heat?"

"No, I'm fine. I just need some fresh air." Johnny glimpsed the signs for CDG and the airport lights getting closer as the car sped towards the exit. Caruthers pulled up to the terminal.

"Thanks so much. You were a real-life savior tonight."

"No worries. See you soon." Paranoia began to take over Johnny as she moved through the terminal. Every time she spotted a man in a suit, her heart took an extra beat. She lowered her head, and quickened her step. Johnny found the check-in desk and waited on line, as she kept checking her surroundings. Suppose the police are waiting for me to get to the desk and then appear.

The closer she got, the little beads of sweat forming on her forehead began to multiply. Airline staff are trained to detect passengers who appear to be unnecessarily nervous. Johnny didn't want to arouse unwanted suspicion, so she closed her eyes, dabbed her forehead, and took a deep breathe before it was her turn. Right before she gave the airline employee her documents. she heard voice come from behind her.

"Ms. Harrington is with me." Caruthers handed them his credentials. As the attendant printed her boarding pass, Johnny tried to keep the astonishment off of her face.

"Merci." He took the boarding pass with Johnny's passport and led her towards a side door.

"I thought you left."

"I told you I would see you soon. Lockwood would never forgive me if I didn't make sure you got out of Paris safely. This is the diplomat's lounge. They will come and put you on the plane right before it is ready to take off."

"I don't know what to say."

"Since you are still in Paris. Á bientôt." He is about to leave when Johnny got the sudden urge to pull him back.

"I thought I was helping Pinky get back to his room. He was so drunk." The words came tumbling out of Johnny's mouth trying to relieve the guilt she didn't allow herself. Caruthers lifted her chin.

"Pinky isn't your problem. He had his own demons."

"Something was on Pinky's desk. A paper with Berlin on it and numbers. Do you think that had anything to do with his death?" Caruthers smiled at her.

"Are you still trying to be the next Mata Hari? Pinky is gone and now you can get a small reprieve in Berlin before Naive comes. Make use of it." He winked at her before he walked out the door.

Chapter 39

———————

23:00 Hotel Adlon Berlin Germany

Berlin wasn't one of the usual stops during Naive's tours, so Hotel Adlon was completely new to Johnny. The bellhop opened the door to a spacious room with a bed enclosed in a modern-day four-poster structure. Across from the bed, French doors opened to a terrace with a direct view of the lit-up Brandenburg Gate. Johnny stepped out onto the terrace and let the cold air hit her face. Caruthers was right—this could be a quiet escape from the madness of the tour. She intended to take full advantage of it. Johnny called the concierge.

"Is the pool open?" she asked, glancing at her phone. She half-expected a negative response, given that it was after 10 p.m. and hotel pools were usually closed.

"No, Ms. Harrington, but you are the guest of Herr Von Bulow, and we will open the pool if you wish." Von Bulow was certainly pulling out all the stops, so why not take advantage?

"Yes, I'd like to do a few laps before bed."

"It will be my pleasure."

Fortunately, Johnny had packed a swimsuit in her suitcase.

She entered the cavernous pool room and eased her body into the warm blue water. Her arms cut through the water's surface as she kept her head submerged, relishing the calm. Suddenly, the underwater lights turned off. She raised her head into the darkness. Only the exit sign and the dim lights along the floorboards illuminated the room. I guess that's the signal they want me out of the pool.

Johnny swam to the far end to retrieve her towel. Her leg violently jerked back. She tried to swim away, but the force of the underwater jet held her in place. Johnny pulled herself up, then dove under the water to free her leg. As she surfaced, gasping for air, a retractable glass floor headed toward her.

"Help! I'm in the pool!" she screamed, thrashing and searching for another way out. She tugged on her leg with all her strength. The glass floor was now just a meter away. "Help! I can't get out!"

The glass was inches from her shoulders when she dove under the water again. Suddenly, the pool lights flickered back on, and the jet turned off. The glass floor reversed direction. Gasping, she raised her head to see a figure leaning over the water.

"Ms. Harrington, are you okay?" The concierge held out his hand. Johnny climbed out of the water, shaking, as he led her to a pool chaise and draped a towel around her.

"I'm okay," she managed to say.

"I don't know how this could have happened. In twenty years here, I've never seen anything like this. We are so sorry." He knelt in front of her. "What do you need? Anything at all?"

"I'm just glad you finally heard me."

"We didn't. The room is soundproofed so that parties here don't disturb other guests."

"Then how did you know I needed help?"

"A gentleman told us he heard someone yelling by the pool."

Johnny dried herself with the towel, slowly regaining her composure. "I owe him a big thank-you. He saved my life. Can you connect me with him?"

"I don't believe he was a guest. After he alerted us, he walked out the door."

Back in her room, exhausted, she opened the door and stepped on an envelope. Inside was a card welcoming her to Berlin from Wolfie and Eva, slipped under the door. Johnny placed the note down and walked around the room, carefully observing. She opened the closet and studied the counter in the bathroom.

To most eyes, nothing seemed disturbed, but Johnny noticed the notepad by the phone had been shifted slightly to the right. The zipper on her suitcase, which she had left slightly open, was now fully closed. Someone had been in her room.

Johnny rifled through her bags but found nothing missing. She double-locked the door before climbing into bed, where she spent a sleepless night.

****

Johnny schlepped into the breakfast room. She wasn't sure if the furtive glances were because of the dark sunglasses hiding her sleepless red eyes or because of her dark skin. She sat at a corner table and ordered a pot of coffee hoping to get a caffeine buzz before her meeting with Wolfie. Johnny sipped her third cafe americano when she observed Von Bulow greeting people at different tables as he walked towards her.

"Good morning Ms., Harrington." Before Von Bulow could sit down, a waiter appeared to pull out his seat and take his order.

"Would you like your usual Herr Von Bulow?"

"Yes, thank you Hans."

"I hope your room is to your liking."

"Yes." She lifted her sunglasses off.

"Your colleague, has been in touch with us and we have everything ready for Naive. He leaned back in the chair and unbuttoned a jacket displaying his matching vest. "I wasn't expecting you so early. He nodded in acknowledgement to the waiter as his demi-tasse was placed in front of him. "I told the hotel to let me know when you arrive. I thought you would be coming with Naive." Johnny hoped he hasn't heard anything about Pinky.

"I decided to come early to make sure everything is running smoothly."

"Good. You know Eva is over the moon Naive will be performing."

"Is this for her birthday?"

"No. I give a big party to mix friends and some business people this time every year. It is wonderful timing Naive is in Paris." The furtive glances have now turned into full gawking.

"Yes. I guess perfect timing."

"Are you in Berlin alone?"

"Yes."

"Well, then I insist you have dinner with Eva and me tonight. My driver will arrive at eight." He rose from the table and gave a European bow before he left. Great, the relaxed evening wearing the hotel's plush robe and ordering room service went out the window.

Von Bulow's driver arrived promptly at eight to pick up Johnny for the ten-minute drive to a luxurious apartment building. She got out the car and right away felt a tightness in her chest. The concierge directed her to a private elevator which went directly to the Von Bulow penthouse. She took a deep breath. The elevator door opened and she stepped inside.

It is the size of a small bedroom but still an elevator. An enclosed space with no windows. Like the closet. Her hand began to shake. She placed her finger on the button. The door and her eyes closed at the same moment. Her chest started to heave. Her breathing got faster. The waves, she thought about the waves soothing her while she laid in the blue waters of Barbados. The calmness of the sea.

The elevator stopped and she opened her eyes to face a butler who led her to a sitting room. Johnny moved around the room gazing at the paintings and art pieces smelling of money. She wasn't an art aficionado but noticed two distinct pieces most people would recognize.

"Ms. Harrington, what are you drinking?" Von Bulow asked as he took a drink from his butler. Johnny still tired from the fretful night wanted to keep alert.

"Club soda with lemon."

"Tea totaler?" Von Bulow asked with a chuckle.

"No. But I'm still a little tired." Eva made an entrance wearing a tight-fitting sheath which left no imagination to what is underneath. Nothing.

"Did I hear you say, you are tired? We have something that can help you with that", Eva said as she slithered her body around Von Bulow. He grabbed her backside and they began to kiss as though no one else was in the apartment. Johnny disgusted by their performance cleared her throat.

"I think I will have a glass of chardonnay."

"Why not some champagne. You wanted club soda, so you will still have the bubbles." Johnny didn't want the champagne but if this is what it will take to stop their PDA, she would pay the price.

"Ok. Thanks. By the way which area will Naive be performing?" Johnny asked as she scanned the area. After she got off the elevator, she noticed several openings without doors which appeared to be hallways.

"Not here" Eva chuckled. She sashayed to the credenza and poured a drink from a crystal decanter.

"This is just our pied- a- terre in Berlin," Von Bulow said as his eyes followed Eva's every move. He turned back to face Johnny.

"The event will be at our country home. It is about 45 minutes away from Berlin. Probably two hours for the American highways but not on our autobahn."

Johnny smiled at his snide remark. The butler announced dinner was ready. As they entered the dining room, she was surprised it wasn't the obligatory billionaire ballroom with the monarchy length table. Instead, an intimate room with a table which could seat only six people.

In most circumstances, Johnny would prefer this setting instead of the ostentatious ballroom dining hall but not with the Von Bulows. The small table and their displays of affections could trigger her claustrophobia if she wasn't so disgusted by them. At one point during the dinner, she had enough and needed a break.

"Can you tell me where I can find the bathroom?"

"I'll show you," Eva said as she jumped out of her seat. As Johnny followed her down a long hallway, she noticed Eva snatched something out of a bowl on a stand. Do they have a bathroom key? They continued until the hallway divided into two different directions.

"Here it is." Eva opened the door and followed her in. She handed Johnny an envelope which felt like it had a key inside.

"Make sure you give this to Naive. Let him know the key unlocks the door to a fun evening. I'll make it special for him." She gave Johnny a licentious smile before she left the powder room. The first thought which came into Johnny's head was nothing worse than an old fool, as Von Bulow's face appeared in her mind, when Eva gave her the envelope.

Naive has no lack of groupies but usually Bobby and the crew handle those situations. Johnny was quite content she never had to deal with them. Now she is not only disgusted from the Von Bulow's performance but also from Eva putting her in this compromising position. If I don't give the envelope to Naive, will Eva be bold enough to ask him about it? She couldn't think about this now. Johnny wanted to find a way to end the dinner early.

As she returned to the dining room, she passed the entrance to another long hallway. Anything to spend less time with them., Johnny decided to enter the area. Along the walls were paintings of people who resembled Von Bulow. Probably family portraits. The sounds of hushed voices emanating from a room pulled Johnny towards a door at the end of the hallway. The closer she got, the hush sounds turned into discernible voices, among the British and German accents, there is one very distinct voice. A voice with the lilt and rhythm of the Barbados accent. A Bimshimian? How could it be?

She quickly tip toed toward the door. Moved her head close, when the knob moved. Johnny rushed to a door on the alternative side of the hallway and hoped it wasn't locked. She slipped inside and closed it right before the voices came out of the other room. Her ear pressed against the door hoping she would hear the Barbados voice.

Chapter 40

21:00 Berlin Germany

The voices stopped outside her door and continued their conversation.

"It would be better if we leave by the back entrance. I believe Von Bulow is entertaining a guest this evening."

"Will he have everything ready for the event?"

"He always does. But sometimes he goes over the top."

"Is it him or is it his wife?"

"More so the wife. It is whatever she wants. The whole Naive production is for her."

"She literally has him by the nose and I mean literally. There were pictures on a dominatrix site with both of them half naked. He had a black leather head mask with a ring around his nostrils. The ring had a chain attached that she was pulling."

"I don't believe you."

"It's true. I don't how they got on the site but he found out and they were quickly taken off."

"How did you see them?"

"Someone sent me a screenshot of course." There were sounds of snickering.

"Of course."

"Everything has to go as plan. Our friend here can get us the final connection we have been waiting for." As they walked farther away from the door, Johnny could hear the Barbados voice.

"It will be quite profitable for all of us." The voices were too far away for Johnny to identify who was speaking, but the accent sounded familiar. She waited a few minutes to ensure they were gone before leaving.

She turned around and froze, face-to-face with a wall filled with whips, S&M attire, and other paraphernalia that looked like a set straight out of Fifty Shades of Grey. Johnny quickly scurried back to the dining room, where Von Bulow and Eva were so focused on feeding each other that they didn't notice her return.

"Thanks for a lovely night, but I think I should head back to the hotel," Johnny said.

"Don't you want to stay for a nightcap before you go?" Von Bulow asked.

"No, thanks. I think the champagne was enough for me."

"My driver will take you back."

"I'll walk her out while you call the driver," Eva interjected. Von Bulow kissed Johnny's hand, and Eva linked arms with her as they strolled to the elevator.

"I hope you had a good evening," Eva said.

"Yes. Thanks so much." The elevator door opened, and Johnny clenched her jaw as she stepped inside. Eva pulled her in close and whispered, "Don't forget to give Naive my message."

Johnny gave her a tight smile that disappeared as the elevator doors closed.

Once she composed herself and the car sped away, her thoughts turned to the Barbados voice. It had sounded familiar. One thing was certain: they would all be at the event. Somehow, Johnny needed to get close to that meeting to identify the Barbados man. However, without an extra burner phone to take pictures, it complicated things.

This was supposed to be a short, uneventful trip. How wrong that turned out to be.

****

The next morning, Naive arrived in Berlin with Bobby and the small crew, looking more despondent than usual. He went straight to his suite without speaking to Johnny.

"He looks awful," Johnny said to Bobby as he checked the crew into the hotel.

"Yeah, he's pretty bad today. A lot needs to be done to get him back up to speed."

"What's going on now?"

"Do you see Chloe?" Bobby asked, not looking up from his iPad.

Johnny scanned the area. "No."

Bobby raised his eyes from the screen. "That's your answer."

"They had a fight?"

"I don't know. You know I don't keep up with that stuff," Bobby said, feigning disinterest.

"Come on, Bobby. I need to know something before I deal with this."

"All I know is he seriously wanted to cancel this gig. He wanted to talk to you this morning."

Johnny winced, regretting her quick exit the night before. "I guess I shouldn't have left."

"What? Thank God you weren't here."

"Why?"

"I told him you went to Berlin early to check on the money and make sure everything was tight. That's the only reason he didn't cancel—because I reminded him of the money. He knew he couldn't get out of it without you around."

"Why isn't Chloe here?"

"I don't know. Who cares? One less headache on the road."

"She's probably the reason for his mood. I'd better head up to his room." Johnny grabbed the extra key card for the penthouse, but Bobby stopped her.

"You, okay?"

"Yeah, sure why?"

"The police were looking for you."

"I know. It was nothing. A friend had some trouble. They wanted to ask some questions I can't answer."

"Okay. Anything I need to know that could derail this tour?"

"No, everything is okay."

"You know I got you whatever it is."

The corners of her mouth lifted. She closed her eyes and nodded. "I know."

Naive was lying on the couch with his sunglasses and headphones still on. Johnny tapped him on the shoulder. He lifted up his sunglasses, gave her a blank stare, and placed them back down. She tapped him again.

"What is the problem?" Naive took off his headphones and sat up.

"I really need Chloe here. That's the problem."

"So, you had a fight?"

"No, she doesn't feel like coming to Berlin."

"Okay. You'll see her back in Paris, right?"

"But I need her here today. How am I going to perform without her?"

"The way you have been performing for all these years without her."

"You don't get it." He moved to the bar.

"I thought you are staying sober?"

"Yeah, that's why I need Chloe. She kept me on the sober path." Johnny took his glass and poured club soda.

"It's only one night. If you go back to Chloe drinking again, what do you think she will say?"

"Yeah, you're right. But where were you? I was calling your cell; it went straight to voicemail. If you were in Paris I might have cancelled."

"Good thing I wasn't. Get some rest. It will be a long night."

Johnny said as she entered the elevator. She checked her phone, trying to calm her fear as the elevator descended, and noticed the missed calls from Naive. The calls were made the same time she was hiding behind the door. Thank God I had the phone on silent. Johnny tried to relax in her room but her mind kept returning to what she heard behind the door. Her phone rang with Bobby informing her the transportation had arrived.

After traveling for an hour, the car pulled up to a manor house. Johnny had to gently nudge Naive awake right before they approached the entrance. As they got out the car, she gaped at the door. Right above it was three prowling wolves sketched into the edifice and below the wolves was written Meute de Loup.

It isn't a person's name. It's a place. Pinky had a place written on the paper. I should have remembered my French. Loup is wolf! Johnny could visualize the paper and the numbers next to the place. 15-1. She is certain the 15-1 was a date - January 15th. Today is January 15th! Bobby was already there to greet them.

"This is some type of gig. No wonder Naive didn't insist on cancelling. I'm sure the money has to be sweet." He took them to the stage area, which was as big as a small theater.

"Everything is set. He only needs to do a soundcheck."

"Give us a few minutes." Naive and Johnny were escorted to a golf cart which took them to a bungalow. Inside the room, the warmth from the lit fireplace took off the chill from the golf cart ride. Naive immediately slumped down in the couch.

"I don't know if I can do this?"

"We are already here and the money is in the account."

"Well maybe we give back the money."

"Now, I know you're kidding."

"No, I'm serious." Johnny sat next to him.

"Is this all about Chloe or is it something else?"

"I don't know?" Naive laid his head back on the couch with his eyes staring at the ceiling. "Maybe. Sometimes I don't know. Do I still have it?"

"Of course you do. Didn't you see how the crowd was going wild last night? You always had stage fright. That's nothing new."

"Yeah, but I think it is getting worse. And this gig. Well, the place is smaller. And you know, I can see their faces. See the reactions." He sat up and bent towards Johnny as he wrung his hands. "Suppose I see someone's face and it ain't good." The fear was penetrating through his eyes and his anxiety so intense it was almost palpable.

"Do you think you need some help tonight?" This is the dreaded question Johnny hated to ask. She would have to talk to Lou and hope he had something.

"Maybe, I don't know. I was so good and strong with Chloe."

"You'll be back with her tomorrow."

"Yeah yeah, I know" Johnny went across the room and took out her phone.

"Lou I might need your help tonight. He's not looking too good. Just have it ready."

During the call, she peered out the window and noticed another bungalow across the field with lights on. Interesting. Who lives in that bungalow? Could it be the caretaker.? Johnny contemplated how she could get to the bungalow while she stared out the window.

"I'm going to take a walk. Get some fresh air."

"Now? It's cold out."

" I know, I need to keep awake."

"Yeah, a good idea maybe I should go with you."

"No, no. You need to rest. I will be right back." Outside was totally dark. The only guide for Johnny was the light streaming from the bungalow ahead and the light from the bungalow she left. She would have to rely on her instincts. She cringed at the sound of the gravel under her feet but she couldn't take off her boots this time.

Johnny scuttled to the rear of the bungalow hoping it had the same back door kitchen entrance like the one she left. She was glad for the grassy path alleviating any noise as she moved to the side door windows. She had the fortune to have a clear view from the kitchen to the main room.

Again, another round table but this time a man was placing papers in front of each seat. This must be the meeting place. Maybe where Pinky would have been tonight. I need to come back here. Johnny hurried back to Naive's bungalow with one thought in her head - getting back to the bungalow.

Johnny stood behind the stage doing her usual scan of the standing audience, but this time for a different reason. Some of the same faces who were at Château Palluau are here. If a meeting was happening tonight, they might disappear when the show begins. Her eyes became camera lens focusing on certain faces.

After concentrating on a face, the blink of her eyes recorded the picture in her brain. She now had a record of where everyone is standing. Walking back to Naive's waiting room, Johnny caught Lou taking the last piece of sound equipment gear for the stage.

"Lou, is everything all set."

"Yeah, no problem. It's at the usually spot"

"Thanks Lou." He grinned, nodded and continued to the stage.

Naive wasn't in any better state than when they were in the bungalow. Then came the knock. The same as the click of the jail door latch, a death row convict hears before his final walk. The door opened.

"Five minutes before the stage," Bobby said as he closed the door. Naive's eyes widened with fear as he stared at Johnny.

"Lou has something for you, if you need it." Naive opened the door and Bobby was waiting to escort him. Bobby snapped his head back to look at Johnny and she slowly shook her head from side to side. No group prayer before the performance since it was only Naive and two backup singers.

Right before he jumped on stage, he moved towards the side, placed his nose on the speaker, and inhaled the white powder which was gingerly placed on top. He pulled his head up, closed his eyes, wiped his nose, and ran on the stage. Naive was now in full throttle. Johnny peeked out to the house and the people were rocking. Eva and Von Bulow are upfront with their close friends around them.

After he finished his first song, Johnny observed one of faces stored in her brain was missing. She scanned the room but couldn't find the missing face. When she looked at the left part of the room, another face was gone. Did they go to the bathroom or for a drink? She would give them a few minutes. Naive's second set was finished and a few more faces were gone. I have to get to the bungalow. It's now or never.

Chapter 41

22:00 Meute de Loup Manor Germany

Johnny went out into the audience and approached one of Von Bulow's staff members.

"How can I get back to Naive's bungalow? He left something he needs for the show."

"No problem, we'll have someone drive you."

"That's okay. Just show me where the golf carts are, and I can drive myself."

"That isn't possible. For security reasons, only staff can drive guests around the estate."

"Okay. I'll meet you at the back entrance."

Johnny took out her phone and called Bobby.

"I need your help again."

"In the middle of the show? This is becoming a bad habit."

"I really need you this time. You know I'd do it for you." Johnny emphasized her point, using guilt to remind Bobby of the times she had saved him from sticky situations.

"What do you need?"

"When one of the house security staff comes to you for a key, send one of your roadies to the dressing room. Tell him to stay there for at least twenty minutes before he comes back to you."

"Where is this key?"

"There isn't one." She ended the call and rushed to the golf cart.

At the bungalow, Johnny performed a quick and fake search, then went back outside to the waiting security guard.

"I can't believe this, but I forgot the key."

"The key?"

"Yes, for Naive's case."

"Okay, I'll take you back."

"Oh, I can't go back without the stuff. He's waiting, and it would look bad. I'd really appreciate it if you could go pick it up for me. I'll call Bobby and have him send one of his guys to meet you."

"I don't know if I should leave you here..."

"Why not? We were left here earlier before the show. Please hurry. You don't want me to lose my job, do you?"

"Okay."

Johnny ran over and hugged him. Flustered, he awkwardly tried to shake off the red tint creeping up over his pale face.

"Thanks so much. Ask for Bobby; he'll be by the stage area."

When the golf cart left, Johnny hurried back inside the bungalow. As soon as she confirmed it was gone, she rushed toward the other bungalow. Running through the complete darkness, with only the distant light of the other bungalow to guide her, she stayed on the gravel path until she got close enough to muffle her steps on the grassy edge.

Peeking through the back door window of the darkened kitchen, Johnny had a clear view into the main room. Seated around the round table were all the missing faces.

Chapter 42

22:30 Meute de Loup Bungalow Germany

Johnny slowly twisted the knob of the door. It was unlocked. She opened it ajar, squeezed through it, and right away, bent down to the floor. Her body laid against the wall. She edged her way to the opening of the main room. The voices were clearly audible. She identified one. The Barbados voice. Johnny glimpsed into the room, the same time someone got out of their chair, and moved towards the kitchen. She fell back against the wall, her eyes darted around the room for another exit. A kitchen table was at the side. She took two steps and slid under the table right before the person turned on the light.

"Does everyone want water?"

"Yes, refill the pitcher." As each drop of water dripped into the pitcher, Johnny's arms wrapped around her knees, pulling them closer to her chest, making her body become the smallest ball as possible. The voice finally completed the task. Feet moved towards the room when water spilt on the floor by Johnny.

"Damn it." The voice placed the pitcher on the table and the wiping motion of hands going up and down passed by Johnny's face.

"What happened?"

"I spilled water on the floor." The voice picked up a napkin, and the figure started to bend toward Johnny's face. She held her breath. Small beads of sweat formed on her forehead.

"Leave it. The help will clean it up. We have to get this over with." The figure straightened, dropped the napkin, and walked back to the room without turning off the light. Johnny couldn't leave without being detected. She was close enough to hear the voices but still couldn't discern what was being said. The door was too far for her to crawl to without being seen. She had no choice but to wait it out under the table.

Time dragged as Johnny sat balled up, cramped beneath the table. Suddenly, another voice entered the kitchen.

"We got a lot done for this meeting. I think it's time to head back."

The voices faded as chairs scraped the floor, and footsteps walked out through a door. Silence. Johnny cautiously began to unfold her body when the door opened again and footsteps re-entered the kitchen. She froze.

The kitchen turned dark, and another door clicked shut. She ran to the back door and scanned her surroundings to ensure no one was around before slipping out. Checking her watch as she ran back, she realized she'd gone over the time limit she had told Bobby. As she got near the bungalow, the golf cart was returning.

"I'm sorry it took so long, but your crew took forever looking for a key they never found," the security guard said.

"I was trying to get a signal out here to call Bobby and let him know I found the key. Reception is terrible." Johnny climbed into the golf cart.

The guard tilted his head and squinted at her. "Don't you need to bring what you came for?"

"Oh, yes. This whole phone business has me off my game." Johnny hurried back into the bungalow, grabbed a satchel with some clothes as a decoy, and returned to the cart.

Back at the stage area, Bobby was in his usual place.

"I don't know what you're up to, and I don't want to know, but you almost got my guy fired," Bobby said.

"What?"

"Yeah, you said 'at least twenty minutes,' but he was in the room for over forty, getting comfortable with his phone. My guys know I don't play with time."

"Who did you send?"

"Tony."

Johnny found Tony slumped by the speakers, looking utterly dejected.

"Tony, I heard I might have gotten you into hot water with Bobby."

He jerked his head up. "You?"

Johnny handed him a fifty-dollar bill. "Thanks for saving my butt tonight."

Tony stared at the bill in bewilderment as Johnny strode away.

Johnny moved to the side of the stage and scanned the audience. The missing faces hadn't returned. *What a waste of time. I almost got caught, and I still didn't see the Barbados voice.*

Naive finished his last set, ran off the stage, and searched for Johnny. She gave him a wink, and he smiled back. The crew loaded the bags onto the bus for their return to Berlin. As Naive and Johnny waited for the car, one of Von Bulow's staff approached them.

"The Von Bulows would like you to join them in the reception area."

"It's late, and we have an early flight tomorrow. Please extend our apologies to them," Johnny said.

The staff member smiled and gestured toward the manor.

"This wasn't part of the agreement," Johnny told him. But with no car in sight, they had no choice but to see the Von Bulows before leaving.

As they were led deeper into the manor, Johnny whispered to Naive, "Whatever you do, stay as far away from Eva as possible. And make sure you're never alone with her."

"Why?"

"What do you think?"

"Another Breckinridge?"

"Exactly. She even gave me a key."

Naive grinned, remembering Katie Breckinridge coming to his dressing room, locking the door, and dropping her raincoat to reveal nothing underneath. Her husband, one of the wealthiest men in England, had been standing just outside the door, while Bobby banged on it, calling the five-minute stage warning. Naive had been tempted but even he had rules: no sex right before a show.

"Don't worry. She's ain't my type."

They entered a room filled with people mingling as waitstaff served champagne on trays. Eva rushed toward them.

"That was a wonderful performance. We couldn't let you go without showing our appreciation," Eva said with a lascivious smile.

So many people are here who would love to meet you." She took him by the hand and pulled him across the room. Naive looked over his shoulder and glared at Johnny following right behind them. When they finally stopped, Johnny's eyes widened.

"It's so nice to see you again," Ashton said to Johnny.

"Ah, you know each other?"

"Yes, we met in Barbados."

"One of my favorite islands in the world. I wish we had more time to get to our place. Do you know Naive?"

"No, didn't have the pleasure of meeting him." Naive's perfunctory smile and dead look in his eyes, assured Johnny of his boredom. But for Johnny, Ashton's appearance had suddenly made this party interesting. Eva snatched Naive away before Johnny got a chance to follow. She surveyed the room and all of the missing faces had return.

"I would never think I would see you here," Johnny said to Ashton as her eyes scanned the room searching for Naive.

"I've known the Von Bulows for a long time. They have a place not too far from my house. Since I was in London, I decided to come to Berlin for their party. They invite me every year."

"And he decided to drag me along," said a voice behind her. Johnny turned to face Henley. "Now, I'm glad he did." He gave Johnny a kiss. She stepped back in surprise. Which one was the Barbados voice I heard? Or was it both? Or was it neither? Is this a coincidence both of them are here?

"This is unexpected. You are the last two people I would expect to see in Germany tonight."

"Yes. It is a pleasant surprise," Ashton said. Both Ashton and Henley were smiling at her. But to Johnny, they were not the same friendly comforting Barbados smile. Now she wondered if they are smiles of distrust and deceit.

Chapter 43

24:00 *Meute de Loup Manor*
Germany

"**A**shton told me you were in London. I tried to catch up with you but I know you were on tour," said Henley.

"Are you a regular guest at the Von Bulow's parties too?"

"No, it is my first time. Ashton said it would be a good opportunity to shore up some business for Barbados"

"For Barbados?"

"Yes, you know tourism with the airline." Johnny didn't know what to believe.

"Oh. When are you going back to London?"

"Tomorrow morning," said Henley.

"How long will you be in Berlin?"

"Just for tonight. Naive has to go back to Paris for another performance." Johnny didn't want to tell them she planned to return to London instead of Paris. She decided she can't take the chance of dealing with the police again. But if I meet Henley, will I get more information out of him? Maybe I can find out if he is the Barbados voice.

"I might have to go to London. I want to go ahead of the crew to get some work done."

"Unfortunately, I will be heading back to Barbados tomorrow. I guess I will miss having tea with you this time. But Henley can take my place," Ashton smiled as he faced Henley."

"That's if she can make some time for me."

"Don't worry. I'll make the time," said Johnny as she walked away to find Naive.

****

Johnny met the small crew at the hotel to go to the airport. She didn't tell anyone yet she planned to go to London instead of returning to Paris. Johnny didn't want to have to deal with questions. Naive wasn't as irritable as usual. In fact, he was fully awake and in a good mood.

"How did you get out of the situation with Eva?"

"The usual line."

"What's that?"

"My herpes has flared up again. It turns them right off." They both laughed at the clever ruse he employed with Eva.

"Finally, you can laugh for a change."

"That's what Chloe has done for me."

"You'll be back with her in a few hours."

"Yeah," he smiled as he's texting Chloe. Perfect time to slip away to London. He will be so involved with Chloe; he won't miss me. But I'll have to deal with Bobby. Everyone was sitting in the private jet lounge area waiting for the luggage and equipment to be placed on the plane the Von Bulows provided. The stewardess announced they are ready for boarding and everyone headed to the tarmac. Johnny escorted Naive to the gangway and stopped him before he climbed the steps.

"I have to leave for London to clear up some media problems in advance."

"What? Now?"

"Yes. I'll meet you in London. You'll be fine. Remember Chloe is waiting for you." He nodded and went up the steps.

When Johnny's plane was in the air, she became aware of the tension she was carrying in her body because the heaviness was lifted with the relief she now felt. But the relief was also accompanied by confusion. All during the short flight she ruminated on the surprise meeting with Ashton and Henley at the Von Bulows event. Ashton, she didn't know but could Henley be trusted anymore?

Who is he? She began to feel guilty about spending so much time with Henley. Could he be part of the reason Winslow disappeared? She was determined to find out. The Uber waiting for Johnny took her straight from Heathrow to the Nottinghill section. This was her safe haven in London, the Portobello Hotel.

"Welcome back Ms. Harrington."

"It's good to be back. I know I called at the last minute but were you able to?" Before she could finish the sentence, Simon had her answer.

"Yes Ms. Harrington, we were able to secure your favorite room. It's quiet at this time of year." He handed her the key for the famous room 16.

"Thanks Simon." Johnny opened the door, placed her bags down, walked past the clawfoot bathtub in the center of the room, and fell back on the infamous round bed. She stared at the draped white canopy, forming billowing clouds above her bed, which lulled her into a peaceful sleep.

When she finally woke up, the sun was setting outside her window. Johnny rose and turned the gold-plated handles on the bathtub to fill with water for a relaxing bubble bath. As she eased her body beneath the warm embraces of the bubbles, she closed her eyes and laid her head on the back of the tub. The ringing of her phone interrupted her zen state.

"Johnny, It's Henley." Johnny immediately sat up in the tub.

"Hi."

"Are you in London yet?"

"Yes. I got here earlier today."

"I'm disappointed you didn't call me when you arrived. I could have picked you up at the airport."

Johnny stared up at the ceiling as she told the lie. "I had to do tour business first."

"Will you be able to make some time for me?"

She moved the bubbles around with her toe. Definitely. How about dinner?"

"Perfect. Where are you staying?"

"Portobello Hotel."

"What time should I pick you up?"

"Give me an hour."

"Okay. See you then." Johnny laid back in the tub with a smile on her face. While getting ready, she dressed as though she was putting on armor preparing for war. But the war she planned to wage was the war of seduction. The phone rang.

"Ms. Harrington, you have a guest waiting for you in the sitting area."

"Thanks Simon. I'll be down in a few minutes." Johnny checked her hair and put on the final touch, Mac's ruby woo red lipstick. Now she was ready. She took the stairs not only because of her claustrophobia but so she could get a view of Henley. Johnny strutted into the sitting room and tapped him on the shoulder. He rose from the armchair as his face lit up. She was so taken aback when they met in Berlin, she didn't notice how handsome he was. He pulled her close to give her a kiss and this time she didn't pull away.

"Are you ready to go?"

"Yes."

"What would you like to eat?"

"Indian food."

"Okay. Indian it is." Johnny gazed out the window, watching the streets change from the Notting Hill area to the center of London. The car dropped them off at Covent Garden, and they wandered past outdoor vendors and small boutiques before arriving at Tandoor.

"Good evening, Mr. Williams."

"I appreciate you accommodating me at the last minute." The restaurant was completely full, and Johnny couldn't imagine where they would be seated.

"Never a problem for you." The maître d' nodded and directed them through the kitchen to a small area in the back. The room was lit by hundreds of small candles. A single table for two, decorated with a short vase of white hydrangeas and roses, sat in the center of the intimate space. It was a perfect setting for seduction. He planned this well, the predator setting his trap.

"The server will be in right away to take your order," the maître d' said before closing the door.

"Thanks, Bindu."

"I hope you don't mind that we aren't sitting in the main dining room," Henley said.

Johnny purred as she stared into his eyes. "This is perfect."

The door opened, and the waiter entered to take their order. As he left, a man in traditional Indian attire entered. Henley stood up to greet him. The man bowed his head and placed his hands in a prayer position.

"Henley, good to see you again."

"Vishnu, this is Johnny Harrington."

He approached Johnny, bowed to her, and said, "So nice to meet you. I hope everything is to your satisfaction so far. If not, don't hesitate to let me know."

"Johnny, Vishnu is the owner of Tandoor," Henley said.

"Everything is perfect," Johnny replied with a polite smile.

"Good. I will leave you to enjoy your evening." Before leaving, Vishnu turned back to Henley.

"By the way, Ashton was here a few days ago. Is he still in town?"

"No, we were both in Berlin yesterday. He's heading back to Barbados today."

Vishnu smiled, bowed again, and left the room.

He knows Ashton too. Is he part of their group? Is this all a coincidence, or am I being paranoid? Johnny wondered, her thoughts swirling.

After they were served, the door remained closed. Throughout dinner, Johnny smiled at Henley, leaned closer, stroked his hand, and stared into his eyes. Her outward demeanor radiated affection, but inside, she felt only betrayal and distrust.

"I love the food. This has been a perfect dinner. I wish it didn't have to end so soon," Johnny cooed.

"It doesn't have to," Henley replied smoothly.

"But it is getting late."

"Let's get a nightcap to complete the evening," Henley whispered into her ear as he pulled her chair back from the table.

She grinned. "Okay, sounds like a good idea."

London is an international city, but it lacks the abundance of late-night spots that New York offers. They strolled around Covent Garden, but most bars and pubs had already served their last round.

"Do you live near here?" Johnny asked.

"Not too far."

"Well, let's go to your place."

Henley's face lit up, his predatory intent unmistakable. The car headed across town, driving alongside Hyde Park, until it stopped at a townhouse facing the park. Airline executives must get paid quite well, Johnny thought as she stepped inside.

Her eyes scanned the room like camera lenses, cataloging every detail. Johnny's brain recorded each observation with precision. Henley took her coat, and as he turned to hang it, she reached for his arm, pulling him close and kissing him passionately.

The huntress has caught her prey.

Henley dropped the coat, took her hand, and led her toward his bedroom.

She unfastened the last buttons revealing her lace bra and slipped off a silk blouse. He lifted and placed her on the bed and gently pulled off the rest of her clothes. His body pressed against her. She could feel his manhood aching. His face leaned close for a kiss. She turned her face away before unbuckling his pants.

He quickly finished undressing and caressed every part of Johnny's body, tantalizing her before mounting and thrusting his manhood, satisfying her sexual yearning. They both came to full ecstasy before he released his body on top of her. He kissed her lightly on her face before getting up to go into the other room. Johnny surveyed the surroundings, her mind again photographing each detail.

He called to her from his living room, "Would you like the drink, you came for?"

"Sure." Johnny followed his naked brown lean body with fainted tan lines as he walked back into the bedroom.

"You remember my drink," she said to him as he handed her a French 45.

"I don't forget anything about you." He kissed her and then said, "Cheers," as they clicked their glasses. They finished their drinks and he took her glass placed it on the bed side table and began to kiss her neck. Her body was now something he is completely familiar with and he took advantage of this knowledge. His manhood called out for her body and she welcomed him.

He mounted her thrusting his manhood until he took them both into rapture. Johnny buried in his arms as he lulled into the deep sexual satisfied sleep. She waited for his breathing against her neck to become deeper before she slipped from under his arms. Johnny went to the desk across from his bed and started to search among his papers.

Mostly airline documents. She opened the drawers. Nothing. When she got to the last draw, it was locked. She scanned around for the key. Where would I put the key? Johnny spotted an empty vase on a shelf above the desk. She turned it upside down but nothing fell out. She scurried across the room to a door which opened into a walk-in closet.

His suits and shirts were color coordinated. Shoes, belts, and accessories immaculately placed. She opened one of the top draws which has his watch collection. Under one of the watches, was a piece of metal sticking out. She picked up the watch and found a key. Johnny's hand hoovered over the key, when she heard movement from the bedroom.

"I would never take you to be a jewelry thief," Henley said as he leaned against the door. Before Johnny faced him, she closed her eyes.

Chapter 44

23:00 Hyde Park London

Johnny turned her head, smiled, and insouciantly dangled the watch.

"It's not my style. But I can see you have good taste."

"Or maybe you were looking for something. I saw you next to my desk."

Johnny's heart began to race. She wondered how long he was watching her.

"I think I know what it is."

" What?" Johnny canvassed the room. Only one exit out and he was blocking it.

"You are looking to see any remnants of a woman." She took a sigh of relief before she chuckled.

"Okay. You caught me. I'm trying to make sure I won't have to deal any drama." He walked over to her and took the watch out of her hand.

"I told you in Barbados there wasn't anyone."

"But that was Barbados. This is London."

"And you are here. Still isn't anyone. Anything you need to know, ask me." He caressed her face and tilted his head toward her lips. She stopped him, pulled his head towards her stomach. He devoured her to the brink of ecstasy and then returned her to the bedroom. They made love again while Johnny's thoughts were on how she's going to get the key.

****

A sliver of light coming through the bedroom windows awakened Johnny. She moved in an empty bed. The faint sounds of water hitting tiles came from a shower. She jumped up and ran to the closet, opened the watch drawer, and picked up the watch. No key. He removed the key. She went to the drawer in the desk, but it was still locked. Damn, I missed my chance!

The water stopped flowing from the shower. Johnny jumped back into the bed and pretended she was asleep. Henley returned with only a towel wrapped around him. She opened her eyes and gave him a contented grin. He sat on the side of the bed and kissed her on the forehead.

"I wish I could stay with you, but I have meetings I can't cancel."

Johnny sat up. "No problem. I need to get some work done also."

"You don't have to leave. You're welcome to stay." She was quite aware if she stayed, it wouldn't be wise for her to do a search. He could have a hidden security system.

"All of my work is on my laptop. You can just drop me off."

During the ride, Johnny kept thinking, What could be in the drawer? Why did he remove the key?

"Will you be available for dinner tonight?"

Johnny bent down to look through the car window. "Maybe. Call me."

She retrieved her key from the front desk without worrying about the dreaded "walk of shame." The Portobello was the hotel of choice for the music industry, so discretion was their specialty.

"Good morning, Ms. Harrington."

"Good morning, Simon."

"Will you be joining us for breakfast?"

"No. Can I have it sent up to my room?"

"Of course. Right away."

Walking to the staircase, Johnny passed the breakfast room where she caught the eye of one of the most famous R&B singers having breakfast with a woman. But the woman wasn't his wife. They both smiled at each other and nodded. After getting out of the shower, Johnny got into the plush terry cloth robe and turned on her laptop to confirm the upcoming press for Naive. There was a knock on her door.

"Breakfast, Ms. Harrington." She opened the door and the wait-staff brought in the tray with breakfast and placed it on the side table. She noticed an envelope placed on the tray.

"Did you forget this?" She handed him the envelope.

"No, miss. It was left for you at the desk."

She poured her coffee and took a sip, then opened the plain white envelope addressed to her. No postage and no return address. Inside was a plain white card, and on the card was written: Be careful! Johnny instinctively glanced behind her shoulder, although no one else was in the room. She called Simon at the front desk.

"Yes, Ms. Harrington."

"Do you know who brought the envelope that was delivered to me?"

"No, I'm sorry, Ms. Harrington. It was brought by a courier."

"Do you know which courier service?"

"No. It was from a service I'm not familiar with."

She went to the window to gaze at the garden. What does this mean? Why would someone send this? Johnny's first instinct was to get in touch with Lockwood, but he wanted her to stop investigating.

Her plan was to call him when she had concrete evidence he could use. She couldn't tell Henley because she didn't trust him. Could he be the person who sent the note? For the first time, Johnny was aware of her vulnerability, and she was alone with no backup.

She got dressed and took a walk to the Portobello Market to shake off this feeling of dread. Johnny wandered among the different vendors, buying a few of the offbeat trinkets the market is renowned for around the world. She was in the middle of haggling with one of her favorite vendors when she got a side glimpse of a familiar figure.

The mysterious man from Barbados!

She dropped the item and started to follow him.

He stopped at a few tables, checked some items, and took the vendors' cards. Johnny made sure she kept a few tables between them. She took out her phone hoping to get a picture of him.

He turned at the perfect angle and she was about to take the shot, when he lowered his head to check his watch, and started a steady pace out of the central market towards the antique shops. Damn it. I almost got him. I can't lose him now. Johnny's previous feeling of dread has been replaced by a determination to follow the Barbados man.

It's harder for Johnny to follow him without being noticed as he walked outside the market. The concentrated crowd and vendor tables made the perfect camouflage. Johnny wheeled her way around people as she kept up with his quick steps. He waited at a crosswalk for the light to change. This was her chance to catch up with him. She quickened her steps and was almost next to him, when the light changed and he crossed the street.

Johnny was almost at the crosswalk, when a baby carriage rushed in front of her and blocked her path. She maneuvered around the carriage and ran to cross the street, when she felt a sudden push. She tried to keep her balance as her feet left the ground and she got closer to the ground.

The screeching sounds of car wheels coming to a sudden stop as voices yelled, shocked Johnny into reality as she laid on the ground. As she tried to sit up, she faced a car a few inches in front of her. People gathered around but one face bent down to her.

"Ms. Harrington. Ms. Harrington are you okay? It is the man from Barbados. Johnny stared at him in confusion.

"Do you need an ambulance?"

"No, I'm fine," she answered as she struggled to get up.

"Maybe you should sit and wait for an ambulance."

"The car didn't hit me. I must have slipped." He helped her up and she brushed herself off.

"Maybe you should sit down for a cup of tea. There is a tea shop not too far from here. Please, let me take you."

"Thank you." Johnny couldn't believe her new circumstances. The Barbados man escorted her a few feet to a quaint tea shop with only 6 tables. He pulled out her chair and guided her gently in the seat.

"You took quite a fall. It was fortunate the car was not going any faster." Before she could thank him for his assistance, she needed to know one thing.

"How do you know my name?"

"From Barbados."

"I didn't meet you in Barbados."

"No, but you were at Mr. Ashton's house with Mr. Henley. I heard you talking to him when I passed the drawing room. My name is Trent. Trent Manley." The waitress brought two teapots and he poured tea for Johnny from her teapot. He definitely was the man at the Hawthornes. Trent had a British accent mixed with a tinged of Bimshimian, so Johnny couldn't be sure where he resided.

"It was lucky for me you were around. Do you live in London?"

"I have a place here but I'm usually traveling for business."

"Does your business also take you to Barbados?"

"Yes. It does." Johnny wasn't getting the information she hoped to get out of him.

"Were you at the Hawthorne's weekend home a few weeks ago?"

"Blenhen? Yes, I was," Trent's head jerked back as he opened his eyes wide. "I was at the skeet shoot with Henry."

"I thought I saw you when I was taking pictures around the estate. But I didn't see you at the dinner."

"No, I couldn't make the dinner. I had to leave early to catch my flight." Manley didn't give the answer to the question going through Johnny's mind.

"What is your business?"

"I'm a curator. An art curator."

"A curator for a museum?"

He smiled as he sipped his tea. "No. I have private clients I work with."

Johnny raised one eyebrow. "Like Mr. Ashton?"

"Yes, among others."

"Were you Pinky's curator?"

"No." He lowered his head and shook it side to side. "I was shocked to hear he was dead. Especially, since I saw him right before he died at the Hawthornes."

"Yes. It was very sad. So are the Hawthornes business or friends?"

"In my world, business and friendship mostly intermingle. But yes, I do advise them on their art collection."

"I initially met them during the tour's first European stop in London. It was so nice of them to invite us to Blenhen. They are such generous and kind hosts", said Johnny.

Manley grinned and gazed out the tea shop window. "European society has a social code that is paramount to their existence." He faced her and then bent close as he focused with a stern face.

"Don't mistake a social façade with reality. It is a lot more behind those brick limestone walls."

"Is this why you were at the bungalow at the edge of the estate?" His angular face became pale as he sat back in the chair.

"How do you know about the bungalow?"

"I was walking the grounds and came up on it."

He leaned forward. "Did you tell anyone you saw me?"

"No."

He sighed with relief. "I wish this can be kept between me and you."

"Why? Is the bungalow off limits?"

"Let's say, it is our secret meeting place."

"So, no one else knows you all meet?"

"Yes. Katherine and I have made it our place." So, Manley thinks I saw Katherine too.

"We try to be as tactful as possible. I'm sure Henry knows but as long as we are discreet, he doesn't have a problem. This is why I hope you will keep our secret." Johnny was disappointed. She thought there was more to Manley's secret than only a pedestrian extra marital affair.

"Sure. Plus, who would I tell anyway."

"I hope you are feeling better," he said returning his face to a placid smile.

"Yes. It was so clumsy of me." Although she was sure it couldn't be Manley, her instincts won't let her tell him she felt she was pushed.

"Can I get you a car?"

"No, thank you. I'm going back to the market." He hailed a black cab and before he closed the door, he gave Johnny a sharp look and said, "Be careful."

"What?" A chill ran down her spine

"Be careful. While you're walking."

"Yes, I definitely will this time." Her body continued to shiver as she watched his cab drive away. Still not sure who she can trust.

Chapter 45

11:00 Portobello Hotel London

London was usually a safe haven for Johnny. But now, while traversing the city she felt paranoia taking over her. She kept watching each person who got close to her. Johnny wasn't particularly happy about being in crowds, but the falling incident, made her claustrophobia kick in. As soon as she arrived at the hotel, Simon ran up to her with a message.

"They sent a car for you. It is waiting outside." Johnny took the note. Trying to get in contact with you. Need you to meet us at the airport. Jerry. She noticed the text messages she missed while talking with Manley. She rushed out the door, jumped into the car, and called Jerry.

"What's going on?"

Johnny heard the cacophony of a crowd in the background. "Where are you, we've been trying to reach you?"

"I was in a television studio, so I had my phone off."

"We need to do an impromptu press conference"

"At Heathrow?"

"Yes The press will be waiting"

"Okay. Spill it."

"There was a misunderstanding about Naive and Chloe's relationship. They are fine and close friends."

"And the real tea?"

The voices from the crowd began to fade away. Jerry moved whispered "They had a big fight in Paris. They trashed the hotel room, the police were called, and she has a black eye."

"Is she pressing charges?"

"No. Her manager was called and talked to Naive's management. They both agreed it wouldn't help either one of their careers."

"And the police?"

"Management took care of it too."

"I can get to the airport in about half an hour. Which terminal?"

"The Private Jet lounge area."

"What?" Johnny stared at her phone and pulled her head back.

"Yeah. Management ordered it. They are determined this doesn't sideline the tour." Johnny began putting talking points together as the car weaved through the traffic. They pulled up behind a crowd of photographers gathered in front of an entrance. Johnny moved through the crowd and entered the building. Jerry was waiting with an escort in front of the VIP Lounge elevator. Johnny held her breath and silently counted to ten.

"Thank God you are here."

"How is he?"

"The usual. Full of denial." They took the elevator down to the lounge where Naive was slumped in a chair, sunglasses on his face, headphones over his ears. Johnny sat down next to him touched his shoulder. He took off the headphones and stared at her. Like a broken doe.

"Naive, the press is outside waiting. I think the best thing to do is to give them a brief statement and leave. I will tell them you will take one question and call on Stephen from The Guardian. He'll ask a soft question about Chloe. He continued to stare at her under his sunglasses.

"You'll just say everything's fine. Chloe is a great actress and a close friend. There is no truth about trashing the Ritz. You can ad lib about how you love the Ritz, it's one of your favorite hotels. They will love that and it will help mend your relationship with them besides paying the repair costs. Naive didn't say a word.

"Do you have any questions?" He took off his glasses and Johnny could see some scratches on his face.

"She wasn't who I thought she was," he said solemnly as he shook his head.

"They never are."

Johnny bent close to him. Johnny spoke to him in the slow steady cadence one speaks to a child.

"Keep on your glasses. After you make your statement, you will get into the car and we will execute our usual plan. You have to get it together. Management needs you to make this work, so this doesn't affect the tour." He sighed and stood up.

"I'm ready." Before they all entered the elevator, Johnny scanned the room and then motioned to one of the roadies.

"Reggie, can you lend Naive your jacket?"

Sure." He took off his camouflaged bomber jacket and gave it to Naive. He put it on as they entered the elevator. When the doors closed, Johnny put on her sunglasses, closed her eyes, and placed her hands on the rail along the elevator wall. Memories from her childhood returned like waves washing ashore. You can't leave her in the closet. She'll be okay. Somebody will find her.

She tried to block out the voices in her head. As the elevator went up, Johnny's hands squeezed the rail so tight she could feel her nails cutting into her palms. The elevator doors opened, and she rushed in front of everyone to exit, leading Naive to face the press. The popping camera flashbulbs were blinding as reporters yelled out questions while they stood outside the terminal doors.

"Naive, is it true you knocked out Chloe during a fight?"

"Is it true the Ritz Hotel in Paris has now banned you for life?"

"Naive! Naive!"

Johnny stepped in front of him.

"Naive will take one question before we leave." She scanned the area and pointed. "Stephen."

"Any truth about what happened at the Ritz with you and Chloe?"

Naive stepped out front and repeated the statement they had discussed. He then veered to the terminal doors with Johnny as the press continued to bombard them with questions. Out of the cacophony of reporters, one question rang out loud and clear.

"Is it true what they say about you, Naive? This tour will be the end of your career. That you're washed up?"

Naive spun around. "What that motherfucker said?"

Johnny took his arm and pushed him back through the terminal doors.

She held him by his shoulders. "This is what they want. To see you go off and have the pictures and footage to go with it."

He shrugged her off and stomped to the door. "Not after I knock his ass out. And it would be worth it."

Johnny stood blocking his path. "Think about it."

He stopped, his jaws clenched and his eyes tight, before making an about-face to the elevator. She returned outside the terminal to talk to the press about the upcoming encore performances in London.

After dodging all the questions about Chloe, she went back inside and asked the escort if she could take the exit staircase leading to the VIP lounge. He cocked his head and squinted at her, not only because she wanted to take the stairs but because most people didn't know about the emergency exit staircase.

"I will have to call my supervisor."

"I know. Tell Stanley it's Johnny."

He took out his phone and made the call.

"Mr. Aldridge, I have a person from the Naive entourage who wants to use the emergency staircase."

"Yes, sir."

He hung up the phone, gazed at Johnny as he scratched his

temple, and led her to a small side door where he tapped a code to let them in. As they descended one flight, he glanced over his shoulder.

"By the way, Mr. Aldridge said to tell you hello. I didn't even have to tell him who was asking to use the stairs."

Johnny smirked. "I know."

Inside the VIP lounge, they were all waiting for her.

"Okay. Is the car outside?"

"Yes," said Reggie.

"Naive, let me have the jacket."

He sulked but took off his jacket and gave it to her. Johnny called Reggie over and handed it to him. After Reggie put it on, Johnny pulled the hoodie over his head and placed sunglasses on his face.

"Now you're ready."

Johnny and Reggie walked out the door to the waiting car. Reggie and Johnny got in.

"Make sure when you get to the hotel, you bend your head low and pass the press quickly. You know the drill."

"Yeah, I got it."

Johnny got out of the car and spotted a solo black press van waiting around the corner. It was the usual Daily Mail TV reporter who pays someone off to get near the VIP lounge. They would follow the car, and all the press would follow the Daily Mail van.

Johnny went back into the terminal. They waited for a work van to pull up to the entrance. Johnny handed Naive a roadie tour hoodie to put on before leading the crew and Naive into the van.

The van drove past an empty entrance where the press had camped out, then got on the M4 highway. Johnny sat in the van contemplating the best way to enter the hotel when her cellphone vibrated. The phone lit up with the name Katherine Hawthorne. Johnny placed her finger on the phone to hit decline but stopped herself and answered the call.

"Hey, Katherine."

Chapter 46

12:00 London

"Johnny, darling. I just saw the press conference on television with you and Naive. The British press can be horrible. If you need to get away from it all, let me know." Perfect timing.

"Thanks Katherine. I would like to take you up on your offer. We are on our way to the hotel but the press will be surrounding it all day and night."

"Say no more. Have your driver take you straight to Blenhen. We'll be in the city for the week but I'll call and alert the staff you will be coming. Anything you need, they will take care of it."

"Thanks so much Katherine. Really appreciate this."

"No worries. I'll call you later after you have settled in."

"A change of plans. We aren't going into London. Do you know how to get to the Blenhen estate," Johnny asked the driver? Naive lowered his sunglasses and stared at Johnny.

****

Lyon, France

Lockwood had finished attending a conference at Interpol Headquarters when he ran into Bérnard.

"Bérnard, it's so good to see you. I was about to head over to your area to look for you."

"I would hope so."

"Ah, my friend, I wouldn't leave Lyon without seeing you."

"When I found out the international conference was this week, I was hoping you would be attending. I know some years you have to skip it because of family matters. How is your wife?"

"The same, but the drug trafficking is getting worse. I can't afford not to attend these conferences. Barbados may be small, but it is becoming a major hub. One of my best officers went undercover, and I'm not sure if he's dead or just gone deeper underground."

"I have some information you may be interested in. I don't think it may help with the trafficking situation, but you still need to be informed."

"Ok. Let's talk in your office."

"No, I think this is something we should discuss over lunch."

Although Etienne was a Frenchman, he had the work ethic of an American and usually ate lunch at his desk. Lockwood was certain the information must be something he wanted to keep top secret.

Bérnard and Lockwood sat at a corner table in a small bistro on the outskirts of Lyon. Most of the patrons were locals on their lunch break.

"I like this place because it is the food of my grand-mère. Fewer and fewer of these bistros are still around."

"I don't think the food is the only reason you want to eat so far from headquarters."

Etienne smiled. "This is what I like about you, Lockwood. We both know each other so well." He took out an envelope and slid it across the table.

Lockwood opened it and read the file. The more he read, the wider his eyes opened in astonishment.

"Are you sure about all of this?"

"Yes. I checked and rechecked."

Lockwood dropped the file, closed his eyes, and shook his head.

Etienne nodded. "I know. I didn't want to believe it either."

Lockwood stared at him. "How could this be? What have we done?"

****

Johnny checked her phone after arriving at Blenhen. She returned the several messages from Bobby and management with a text informing them of the new location. The other texts were from Henley.

She noticed his missed calls in the car but waited until she had privacy to call him back. Although, she was in a room, a lot of work had to be done before she could call him. She hoped he heard about the press conference and would understand why she didn't return his calls. Johnny's phone vibrated.

"What the hell happened? Where are you?" Johnny could imagine the Bobby's angry face from the tone of his voice

"Calm down Bobby."

"Calm down, we are so off schedule." Johnny pulled the phone away from her ear to keep the sound level from hurting her eardrum.

"Naive is supposed to be rehearsing right now. We have everything set up."

"I decided to make a change of plans. Paparazzi would make it too difficult to stay at the hotel. So, we're staying in Blenhen."

"Blenhen? Who gave you the authority?"

"I took it on myself. Management wanted to make this tour work, right? He won't be in the right state of mind at the hotel."

"How is he going to rehearse? Do sound check?"

"Blenheim has the space for rehearsals. Have the crew come out here. Sound checks can be done when he goes to the venue. I'll make sure, we are early to give you enough time for sound and lighting."

Tension was in Bobby's voice. He said each word with deliberation. "I hope you are correct about the space. I'll call you when we are on our way."

Johnny hoped she was right too. She hasn't seen it yet herself. Before she checked the space, Johnny had to check on Naive.

Blenhen was like a maze so although the staff placed them close to each other, it was still possible to get lost. Fortunately, for Johnny her photographic memory served her well. She knocked on Naive's door, before opening it. He had his headphones on so he couldn't hear anything else.

"How you feeling?"

"Like a prisoner. Why did we have to come out here?"

"Would you rather be a prisoner in your hotel suite? That's the only place you would be without the paparazzi hounding you."

"At least I could sneak and hang out in London."

"Oh sure, I can see the headlines now. Naive gets arrested for knocking out cameraman. You can walk around here without any hassles."

"It's boring here. They don't even have a cute maid to talk to."

"Bobby is bringing the crew, so you will be able to do rehearsals. What about your writing?"

"I'm not feeling it anymore. I'm not even feeling the show." He laid down in the chair.

"Don't start talking like that." Johnny pulled him up.

"Let's go look at the space for the rehearsal. Walk around. We're lucky the weather is nice, at least for England." They found the head butler who took them to an empty area on the other border of Blenhen.

"The Hawthornes usually use this area when they have philanthropy events for their foundation." The empty room was the size of a small theatre with a stage set up in the front.

"There is another area I could show you."

"No, this will be fine." Johnny glanced at her watch and remembered Bobby texted they were fifteen minutes away.

"The rest of the crew will be here soon."

"I'll be sure to have the staff escort them here," said the Butler.

"Thanks." Naive wandered around and gazed out the floor to ceiling windows encased around the room.

"Bobby will be coming with the crew." Naive kept staring out the window and didn't say a word.

"I'm going to make sure they tell the equipment van to park on this side of the estate." Johnny started to walk towards the door.

"I would have made her my wifey." Johnny stopped, closed her eye, and bent her head before facing him. *Damn I was hoping this conversation wouldn't happen. I'm really not in the mood to listen his whining.*

Johnny sighed. "Ok, Naive, what happened?"

"She saw a naked photo some girl sent to my phone."

"Some girl?"

Naive shrugged. "Yeah, I don't even remember her. It probably was some groupie I banged while I was touring."

"You give groupies your number?"

"Only if it was good."

"Did you hit her?"

Naïve lit a cigarette. "No, no. I tried to explain, I didn't know the bitch and she went off. Like a wild cat."

Johnny's eyes tightened. "Then how did she get the blackeye?"

He took a deep drag on the cigarette. "She jumped on me and started to scratch my face. I pushed her off. I can't have scratches all over my face."

Johnny pulled the cigarette out of his mouth and stomped it out on the window. "You pushed her off or punched her off?"

"Whatever. I had to get her off of me. I guess it was an automatic reflex." Johnny rolled her eyes. "I think you could have handled it better. You are lucky her career is on the brink."

"You think I might still have a chance?" Johnny shook her head and made an about-face.

"I am going to make sure the van is parked on this side." She strolled out the door, still shaking her head. *What is he thinking? No, I'm crazy to think he would have a rational thought.*

Before Johnny could get halfway down the path, the equipment van was already heading toward her. Bobby jumped out and stood next to her, scanning the area.

"Yo, I don't know who's more trouble—you or Naive."

"You have to admit this is much better. He'll be on time, and everything will run like clockwork here."

"I don't know. I haven't seen the rehearsal area yet."

"You'll love it."

Johnny climbed into the van with Bobby to show them where to park. As they drove back up the path, she caught a glimpse of a side door where people were entering. She snapped her head around to get a full view but only saw the door closing. *Katherine said she would be in the city. Isn't the house supposed to be empty?* From what she could tell, the people didn't look like servants.

"Johnny? Johnny, is this the space?" Bobby's voice snapped her out of her thoughts.

"Turn right and pull up over there."

They entered the rehearsal area, and Bobby immediately got into his road manager mode. Meanwhile, the head butler marched toward Johnny, carefully navigating around the chaos of roadies bringing in equipment.

"Anything more you might need?" he asked.

"No, I'm sure Bobby has it under control."

The butler nodded and was about to leave when Johnny stopped him.

"Katherine told me the house would be empty, but I thought I saw some people entering the estate."

"What you were told is correct. No one else is staying at Blenhen at this time."

"Maybe what I saw were workers."

"I doubt it. When the Hawthornes are not staying here, only a handful of staff are working, and they would never enter the estate except through the service entrance, which is on the other side of Blenhen. Anything else?"

"No, I probably made a mistake."
The butler gave a faint smile, nodded, and walked away.
It wasn't a mistake. Why is he lying?

Chapter 47

16:00 Blenhen Estate Herefordshire UK

Johnny sidled over to Bobby as he is about to yell at one of the roadies.

"You don't need me for anything, do you? I'm going to take a walk around the estate." The sound of her voice barely reached him through the cacophony. He snapped to attention to glare at her.

"What?"

"I'm leaving."

"Yeah, Ok," he said before he jumped up to look at the staging. She left the rehearsal area, traversed the grounds, and backtracked to where she saw the door. Her eyes darted around before she tried to open it. It was locked. No windows. She moved further down the path and peeked through a French door.

Johnny turned the handle and it opened. It was one of the many drawing rooms in the Blenhen house. She surveyed the room and became aware this was where Katherine had the afternoon tea. Johnny left the room and moved back in the direction of the door.

She scurried along the corridor hoping not to run into one of the servants. The corridor came to an end. Turn left or right. The click clacks of high heel shoes hitting the tiles coming from the left, determined Johnny's decision. The high heels were behind her and getting closer. She opened a door and tilted her head in. The room was empty. She placed her ear on the door and the sounds of footsteps were now accompanied by voices.

As the voices got closer, Johnny's eyes darted around the room for an exit. A door on the other side of the room. She rushed and pushed it open. A small closet with shelves. The voices are clearly audible to Johnny. The door handle began turning. She had no other choice and went inside. The voices entered the room. Sweat beads started forming on Johnny's forehead and hands.

Her racing heart was in sync with the throbbing in her head. She sat on the floor with clasped arms around her knees pressing against her chest. Johnny's eyes were closed as her body swayed back and forth. She's back in Barbados. In the closet, crying herself into a fetal position. Waiting for someone to open the door.

Aunt Vera and her married lover 's voice streamed into her head. "That quirky memory of hers is a problem. We'll be gone by the time, they find her." Johnny shook her head from side to side. I have to focus. *I can't let them hear me breathing.*

Her mind returned to the beach in Barbados. She counted to ten. Imaging blue waves rolling back and forth calmed her. Slowly she unfolded her arms and opened her eyes. Crawling towards the door, she placed her ear against it. The voices were now audible.

"When will the connection be complete?"

"We came across a problem. We believe we might have been infiltrated."

"How is this possible?"

"We think it is someone from the Barbados side." The sound of the rhythmic Barbados accent interrupted the conversation.

"We eliminated the problem we had. So, you have to be wrong. Our circle is smaller than yours. You better look among yourselves." Johnny turned the knob and gingerly cracked open the door. One eye squinted through the crack. All the voices were sitting with the back of the chairs facing Johnny. She moved her head to the side to try and get a glimpse of one of the faces. A woman rose and faced the chairs.

"This is no time to start fighting among ourselves. We can't afford any other disruptions. We have another big shipment coming through Barbados in two days. The Barbados -Carolina connection is the perfect route for the US distribution." A man stood up next to her.

"The connection wouldn't exist if we didn't think of the old slave trade route. That idea came from Barbados, so I take offense with the suggestion the leak stems from our side." Johnny slid away from the door. Leaned against the wall with her mouth agape.

Eyes opened wide in astonishment. Her chest began to heave. *Eva and Ashton?*

"We can't start fighting among ourselves. This won't help us find the mole," said Eva. "We have one of our people working on it. They apparently have a lead. We have to take extra precautions." Johnny moved off the wall to peek back through the door and her foot knocked over some papers.

"Did you hear that," asked Eva?

"It sounds like it was coming from behind that door." Footsteps moved towards the door. Johnny retreated behind some boxes. The darkened closet was washed over with light as the door opened. Johnny held her breath. She hid against the wall. The door closed and the footsteps walked away.

"Nothing."

"Since this isn't our regular meeting, we need to keep it short," said Eva.

"I want everyone to be extra vigilant since the mole is still among us. Let's keep to our schedule, everyone knows what they need to do."

"What about the European connection?"

"It's being solidified as we speak."

"We will have a full update at our next meeting. Any other questions?" Silence

"Okay, Gentlemen." The sound of chairs scraped across the floor and footsteps traversing the room as voices faded away relieved Johnny. A door closed.

"I don't trust him."

"Why not?"

"Something about him."

"Ashton brought him in, so I'm sure he was well vetted."

"Ashton thinks everyone from Barbados is beyond reproach."

"Well Lord Belacorte, what do you expect from the colonies," Eva said with a snicker as she closed the door behind them. *Belacorte too?* Johnny sat for five minutes to make sure no one else was in the room before she exited the closet. She moved in silence with stealth and peeked out the door before leaving. Johnny returned to the rehearsal area. Her thoughts were consumed with all the information she heard and how to get it to Lockwood.

"I was wondering if you had left the estate. Naive is looking for you," said Bobby before he walked off to fix a microphone. Johnny headed to the side room set up for Naive.

"You know what?" *Whenever he starts off with this question, it will only lead to a headache.*

"What?"

"I think I spoke too fast about Eva."

"Uh?"

"She texted me she is in London and would like to see the show. She'll need tickets and a VIP pass for backstage." Hearing her name brought a chill down Johnny's back.

"Isn't it too soon? This could hurt your chances of getting back with Chloe."

"She'll never know. This will be a backstage thing. You know. Something quick." *Something for his ego.*

"I probably will have to go into the city early, to make sure about the comps. I'll put a package together for her." *Perfect timing. I can get a burner phone to call Lockwood. I have to let him know about the shipment.* Johnny went outside to find all of the equipment vehicles and trucks have left. She stopped the sound engineer who was walking back into the rehearsal area.

"Where are all the vehicles?"

"They went back to the venue."

"I need to make it back to the city."

"They will be back by five o'clock" It will be too late for Johnny to obtain a burner phone. Unlike New York City, Johnny was aware London isn't a twenty-four-hour town. She made the decision to use her phone to call the one person who can contact Lockwood.

"Ms. Harrington, how are you doing? Are you in London?" asked Caruthers in his usual clip British accent.

"Yes. Well not in central London. I'm at Blenhen."

"How nice. Didn't realize Katherine stays around during the week."

"She doesn't. Naive got into a little mess, so Katherine was kind enough to let us stay here to avoid the press."

"Katherine is a very gracious hostess. But I'm sure It's not why you called me."

"Yes, you're right. I need to give some information to Lockwood. I don't have a burner phone."

Caruthers took a sip of whiskey from his cut crystal tumbler and cocked his head "Burner phone. You have been using burner phones."

"Yes. When I call Lockwood with information."

"I think it would be best for us to meet to discuss this further. I'll drive up to Blenhen."

"No, I will be leaving soon to return to London for Naive's show tonight."

"He is performing tonight?"

"Yes. At the O2 arena."

"I'll come to you."

"I'll have a VIP backstage pass for you at the box office. Call me when you pick up the pass."

"I won't need the pass. I'll find you."

Chapter 48

19:45 O2 Arena London

The arena was buzzing with the roadies and tech people swarming around backstage as people are entering the arena. Johnny kept a close eye on her watch and glanced around wondering when and where Caruthers would appear. She checked her phone again and returned to Naive's dressing room. As usual, the sycophants and groupies were circling around him, as he absorbed their adulation along with the weed. Naive motioned for her attention.

"Did you make sure Eva will have access to my dressing room."

"Yes. Everything is set up."

"I want to make sure she is in here as soon as I get off stage. Make sure Bobby keeps the dressing room clear except for her," he said with a lascivious smile on his face. He was almost salivating in anticipation of the delights he expected after the show.

"I'll make sure Bobby knows." Naive returned to inhaling the joint passed to him.

As soon as Johnny exited the dressing room, Bobby appeared walking towards her.

"Bobby, make sure no one is in his dressing room when the show is over except for Eva Von Bulow."

"For the entire night."

"Nah. Just the first 45 minutes. Maybe only thirty minutes, the way he is going."

Bobby grinned and said, "I'll have Reggie put security in front of the room." As soon as Naive jumped on the stage, Johnny's phone lit up with a text from Caruthers.

I just arrived.

Where are you?

I'm on the upper level of the backstage area, by the cables. Take the steps on the far left.

OK.

Johnny rushed pass the record executives and managers flexing their importance. Everyone else's full attention was on the stage, so no one noticed when she climbed the steel steps to the upper level.

She moved along the rafters surrounded by cables which held the lighting and other equipment for the stage. Only the lights from the stage cleared her path. When one of the special effects lit up the stage, it revealed Caruthers standing at the top of the rafter.

"Why did you pick to meet here?"

"I wanted a place where you can watch the show and be discreet. This serves both purposes."

"I think I found the center of the drug ring while I was at Blenhen."

Caruther's snorted "At Blenhen? That's absurd."

"I don't think so. Katherine told me the estate would be empty but I saw people entering into a side entrance. When I asked the butler, if any other guests were arriving, he told me no one."

He shook his head. "Maybe it was extra staff."

The muscles in her neck became tense as she shook her head side to side. "No, please listen."

"I found the area they entered and hid in the room where they had their meeting."

"Who were they?"

"It was Howard Ashton from Barbados and Eva Von Bulow. Eva was conducting the meeting. They were discussing the Barbados-Carolina connection and about a steady shipment. They believe there is a leak but it will not stop the shipment coming to Barbados in two days. Lockwood has to get this information." Caruthers grinned and shook his head.

"What? You don't believe me?"

"No. I do."

Johnny gave a sigh of relief.

"I can't believe I underestimated you. I thought you were this silly young woman who had too much time on her hands. But you are so much more than that. You are not only smart but resilient. Not easily dissuaded. All the perfect attributes for an agent. Even when I pushed you into the street, you still continued with your quest"

Johnny took a step back as her eyes widened. "It was you who pushed me?"

"Yes. Last time we talked, I felt you were getting a little too close. I figured after Pinky's death; you would get the hint."

"Pinky?" Caruthers' words were audible and quite clear but they were racing through Johnny's mind, forming a puzzle where all the pieces were scattered.

"Pinky, talked too much. He became a liability we couldn't afford to keep."

"So you are part of The Firm?"

"No, they are too pedestrian for me."

Johnny wanted to keep him talking while her mind raced to figure a way to get out. "Why did you kill Pinky and tried to kill me."

"You were getting in the way of my financial arrangement. Do you think working for governments, could afford my lifestyle? I always needed a supplement. So, I made sure their connections connect and they supplement me very nicely."

"But Lockwood trusted you."

"Yes," he shook his head. "He is such a good friend to send you, my way. But I can't afford to have a conscience. Johnny's eyes darted around to find an exit but the only way out is down the steps or jump off the rafters. He grabbed her arm and pulled her towards him as a sharp object stabbed her side.

"Now walk slowly down the steps. We are going to take a little walk. If you make any sudden moves, this knife will quickly carve out your kidney." As Johnny placed her foot on each step, her mind sank deeper into her fear. They passed the people she worked with every day, but no one noticed her or the fear in her eyes above the roaring music coming from the stage. The world seemed to move in slow motion as Johnny's eyes glanced at each person she passed.

"Johnny." Bobby's voice pulled her out of her trance.

Caruthers hissed in her ear. "Get rid of him or you'll see the blood spewing out of his throat before I carve you up." He let go of her arm and she turned around to face Bobby.

"Want you to know Eva is in his room asking for Champagne. That wasn't part of Naive's rider."

"Can we send someone out for it?"

"At this time? You know the stores are all closed."

"May I give a suggestion?" asked Caruthers. Johnny faced him with a faint smile.

"A pub is not too far from here. They might have a bottle or two. It won't be Veuve Cliquot but it should suffice."

"Bobby, they may have Bollingers, you know how we all loved that one."

"Thanks. I'll send Reggie for it," Bobby squinted his eyes. He scanned Caruthers from his bowler hat to his brogue shoes as they walked away.

. . .

"Where are we going?" asked Johnny as they stepped outside the arena.

"It's a nice night. Not too cold for London. How unmannerly of me" He took off his raincoat and placed it around Johnny's shoulders. They moved towards the wharf. Stopped at the railing which separated the walkway from the Thames River. Johnny was surprised the coat around her arms along with the walk had put her at ease. *Maybe he has changed his mind about killing me. Maybe he does have a conscience.*

She stared at him. "Can I ask you a question?"

"Sure, why not," said Caruthers. He lit a cigarette.

"Why did you send the note to my hotel telling me to be careful?"

He chuckled, "My dear, it's not my style. I never sent you a note."

He stomped out the cigarette. "This is where unfortunately; we will have to say our last goodbye." He took off the raincoat from her shoulders and placed it on.

His ubiquitous black string bracelet missing from his wrist. *He did change his*——— A cord tightened around her neck. Her head jerked back. Johnny's breathing became constricted. Her body involuntarily struggled. Her hands reached behind clutching at his face.

"It will be much easier, if you don't struggle. It's better for you to be dead before you hit the Thames," Caruthers calmly whispered in Johnny's ear. The view of the lights on the pier began to fade. Movements became slower and weaker. Her eyelids steady flicker slowed down.

They were about to make a final closure. The cord in one abrupt movement loosened from around her neck. She fell to the ground, and for a few seconds her eyes were shut, before they opened to reveal a blurred vision of two figures moving around.

Johnny struggled as she pulled herself to sit up against the wall of the railing and focused her eyes on Caruthers fighting with a man. Caruthers blocked her view of his opponent. He stopped and jerked his arms upward. Moved backwards and then halted. In a split second the whole world came to a stop. The only sound was the quiet movement of the water from the Thames River slapping against the wharf's boulders. Caruthers turned to the rail and in one movement, lifted his body and jumped over the rail into the Thames River. Johnny tried to get up, when a firm but gentle grip helped her. When she lifted her head, she faced Lockwood.

Chapter 49

20:15 Thames River London

"Are you okay?" Lockwood said as he wrapped his coat around her. She didn't realize her entire body was trembling until Lockwood's coat covered her, and they were both sitting in the police car on the road to the hospital.

Johnny laid on a gurney in the emergency room while Lockwood talked to men in blacksuits. At one point, they turned and stared in her direction while they talked. A doctor approached the gurney and closed the curtains around her.

"You are very lucky Ms. Harrington. By the look of the wound around your neck, you might not have been with us tonight." He checked her pulse. "How are you feeling?"

"Much better now."

Lockwood poked his head through the curtain. "May I come in?" The doctor looked to Johnny for approval. She gave an affirmative nod.

"How is she?"

"I'm right here. Why not ask me?"

"Because I want the truth from a doctor."

He checked the pupils of her eyes. "As I told Ms. Harrington, she is lucky to be with us tonight."

"I feel much better."

"Your body is still in shock. I suggest you take a few days of rest. I'll give you a prescription for medication to make sure the wound on your neck doesn't get infected," the doctor said as he exited outside of the curtain.

"I hope you take his advice, since you don't take mine. Do you want me to call your family?"

"No. I told you I'm okay. I'm glad you found me. What were you doing in London?"

"I was at an Interpol conference when I found out Caruthers was an agent for hire. I couldn't leave Europe without finding you, so I tracked down the tour."

"What made you look by the wharf?"

"Because I didn't know what hotel you were staying, I came to the venue. A man backstage said he saw you leave with a gentleman wearing a raincoat." *Thank God for Bobby.* "I knew it had to be Caruthers."

"I can't believe he was going to kill me. Although he had a knife to my back, he was still a gentleman to the very end."

"I couldn't believe it either. I've known him for over twenty years, but I guess I never really knew him." Johnny sat up in the gurney.

"Eva and Ashton are behind the drug shipments. They are planning a huge shipment to come through Barbados in two days. I heard them talk about it when I was at Blenhen."

"Eva Von Bulow and Howard Ashton? What were you doing at Blenhen?"

"Long story. You have to let Barbados know about the shipment. Ashton talked about the Barbados -Carolina connection."

"The slave route."

"Slave route?"

"Yes. Barbados was once one of the richest countries in the world because of the slaves and sugar cane commerce between South

Carolina and Barbados. No one sails that route anymore because of modern technology with ships."

"I couldn't get a burner phone before the show, so I called Caruthers hoping he would contact you with the information."

"Can't believe I sent you right into his trap," said Lockwood. He shook his lowered head. "I trusted him with your safety. What would I have done if I didn't get here in time?"

Johnny placed her hand on his arm and said, "But you did."

"Johnny, we can't let anyone know Caruthers did this. It could jeopardize us finally picking up Eva. We found out about her connection after you told us about the party at the Château. You will have to tell people you got mugged."

"Sure, anything to catch her."

"But it also means you will need to leave."

"How? I still have the rest of the tour."

"You got mugged, right? You need some time off. The time off is true. Get some rest. I'll let them know you have to leave because of the incident."

Johnny began to wring her hands. "One more thing, I think you need to know. I think Henley is involved with them also."

Lockwood cocked his head and squinted his eyes." Was he at the meeting with Ashton and Eva?

"No, I don't think so. But he was at the party at the Château."

"He would be at the party because of his company's business connection. They would invite him as well as other people to make them seem more legitimate."

Johnny still felt uneasy about Henley. "I need to call him."

"If you do, don't tell him about Caruthers. Don't tell anyone."

"Okay but what did you tell those men you were talking with?"

"They are with Interpol, I told them what happened to Caruthers," he said before he went outside the curtain area. Johnny laid back down on the gurney and closed her eyes for a minute. A hand brushed against her cheek. She opened her eyes. Jumped to sit up. He placed his finger to her mouth.

"I wanted to be sure you are okay," Winslow whispered as he held her hand.

The words rushed out her mouth. "What are you doing here? Where have you been?"

"I've been everywhere."

"Everywhere? Even Lockwood doesn't know where you are?"

"I know. I couldn't get in touch with him at that time. After I intercepted the cadaver from the medical school and planted my chain, I knew it was too risky. When I got to London I finally contacted Mr. Lockwood. He told me about what you were doing and how he tried to talk you out of it. I needed to know you were okay since you are so hard headed. Didn't you understand my note."

"What note?"

"The note I left at your hotel."

Her eyes widened. "You left the note?"

"Yes. You were getting too close. This isn't a game. You could have gotten yourself killed." At this point, Johnny didn't know whether she was more relieved to see Winslow or angry he let her wonder whether he was alive all these months.

"How could you let me think you were dead all this time."

"I sent you a clue. In the Barbados newspaper."

"I figured it out but when Lockwood confessed you didn't contact him, I had to find you." He placed his face close to her.

"You missed me that much?"

"I never believed you were dead. Now you can go back to Barbados. I'm going to take some time off. He kissed her before she finished her sentence.

"I have to go.

Chapter 50

Barbados Two Weeks Later

Johnny sat in a half lotus yoga position, at the edge of the shore, gazing out towards the calm blue waves. Although Lockwood told her they stopped the shipment and had enough evidence to pick up Eva and Ashton, Johnny couldn't shake her insecurities.

The only thing that made her feel whole was sitting on this beach. She came every day at the same time hoping Winslow would appear, and take her out on Teamie. But each evening she left, right before sunset, without seeing Winslow, her hopes dwindled.

Barbados might be a small island but Johnny managed to rent a bungalow without anyone knowing about it. The bungalow was in a secluded area, behind the ruins of a half-built hotel, on Paradise Beach. She couldn't bear to see her family because she was still raw from the incident in London. Johnny wasn't ready to answer their questions about her sudden return to the island.

The cool soft white sand under her body and the warmth of the sun ray's hitting her face were the healing element she needed. Barbados was the place she came to find peace. Johnny closed her eyes and lifted her head to the sun falling into a meditative trance when she felt a hand on her shoulder. She opened her eyes and spun around with a smile expecting to look into Winslow's face.

You always seem to get away from me," said Henley. Johnny's smiling face turned to a mouth agape.

"How did you ——"

"Know you were here? I didn't I was back in Barbados on business and Lockwood told me you were here."

"Did he tell you everything?"

"Yes, I'm so sorry about the mugging. I thought I hadn't heard from you because of the tour. I'm going to have to keep better tabs on you." He kissed her forehead.

Johnny was glad Lockwood was keeping to the story. She didn't want Henley to know what she had done.

"When are you leaving?" he asked as he gently pulled back a stray hair by her eye.

"In three days."

"Good. I'll pick you up for dinner tonight."

"No. I can't. I just want to stay by the house."

He stooped down next to her. "You need to get out some time. It will be good for you."

"My family doesn't even know I'm here."

"I have the perfect place. No one will ever know you were here"

"I don't have anything to wear. I bought two bathing suits from a boutique on the way to the house from the airport and that's all I have."

"No problem. I'll get you something."

"See you at eight." He kissed her forehead, moved down to her cheeks, and then to her lips before he stood up and trekked down the beach.

Johnny sat on the porch of her rented house drinking the local mauby drink when a man on a motor bike approached the house and handed her a box. She went inside and opened it to find a midi length white cotton sheath dress. Johnny read the note.

I saw this dress and thought of you. Can't wait to see you in it.

Henley Johnny smiled and took the dress out of the box. It was the first time she smiled since she returned to Barbados. She checked the time and began to get ready for her date. The evening is humid and since the house had no air-condition, she sat outside on the porch to wait for Henley. After a half hour and he hadn't arrived, Johnny began to feel worried. Henley was always prompt so this is not like him to be late. Her phone lit up with a text.

> I'm so sorry but I had to deal with a business situation and won't be able to make it tonight. I can't change it for tomorrow because I have to leave in the morning. Will catch up with you soon.

After getting Henley's text, she spent the rest of her days strolling along the beach, hoping to see the Teamie sailing by.
****

Johnny gazed out to the shore one last time before she entered the cab for the airport. Although she was disappointed, she didn't have dinner with Henley, she was glad to spend her last three days alone. She needed the time to center herself before she jumped back into the hectic world awaiting her.

As Johnny trod along with the other passengers on the tarmac, she glanced over to where the private planes are stationed. Johnny loved to spot the different celebrities who are either leaving or arriving at Barbados.

She watched a group of people walking towards a private gulf stream jet. Johnny stopped on the tarmac while the other passengers moved past her. She moved away from the area and tried to head to the private jet but was stopped by security.

"Can I get a little closer? I think I see someone I know."

"No, Miss. You need to go back to your plane." Johnny didn't need to get any closer. She could see the person clearly. It was Henley.

"Would you happen to know where that flight is going?"

"No, Miss. But most likely London." While Johnny sat watching the Gulf Stream taxi down the runway, with the speed lifting it in the air, it also took away her trust in Henley. Another call to Lockwood when she landed.

Before she was a spy, Johnny Harrington had a secret of her own. Get her free origin story-*The Making of a Spy*-and be first to know when the next thriller arrives.

Scan the code below to claim your free story
https://read.judyhutsonwrites.com

About the Author

Judy Hutson began her career as a freelance writer for magazines including *Rock-n-Soul*, *Spin*, and *People* before stepping into the music business during the early, electric years of hip hop.

Hired as publicist for the iconic rap group The Fat Boys, she traveled with them on the historic Fresh Fest tour, working alongside legends like Run-DMC, LL Cool J, and Kurtis Blow. That tour led her to one of hip hop's first feature films, Warner Bros.' *Krush Groove*, which she worked on with The Fat Boys.

Over the years, Judy has worked with artists such as Bobby Brown, Jill Scott, and Kanye West, and with actors including Lance Reddick, Pam Grier, and Michael Michele. Those experiences—and the places they took her—became the muse for the stories she now tells.

Her debut novel, *Spy Notes*, follows a music publicist who's pulled into the world of espionage to save a friend, taking down an international drug ring while on tour with an iconic artist.

Judy loves hearing from readers. Connect with her at judyhutsonwrites.com.